THE EARTH AWAKENS

ELEMENTAL ACADEMY BOOK 2

D.K. HOLMBERG

ASH
PUBLISHING

THE AIR WAS HOT THIS FAR TO THE EAST. TENSION ROSE within Tolan Ethar, the kind of tension that came from approaching the waste, a place devoid of all life. It was a place that created a separation for Terndahl, a place where the shapers kept themselves safe from those who served the Draasin Lord.

Tolan had only seen it in his dreams.

He'd come close before, but never as close as now. Within Ephra, his hometown, there was an annual festival where the master shapers led people up to the border of the waste and the master shapers would stay there, staring over the vast expanse of nothingness and attempt to shape into it. It was a demonstration that served a purpose: to show the shapers weren't afraid of the waste and the power that supposedly lived out in it.

"Can you believe we're here?" Jonas whispered.

Tolan glanced over at his friend. They were dressed in

their traveling cloaks, prepared for whatever they might encounter, but the cloaks were far too warm for the heat radiating from the waste. Jonas stared out toward the waste, his eyes wide and excitement written on his face. Wind fluttered his brown hair and a sheen of sweat lined his forehead.

"I've never really wanted to see it before."

"Why not?"

"Because beyond the waste is the Draasin Lord," Tolan said.

"We don't know that. No one really knows where the Draasin Lord is. Rumors speak of him beyond the waste, but there's nothing there."

"We don't know that either."

"I'm sure someone does. There are shapers powerful enough to attempt a crossing."

"There aren't any strong enough to make that crossing." Ferrah tucked a loose strand of curly red hair behind her ears, shielding her eyes from the sun. She had been listening near them and been silent as they approached the waste. Much like the other students, she whispered. With so many students approaching, it was a soft and silent murmuring that drifted into the air and disappeared into the waste. "There aren't any Shapers Paths that cross over the waste, and it's so vast that every attempt to shape across it fails."

The Shapers Paths were roads in the sky, formed out of power and meant as an easy way to reach faraway places. They had traveled along several of the Shapers

Paths on their way here, using them to navigate quickly. When they had neared the edge of the waste, they had been forced off the Path. As Ferrah suggested, the Path did not extend this far out.

Before heading to Amitan and the Academy, Tolan had no experience with Shapers Paths. They didn't have any in Ephra, and though there might be some in other places, he had only heard about them since being selected to attend the Academy and had only used them once: to arrive there. Then again, Tolan had never believed he had any ability to shape in the first place, so believing he was capable of traveling along a Shapers Path would have been beyond him.

"Why would shaping fail with the waste?" Jonas asked.

"The entire waste is devoid of the power of the element bonds," Master Barry said. He was older man, and held a handkerchief in one hand that he continued to dab at his forehead. "Many have attempted to shape into the waste, trying to push against the borders, but they have failed. The most we manage to do is keep our borders intact."

"What would happen if the waste started retreating?" Jonas asked.

One of the students nearby laughed. "The waste won't retreat. The Draasin Lord is too powerful," Draln said.

"The waste existed long before the Draasin Lord and will exist long after he is gone," Master Barry said. "All we know is that it's a place where there exists no connection to the elements. The bonds fail. It's been like that for hundreds of years, and in those hundreds of years, every attempt to change it has failed. Perhaps your class will be the one who changes that."

"Not likely," Jonas said.

A shaping built from him and he pressed out, letting it roll out over the waste. As he did, it dissipated, striking some invisible thing and failing.

Others tried the same thing near him, and with each, the sense of shaping failed, no differently than Jonas's had.

Tolan didn't even bother trying. He might have an ability to shape, but his ability wouldn't have done anything and would require revealing his furios, the bondar for fire that granted him an attachment to the fire bond.

"Aren't you going to try?" Jonas whispered.

"I've been near enough the waste before to know what happens when people try," he said.

"How often would you come here?"

"This close to the waste? Never. The master shapers did. The rest of us from the city would follow them, but we stayed a reasonable distance back."

"What's considered a reasonable distance?" Ferrah asked.

"Far enough away that you can glimpse only the beginning of the waste and nothing more."

Tolan thought about the first time he'd been here. His parents had still lived with him then. He'd been young, no more than seven or eight, and terrified. Most who came to the waste were a little bit older for their first time, but his parents had attempted to reassure him, telling him there was nothing to fear here, that there was still much life around him, and that it was just one more part of the world.

He should have known then that something was wrong.

Others feared the waste the same way as the students around him did, and for good reason. Most people within Terndahl recognized the innate power of the element bonds. That was part of their connection, part of their heritage, and connected as they supposedly were to the various element bonds, they should have been able to remain safe, but there was a sense of emptiness when it came to approaching the waste, a certain fear their power would be taken from them.

"What would happen if we attempted to cross?" someone asked.

Tolan glanced down the line and saw another of the first-year students, Sarah, looking out. She had come from the eastern edge of Terndahl, the same as him, though she wasn't nearly as close to the border as he was. Ephra was near enough to the waste that they could make the journey in a day by foot, whereas most other places within Terndahl required a several-day journey. Either that, or they had to shape themselves there.

"Some have tried. There are stories of men and women who have packed water skins and food and have headed out over the waste," Master Barry said.

"It doesn't kill you?"

Master Barry shook his head. "The waste is a desert, an empty wasteland, but it does not actively kill you. The hardest thing for you would be the fact you would be severed from your connection to the element bonds. Most who have the ability to reach the element bonds fear losing that connection, and that is why so few have attempted to cross it."

"I thought some had tried to shape their way across."

"Very powerful shapers have attempted to make a crossing before," Master Barry said. "Very few get very far."

"Beyond the waste?" Ferrah asked.

"We have attempted to circumvent it, to circle around it, but it's incredibly vast, and traveling by sea has failed, as has attempting to circle around the north. There is nothing but an endless swathe of the waste. For all we know, it continues forever, though none truly believe that to be the case."

"Your people couldn't sail around it?" Jonas asked, looking at Ferrah.

She glared at him. "The people of Par don't really care about sailing around the waste. Most are more interested in fishing."

"You're just saying that because they can't do it."

"The people of Velminth are certainly welcome to try, too. I thought you were something of a mountain man."

"I've spent plenty of time in the mountains, but I have no interest in crossing."

"What do you think is beyond it?" Tolan asked.

Master Barry smiled. "I think there's nothing behind it. I think the waste extends onward and onward, a place we aren't meant to go. Man, and his connection to the element bonds, belongs this side of it."

"What about the stories that the Draasin Lord is on the other side of the waste?" someone called.

Master Wassa approached the group and smiled. "They are nothing more than stories. As I said, there is no way for anyone to travel across the waste. We have tried and failed, so for those of you who believe the Draasin Lord has somehow managed to not only bring himself but all of his followers across the waste, you would be mistaken."

There were several long moments of silence.

"This is it?" Draln walked up to the edge. Near the edge of the waste, the grass changed from a bright and vibrant green to dry and nearly lifeless, and there was a rapid transition, a point where life suddenly stopped and changed over to rocks before eventually becoming a bleak and barren expanse of darkened land. Flowing sand rolled in the far distance, but not near them. The sun shone brightly and it was warm, but not excessively so. "I don't get why this is so impressive. Why did we get dragged out here?"

"This is part of every first-year student's journey," Master Barry said. "You must know about the waste, and you must know what it feels like to have your powers suddenly separated from you."

"Do we have to do this?" Jonas muttered.

He didn't say it quietly enough and Master Wassa came

up behind him, chuckling. He was a larger man and despite the heat, he didn't seem to be sweating at all. His enormous, flowing robes swept around him. "All must experience the separation."

"Why?" Jonas asked.

"You were selected. And now you must be separated. Consider it a part of your journey. When you return, you will have faced something all young shapers fear. At this point in your shaping career, you have embraced you power. Many of you have become dependent upon it. Some of you have begun to show great potential. All of you fear losing it."

He swept his gaze along the line of students. Tolan suspected the master's voice had been shaped to carry, and though Master Wassa was a water shaper, he was also something of a skilled wind shaper as well.

"When you're ready, we ask that you approach the border and take at least a dozen steps across. When you're there, you will remain for one hour."

"Why an hour?" someone else asked.

"An hour is long enough for you to be tempted. Everyone must feel the sense of the separation. At first, you will have some residual connection to the element bonds. For those of you who had been drawing upon that power when you cross the waste, that will linger within you, and the sooner you attempt to use it, the sooner you will find it separated from you. Some will wait. Those of you who continue to wait will find that power difficult to reach, but we have learned that the most powerful shaper can still draw upon their element bond connections within that hour. What we want is for you to find yourself separated. It needs to be enough of the separation for you to experience a moment of panic but know that it will return when you cross back over to Terndahl once again."

Master Wassa turned away and the students along the line all glanced at each other, including Jonas, who looked at Tolan before turning his attention to Ferrah.

"Who's going first?" Jonas asked.

Tolan took a deep breath. He had only recently connected to his power, but he also didn't fear losing it, probably not the same way others did. His identity wasn't wrapped up in it. He reached into the pocket of his cloak, tapped on the furios, and took a step across the border.

"Look who's chasing after the Draasin Lord," Draln shouted.

Tolan hesitated, his back stiffening, before continuing onward. He had heard such taunts before, and Draln couldn't know what that meant to him. No one in the Academy knew. He forced himself to ignore the taunt, heading deeper and deeper into the waste. As he went, he felt nothing other than heat. Tolan didn't know if he should be afraid, especially as from what Master Wassa said, his connection to the element bonds would be separated—though he still didn't know exactly what his connection to the element bonds was. He could reach for fire, but when he did, his connection to it was so different than what it was for others. How could it be, when it required he visualize the elementals in order to create a connection to power?

He glanced back and saw he was the only one out in the waste.

Would others follow? This was required of them, at least Tolan had thought so, so he expected they would. But maybe he was the only one willing to venture this far out into the waste.

A dozen steps. An hour. None of that sounded terrible.

Only, he'd once had visions of the waste. Those came racing back to him now.

When he had been selected for the Academy, he had seen the waste in a way he had never seen it before. He had chased the elemental power in his vision, letting it follow him, and in that vision, the elemental had trailed after him, heading into the waste itself. That went against what he believed about the waste and went against his belief that whatever power existed out here was minimal. Supposedly, the waste was a place of emptiness, a place where there was nothing. There was no connection to the element bonds out here. Without that connection, there would be nothing for him.

It was a good place to test what he could do.

If he had a connection to power in the element bonds, then he wouldn't be able to shape. If his power depended upon the elementals the way he thought it might, maybe it would be different.

When he was far enough, he stared outward. Rocks spread all around him, bleak and dark. Every so often, he thought he caught the edge of a shimmering sand dune, but that was difficult to tell. Likely it was nothing more than his imagination, especially as he wasn't deep enough into the waste to see the sand, and unless he ventured farther out, he wouldn't encounter it.

How far had he walked? He turned and realized he had to be a hundred paces or more out into the waste. Others had begun to follow, but they did so cautiously, only a few steps over the border, before pausing.

Tolan stood, staring out into the waste, and reached into his pocket and ran his finger along the furios. When he encountered the runes along it, he squeezed them, as he often did.

In order to reach for power through the furios, he had to draw upon an image of an elemental, feel the power of the fluttering within him. Traveling on the Shapers Path had required he draw upon a shaping of fire, and he had only enough control to blast himself onto the path. He didn't have enough to reach it with any sort of security, not like so many others within his class. Most were able to control their travel to the Shapers Path using their connection to shaping to guide their way, often using more than one element in order to do so.

Eventually, Tolan had to hope he could reach another of the elements. It had failed him so far.

He was to stand here, but what was the point in that? He settled onto the ground, crossing his legs, sitting, connected to the waste.

With his hand on the furios, he focused on fire, trying

to reach for that elusive element, focusing on one of the elementals. Hyza came to mind as it often did, mostly because it was the one he had seen first—and the most often. Hyza was a mixture of fire and earth, a combination of power that should not exist, and yet somehow still did. With that combination of power, the elemental was unique. Somehow, when he connected in that way, he thought he could reach for hyza and power, but today it wasn't there.

And why should it be? He was out on the waste.

Tolan continued to trace his finger along the furios. He was the only student he knew of who had a furios. The bondars were used in their classroom, an opportunity for them to try to connect to the element bond they struggled with otherwise, but this furios was his. Without it, he would never have developed the way he had.

There was no sense of separation from anything. There was no sense of anything, for that matter.

It reminded him of when he had traveled into the northern mountain range with his parents, though it might be a bit hotter and windier. In the mountains, they had reached a point where they climbed above the tree line and it looked awfully bleak. It was colder, and he had been dressed in a heavy cloak when he had traveled with his parents, their attempt to see how much he might be able to connect to earth. But that hadn't brought him any closer to the element. He had known about his connection to earth-sensing since he was young, and they'd hoped to elicit a greater connection, to draw forth an ability to do more than just sense earth, and be able to shape it. But that had failed.

There came the crunching of boots and Tolan looked up. The Grand Master approached and took a seat next to Tolan. He was an older man, thin but with dark eyes and a heavy gaze. There was an intensity to him, and normally when Tolan was around him, there came the sense that he shaped power at all times. That sense was absent. The realization left Tolan with the first understanding of how he'd been separated from the elements.

"You have come farther than most choose to come when they first encounter the waste."

Tolan turned his attention back, staring out into the distance. "I didn't know you'd come."

"I accompany the students each year. There's something strangely peaceful about it. It's a matter of testing yourself, allowing the separation and then reclaiming power once again."

"You didn't travel with us."

"There was no need to travel alongside you," the Grand Master said.

"You shaped yourself here."

"Students can only travel so fast, but I have some experience with expediting my journey."

"Why do you come out here?"

"For the most part, it allows me to understand."

"Understand what?"

"The reason we train. We must be strong in order to handle what we do. We must recognize the purpose of our shaping and be ready for how Terndahl might need us."

Tolan could only nod. He wasn't sure he would ever be needed by Terndahl. His ability wasn't quite enough to truly be useful, though at the same time, he had been instrumental in preventing Jory from succeeding at raising a draasin.

"Do you believe the Draasin Lord is beyond the waste?"

"I believe people feel the need to claim the Draasin Lord has hidden somewhere, and where else could he have hidden but on the other side of the waste? Unfortunately, the Draasin Lord cannot be there. Not if what he aims to do is accurate."

"Release the elementals."

The Grand Master nodded. He pressed his fingers together, his mouth pinched in a tight line. He sat like that for a moment before letting out a heavy sigh. "Unfortunately, he must be hiding someplace we haven't discovered, but it cannot be on the other side of the waste. Nothing exists in the waste. Nothing connected to the elements does, at least."

"That's not entirely true though, is it?" Tolan said.

The Grand Master arched a brow at him. "Why would you say that?"

"Well, we're sitting on earth, the rock and the sand and whatever else might be out here. I've felt the effect of a breeze, so wind is here. The sun shining overhead casts some heat, and if the vast expanse of the waste represents a desert, then there definitely is heat. With that being said, I still wouldn't be surprised to find water. So, in that regard, there are aspects of the various elements here."

The Grand Master studied him for a moment before chuckling. "I suppose you're right, but there is no connection to the power that birthed these things. Perhaps that's a better way of phrasing it."

"None has ever been able to pull upon that power?"

"Not here. It's the reason I walked to follow you."

"What do you think formed the waste?"

"Who can say? We know the waste has been here for hundreds of years. Perhaps thousands. It's a place where the power of the element bonds has been separated, as if we weren't meant to travel across here."

"At least, not with the power of the bonds," Tolan said.

"Perhaps that's true. Perhaps that's all this is, a way of separating us from the bonds and creating a different experience. If that's the case, then one must ask why."

Tolan could only shrug. "I guess that's why I'm at the Academy."

"Unfortunately, those answers won't come at the Academy. We can theorize, and the longer you spend studying with us, you will come up with your own suggestions as to why it's like that, but I don't know you will find definitive ones. But then, as Master Wassa said, perhaps your class will be the first one to uncover truths about the waste."

Tolan and the Grand Master sat in silence. He rested his hands on either side of himself. Why had he ever been nervous about this place? This wasn't anything to fear, though the longer he was here, the more he was aware of the absence. It was a void of what should be here, the *sense* of the elements he should be feeling but did not.

"Do you intend to stay longer than the hour?" the Grand Master asked softly.

"Has it been that long already?"

"It has. Most are eager to return, though most don't venture this far into the waste, either. In that, you surprise me, Shaper Ethar."

Tolan glanced over his shoulder and realized the line of students who had ventured over the border of the waste had retreated, returning back into Terndahl, as if they had gone at the first opportunity. Did they really fear it out here? Did they really think there would be such danger?

And did he not?

"Probably because most of them never lived so close to the waste growing up."

"Even living close to the waste doesn't mean you would always be so fearless. There are plenty of master shapers who serve near the waste and don't come so far out into it. What is it you have come to see, Shaper Ethar?"

Tolan tore his attention away from the Grand Master. What was he here to see? He wanted to know who he was, but as much as that, he wanted to know what he was meant to do. Having lost his parents, having them disappear—or be killed, as difficult as that might be to acknowledge—had put him into a place where he hadn't known just what he wanted for himself.

And if he was honest with himself, he still didn't really know what he wanted.

An opportunity. A chance to do something valuable. A chance to prove he was more than he had believed himself to be.

But he wouldn't be able to do those things here. That required he returned to the Academy, and that he continued to pursue his training, gaining skill—if that were possible for him.

Tolan got to his feet, dusting his hands on his pants. "We can return."

The Grand Master looked over at him. "Only if you want to."

"I think we should... What was that?"

He stared into the distance, convinced he'd seen movement. There had been something more than the sand shifting on the far-off dunes. Whatever it was out there had moved more quickly.

"I didn't see anything." The Grand Master climbed to his feet and peered into the distance.

There came a flicker, barely more than that, and Tolan had a sense that the Grand Master either attempted to shape—or had managed to. If he had managed it, then somehow, he had done so despite the fact there were limitations here that should have prevented him doing so.

"There was movement."

"There would be none out here, Shaper Ethar."

"Are you sure?"

"We have many master shapers who spend time along the borders of the waste. All patrol, watching for signs of movement, and spend their time trying to ensure the waste doesn't move, that the borders don't change. In all that time, there has rarely been anything out on the waste. Our shapers, those who don't fear it, will occasionally come out here, but even that is infrequent and rare."

Tolan continued to stare. He didn't think it was his imagination and having seen the waste in his vision prior to his Selection, he wondered how much of that was real? In that vision, there had been others out on the waste. It had been more than shapers, but why should that be? Could it be the Academy and the Council of Terndahl didn't know nearly as much about the waste as they thought?

Or more likely, it was nothing more than a vision. While it had come to him during the Selection, nothing about it suggested it was any more real than anything else in his Selection. As far as he knew, everything had been imagined, nothing more than visions of his tired mind. He needed to treat them as nothing more than that.

As he started to turn, he caught sight of movement once again.

Tolan froze. This time, he was certain he'd seen it. It was more than a shadow. It had been movement deep into the waste, far enough away that he couldn't see it clearly, but he had been sure it was real and had been there.

Tolan glanced over at the Grand Master, not wanting

to say something until he knew whether or not the other man had seen the same thing. He didn't need anyone else questioning him; he'd had enough of that as it was.

But the Grand Master seemed not to have noticed.

"Are you ready, Shaper Ethar?"

Tolan studied the Grand Master, watching him, debating how much he should say, before nodding. There wasn't anything to say. The Grand Master hadn't seen the same thing, and Tolan wasn't about to cause trouble.

They started back toward the distant line of students. As they neared, he could tell how Jonas and Ferrah watched him, the concern in their eyes. There were other students he was friendly with, people like his other roommate Wallace or even Sarah and Elizabeth, but for the most part, he spent his time with Ferrah and Jonas.

As he approached, their gaze flickered from him to the Grand Master. Tolan already knew tongues would be wagging and questions coming about why he had spent time sitting out in the waste talking to the Grand Master, but he was used to things like that.

When he stepped across the border between the waste and Terndahl, a surge of shaping power flooded through him.

He gasped involuntarily. It was a sudden change, and as that power swept through him, he could tell it was building. But strangely, there came a sense of it from behind him as well.

He spun around, looking out into the waste while everyone else continued to head back toward the heart of

Terndahl, returning toward the access point for the Shapers Path. Tolan alone stood, lingering as he stared out into the waste. There wasn't movement as he had seen before, but there was the strange sense of power.

He couldn't shake it. It was real, and if it was out there, where was it coming from?

It couldn't be imagined, could it?

He glanced over at the others, turning his attention to the master shapers, but none seemed to be paying any attention to him or the direction of his interest.

Maybe it was imagined.

Power continued to build and Tolan maintained his focus outward, staring into the waste.

The ground suddenly trembled and he was thrown, landing on his back, his breath knocked out of him. As he lay there, the power of a shaping surged.

And then it exploded.

2

TOLAN ROLLED TO HIS FEET, REACHING FOR THE FURIOS. HE struggled to gain control over himself, straining for a connection to his shaping. Something had thrown him backward, but as he spun around, trying to take stock of what had taken place, he couldn't tell what it was.

The other shapers had been knocked down as well. Most were students, though Master Barry lay motionless. Master Wassa leaned over him, and Tolan imagined a powerful water shaping building, checking to see what might have happened to Master Barry.

Someone shouted, and Tolan turned his attention toward them. The ground surged, rolling violently near the edge of Terndahl.

Not just the edge of Terndahl, but along the border of the waste.

An elemental. He was certain of it.

Why would there be an elemental out here?

As far as he knew, the elementals were never found near the waste. There was no power out here for them, and they had remained deeper within Terndahl when they did appear. He started forward, stumbling as he neared the others, and grabbed for Jonas and Ferrah. Both were getting to their feet unsteadily, and Jonas in particular looked around, his eyes wide.

"What was that?" Ferrah asked.

"Is it some part of a test? Were they trying to scare us?"

Tolan shook his head. "I don't think this is a part of it. Look," he said, pointing toward the surging ground. It was strange the way the ground seemed to undulate, moving. There was something there, deep beneath it, and as he stared, he realized he could *feel* it.

He shouldn't be able to feel anything moving beneath the ground, not from here, but there was no question that was what he detected.

And if that was what he detected, then it was certainly an elemental. There was no shaping that would perform like that.

All of a sudden, the ground erupted.

Master Shorav raced forward, a shaping starting to build, and the ground collapsed. Master Sartan was there, adding a rising heat. Tolan could only stare. The power between the two was enormous. It seemed as if Master Shorav added a hint of fire to his earth shaping while Master Sartan used some earth, complementary elements when it came to overpowering the other.

"Keep moving, students," a voice said behind him.

He glanced back to see Master Marcella, a young and lovely master shaper. She was only a few years removed from the Academy, and reportedly incredibly powerful. She had stayed on to continue her training with Master Shorav, and he was surprised she guided the students away rather than going to help her mentor.

"What's happening?" someone asked.

"Keep moving," Master Marcella said, guiding them away. "We can deal with this when it's over."

"Is that an *elemental*?" someone screamed.

Tolan glanced over to see that Matthew, a shaper nearly Tolan's own age, and one who—like him—had really only connected to a single element bond, pointed toward Master Sartan and Master Shorav, who continued to hold their shaping. Despite that, there was ongoing surging, power that pulsed as if trying to rise from the ground.

"If it is, does any of you want to be near it?" Master Marcella asked, her voice far calmer than Tolan would have expected.

The students began running. He hesitated, his gaze lingering on where the master shapers were working. He felt someone pulling on his sleeve, only to realize it was Ferrah. She looked at him, trying to urge him with her gaze.

"I'm just trying to see..."

"I know what you're trying to see, and you need to get moving."

Strangely, there was a sense of power within him. It

was a pressure, yet more than just a pressure, it was like a reverberation. A calling.

Why should he feel that?

Stranger still, the sense of reverberation came through the bondar. There was no question that was what he felt.

When he let go of the bondar, the sense faded but did not disappear completely. Either the fact that he held onto it connected him in some way, or the power was enough that he was able to feel it regardless of whether he was holding onto the bondar.

"Tolan!"

He glanced over at Ferrah. "I'm coming," he said, backing up a step.

He couldn't take his eyes off Master Shorav and Master Sartan, whose shaping was incredibly powerful, the power rising from it and slamming into the ground, though despite that, the earth still trembled. Was that the nature of the earth elemental straining to escape or was there something else?

The winds shifted. Whereas before it had been comfortable, warm and typical for Terndahl, now it was hot. It came out of the east, and as it did, it carried with it the heat of the waste, but there was more. Sand came with it, blasting against him, and it forced him to throw his arm up over his face to prevent the sand from slamming into him, from burning through his eyes and mouth.

The wind was shaped. Tolan could feel it, and he worried why it would be shaped?

Master Wassa, who had been still bent over Master

Barry, stood and held his hands outward. The shaping that built from him was an enormous, powerful surge causing the skies to darken and clouds to form. Thunder rumbled.

As rain began to fall, it struck the sand in the air and forced it down to the ground. Master Rorn pulled on a wind shaping, sweeping away from them. As he did, the pain from the sudden gusts waned, but it seemed as if the wind swirled around them, coming from behind them to slam into him with just as much force from the back as it had from the other side. Sand seem to get everywhere, crawling down his cloak, along his spine, working down his shirt and mixing with his sweat.

Screams reverberated as everyone panicked, sprinting away.

Was this an elemental or a shaping?

Tolan didn't move, remaining transfixed. In the time he'd come to the edge of the waste, he had never imagined it would be so active.

If this all was some sort of shaping, there would have to be shapers.

More than that, they weren't nearby—which meant they were in the waste, but the waste was devoid of the power of the element bonds.

Perhaps it wasn't as devoid of the elemental power, though.

Ferrah grabbed him and pulled, and this time, Tolan didn't resist. He staggered back and they chased the others as they retreated, racing backward, heading deeper into Terndahl. The master shapers, including Master Marcella, had all abandoned herding the students and now they focused on shaping, opposing whatever was taking place. They stood in a line, nearly a dozen master shapers, and the power surging outward from them was like nothing Tolan had ever seen. Even when they had been in the Convergence, connected to that deep power from which Jory was trying to raise an elemental power, he hadn't felt anything quite like that.

"What's happening?" Jonas asked. His voice was high-pitched, his eyes were wide, and he jerked his head around with each movement near them.

Wind continued to howl around them, and every so often, the ground rumbled, forcing Tolan to focus on his footsteps to ensure he wasn't tossed to one side while rain continued to pelt down on them. The wind continued swirling around. He was no longer certain how much of it came from the master shapers attempting to resist whatever was taking place and how much of this came from the shaping or the elementals that were attacking.

"Keep moving," Ferrah said.

Tolan knew that he should be moving, but a part of him wanted to know what was taking place. That part of him wanted to experience the majesty of this power.

He could feel it. After returning from the waste, the sudden return of his ability to detect shapings was incredible, and he held onto it, clinging to that sense, afraid he'd forget what it felt like.

Maybe that was why shapers feared going out into the waste.

Was there anything he could do?

"We need to help," he said.

"Help with what?" Ferrah asked.

"I don't know, but the master shapers need us."

"We're students. We're *first*-year students," Jonas said.

"We are, but that doesn't mean that we don't have some abilities."

As he watched, the master shapers were forced back a step.

He jerked his arm free from Ferrah and raced forward, taking up a position near the Grand Master. "We can help."

The Grand Master had his jaw clenched and glanced over at Tolan before finally nodding. "Any additional power would be helpful. Search for what you feel. Resist it."

"How?"

"There is a connection within you to the elements, Shaper Ethar." Despite how strained he looked, he sounded far calmer. "Use that connection."

"I can only reach fire."

"Then counter earth."

Tolan gripped the furios and focused on what he could detect. He had felt the earth rumbling first, so finding where that was taking place wasn't difficult. It rumbled all around them, though now it was in front of him.

It seemed as if the ground strained, trying to throw them back, pushing them. Almost involuntarily, he took a step backward and realized he wasn't the only one. The line of master shapers all backed up a step, withdrawing from the power of the shaping.

As he focused on the rumbling, he used the furios, connecting to fire, feeling the way it surged within him. It came slowly, a fluttering, then it burst out from him.

Tolan kept his focus on the ground, letting the power of the flame strike it. It seemed to him that his shaping took on the form of hyza, an elemental of fire, but also of earth. Each of his shapings seemed to take on aspects of elemental power, and this was no different. Sometimes, it seemed to him that he was the only one who recognized that. In this case, it was difficult to tell whether it was his shaping that took on the form of an elemental or whether it was more the fact there were elementals that seemed to be attacking him.

Tolan held onto his shaping, letting that power flow from him. He focused on his intent, using the knowledge they'd learned over the last few months, pushing it against the sense of earth.

Additional power began flickering near him and he hazarded a glance down the line of master shapers, realizing other students had joined.

Not all of them. Tolan couldn't blame those who avoided it—he was just as afraid, only he feared doing nothing more.

Still, the additional power pushed back against the shaping. It happened slowly—too slowly—and finally, the ground gradually ceased rumbling. The wind began to slow, then shifted directions. The heat dissipated. Only the rain persisted, but it rolled up to the border of the waste before stopping. Tolan continued to hold onto a shaping and realized he might be one of the few who still did.

He released his connection, and the image of the hyza elemental flickered before disappearing completely. It seemed to him that the elemental—at least the shape of it, as he wasn't completely convinced it was an elemental—glanced back at him before it disappeared. That had to be his imagination, didn't it?

He looked around. Most of the students who had joined the master shapers had collapsed to the ground. Ferrah still stood, and Draln, but the others had sunk to their knees or their backsides, staring out into the waste. The master shapers remained standing, and Tolan wondered if it was a matter of strength that allowed some to stand while others no longer could. That didn't seem quite right, especially as he didn't view himself as particularly strong with his shaping, though perhaps it was the fact that he had been shaping through the bondar.

"Gather the students," the Grand Master said.

The master shapers all began to move the students, helping some on the ground to stand while a few needed to be carried. Tolan stared out at the waste and pondered what had just taken place.

It had been an attack, but why here and why now?

"Keep moving, Shaper Ethar," Master Wassa said.

Tolan glanced over at him. Sweat beaded across his brow, more than he'd ever seen on the man. Worry lines wrinkled his forehead and the corners of his eyes. There was a stoop to his back.

How much energy had Master Wassa—and the other master shapers—expended in order to stop whatever this had been?

"What was this?" he asked.

Master Wassa didn't answer. He only pushed Tolan to join the other students. Tolan followed, and when he reached Ferrah, he slid his arm under her shoulders, keeping her upright. Jonas stumbled more than Tolan expected he would.

"What was that?" Ferrah whispered.

"I don't know. It felt like a shaping, but there were elementals." Tolan cast a glance back. The master shapers were all congregated together, and many looked out toward the heart of the waste, though none was shaping. If they were attacked again, Tolan wondered if they would have enough strength to resist it. Could the attack this time have been almost too much?

"I didn't think the waste was supposed to have shaping like that," Jonas said.

"I didn't come from the waste. It came from Terndahl," Ferrah said.

"It may have attacked us in Terndahl, but I think the first one came from the waste," Tolan said.

There was a distinct sense that whatever strange attack he had observed first, the strange rumbling had emanated from the other side of the border of the waste. There was no question in his mind it had come from there. But then, there was also the wind that had gusted in, blasting them with the heat and sand from out in the waste. That had to have been from the other side. It shouldn't have been possible, not with what they knew about the waste.

"There's nothing out there," Ferrah said.

"I saw movement when I was out there," Tolan said.

She looked up at him, a question in her eyes. It was almost an accusation, the kind of thing that he was far too familiar with from his time in Ephra. It was the same way people had looked at him when his parents had disappeared. It was an accusation that said he sided with the Draasin Lord.

"I don't know what it was, and the Grand Master didn't either," he said hurriedly, wanting to point out that he hadn't been alone out there. It hadn't been his fault, and he didn't need his friends to believe it somehow had been.

"What kind of movement?" Ferrah asked, glancing over her shoulder to look back. They were far enough away now that the masters were difficult to make out clearly. Pretty soon, they would be able to shape their way up to the Shapers Path, and from there, they could focus on returning to Amitan and the Academy. It was where they wanted to go. After everything else, Tolan wanted nothing more than to get back to the Academy and resume the normalcy of his studies.

Since his arrival at the Academy, there hadn't been any normality. First, there had been the elemental attacks, and then there had been the students who had been injured, and then he had discovered Jory had been a part of it. That wasn't what time at the Academy was supposed to be like. He was supposed to have a chance to focus and learn —and see if he could reach for various different element bonds.

"I don't know. It looked like a shadow, but it moved far faster than any shadow should have been able to move," he said.

"If it wasn't a shadow, then what do you think it was?"

"Like I said, I don't know. The Grand Master didn't, either." The Grand Master hadn't seen it.

"Someone must have released the elementals when we were on the other side of the border," Jonas said.

Tolan didn't want to continue arguing the point, but that wasn't what he thought about it at all. He didn't think it had come from their side of the waste. Whatever had happened, it seemed to him that it had come from the other side.

Only… The other side of the waste was not supposed to have any sort of connection to the element bonds, so how was that even possible?

He looked ahead. Several of the students had already begun to shape their way up to the Shapers Path. It took a burst of power, and prior to his time in the Academy, Tolan wouldn't have been able to reach the path on his own. Even now, he wasn't entirely sure he had the necessary strength, especially after having spent so much of himself. Several of the students must have been in the same situation, as they sat, arms resting on their legs, heads propped up, and as he approached, he saw glazed eyes.

"Are you able to reach the path?" Tolan asked Ferrah and Jonas.

Ferrah nodded and then let out a heavy sigh. "I think I can."

"I... I don't know." Jonas looked from one to the other. "I might need one of the master shapers to help."

"I can help you," Ferrah said. She turned her attention to Tolan. "What about you?"

"I think I can manage."

"If you get off course..."

"Then I'll fall."

"You could wait."

"I think I would like to be above all of this," he said. Once he was above the ground, it was much easier to hurry along the Shapers Path. There was something about it that expedited movement so that distances didn't matter. Reaching Amitan would take the better part of the day, but once he was on the Path, he didn't need to fear the elemental attack.

Ferrah began to shape, wind and fire swirling around her, lifting her and Jonas up.

Tolan dipped his hand into his pocket, gripping the furios. Focusing on it, he imagined saa this time, rather than hyza. Each time he connected to the elementals, he imagined a different one, though most of the time, he defaulted to hyza. Saa had a different connection to him, and using that, he was able to launch himself into the air.

There was more control within it than there would be had he used hyza. After what he had just done, he wasn't sure he wanted to draw upon hyza.

The students lining the Shapers Path overhead gave him a target, and as he rose higher and higher, he realized he hadn't angled himself quite right.

He tried to shift the connection, but something pushed against him.

Great Mother!

Tolan focused, straining to redirect, but he was going to overshoot the Shapers Path.

And then something grabbed him. It seemed like a rope of wind wrapped around him and it pulled him, drawing him toward the Shapers Path and Ferrah. When he landed, he released his shaping and let out a shaky breath.

"Thanks," he said.

"That was Jonas," she said.

Jonas shrugged. "I might not have had enough strength to reach the Shapers Path, but to pull you in doesn't take a whole lot."

Tolan turned his attention to the distance, looking out toward the edge of the waste. From here, it was difficult to see, but the vantage had some benefits. He could make out the boundary, and it was quite clear the way the green grass shifted to brown and then quickly to rock. The waste was bleak, an emptiness, and made him feel as if all he wanted to do was run in the other direction, especially after what they had just gone through.

There was something else about it though.

"What do you think of it?" he asked Ferrah.

"I think I don't want to return. I can't believe you grew up so close to it."

"It wasn't like that when I was growing up," he said.

"You mean the waste didn't attack you?"

"We didn't spend that much time near it. Something about it seems off, though."

"Ever since we came here, something's seemed off, Tolan," Ferrah said.

"This is different."

He stared at it, trying to determine what gave him that feeling. Maybe it was simply the fact he had just been attacked out there, or maybe it was that the master shapers still stood, now in something of a line. They were staggered, and from here, Tolan could feel just the beginnings of a shaping and wondered what they were doing and why they felt the need to continue shaping. Was more happening?

He didn't think so. There was no shifting wind and no rumbling of the ground, nothing else suggesting the shaping went awry. There was nothing other than the vast emptiness of the waste.

Why then did he feel as if there was something out there?

"The border seems different," Jonas said.

"What?" Ferrah said.

Jonas frowned. He was holding onto a shaping, enough of one that suggested to Tolan he was using it to peer out toward the waste. What sort of shaping would allow him to do that?

"The border. There's something about it that doesn't seem quite the same."

Tolan stared. "I don't see it."

There came a fluttering in front of his face and everything suddenly surged closer.

"A trick I learned in Velminth."

Tolan stared through the shaping of wind and realized what Jonas said was true. Something about the border of the waste was different. It was a little irregular, whereas before, it had been nearly a complete line. And as he watched, it seemed to him that it continued to creep inward, pushing toward the heart of Terndahl.

His breath caught. The intent of the shaping suddenly made sense to him.

"How long had they said the boundary with the waste had remained the same?" he asked.

"For centuries," Ferrah said. "The waste hasn't shifted one way or the other for countless years. That's why the people of Terndahl feel comfortable having cities like your home near it."

"Whatever that was, it seems it just changed," he said.

And from the way the masters were shaping, Tolan suspected they knew, but if they knew, was there anything they could do about it? From what he'd already heard, there was no way to push back the boundary of the waste, regardless of how strong a shaping someone used.

3

THE AIR WAS HOT AND ALMOST SHAPED, THOUGH TOLAN wasn't certain that was what he detected. His ability to sense shapings wasn't honed very well yet, though the more he continued to work with the furios, the better acquainted he became with ways of detecting shapings that he had never known before. It wasn't that he was skilled—far from it—but with the furios, he was able to be so much more.

"What do you detect, Shaper Ethar?"

Tolan glanced over at Master Marcella. She had more patience than others when it came to working with him. He was thankful for that, if only because she allowed him the opportunity to practice without any judgment over the fact he needed his furios in order to succeed.

Then again, Tolan hid his use of the furios, not wanting others to know he was so dependent upon it, almost as if he was afraid of others discovering the fact he didn't necessarily shape the same way they did.

"I don't detect anything."

She frowned, the expression souring her attractiveness. Since working with her, Tolan had to try to ignore that, but seeing as how she was only a few years older than him—and much younger than many of the master shapers—it was difficult. She had dark hair, which she made no attempt to bind behind her head as most master shapers did. She wore a jacket and pants, preferring the style of the men over the flowing gowns of the women. When she pressed her lips together as she frowned at him, there was something almost angry to it—and he'd do anything to keep her from getting angry.

"We've been out here the better part of an hour and you don't detect anything?"

Tolan swept his gaze around. They were well outside of Amitan, the city that was home to the Academy, making exploring shapings too easy—at least, according to Marcella. She preferred to step outside of the boundaries of the Academy and test him in a different way. In the days since they'd been back from the edge of the waste, everything had gotten back to normal—or as normal as they could be. He and Ferrah had been researching the waste, but they hadn't come up with any answer about how the border could have shifted.

He and Marcella were near a narrow stream, the water moving slowly, all part of her desire for him to use that in his shapings. A wind gusted, blowing across the landscape.

With the heat in the air, it seemed almost as if this was her way of trying to ensure he would detect each of the elementals, though he didn't know how much of this was from the elemental bonds and how much shaped by Marcella in her attempt to instruct him.

"By now, you should have detected something," she said.

Tolan closed his eyes, squeezing them shut as he focused. He strained to reach the element bond, searching for some way of calling on that power. It should be there, but for whatever reason, it simply didn't come to him the way it came to so many others.

Using the furios, he called on that power, pulling through it, and felt the familiar stirring within him. It still troubled him that he should have that connection to the elementals, and to fire elementals in particular. And yet, the longer he focused through the furios, the easier it became to do any sort of shaping. Wasn't that what he was after?

He had discovered the more power he put through the furios, the likelier it was he would call upon an elemental. In this place, the dangers of summoning an elemental weren't nearly as significant as they would be in other places. Nothing like when the elemental had been freed within the city or whatever had happened on the edge of the waste, but still, he had no interest in releasing an elemental from the bond again.

"I feel each of the elements, if that's what you are getting at."

Marcella studied him, and Tolan worried he'd offended her again. It didn't take much to upset her, and it seemed he had a knack for it; everything he'd done seemed to irritate her.

"That is what I'm getting at, Shaper Ethar. What can you tell me about the various elements you detect?"

"I can feel the presence of each of them."

"That's too easy of an answer, and something I would expect the earliest students just learning of their sensing to answer. From you, someone who approaches the second year at the Academy, I would expect a much more robust response. In order to progress through your second year, you need to be able to describe the elements. That is why I have you out here, Shaper Ethar. If you aren't able to describe the elements and are not able to describe in detail what you're able to sense, you won't be able to move on."

Tolan nodded quickly. There were several different tests along the way through the Academy. Getting in was hard enough, but there were other tests, and he didn't know what they were. Older students were forbidden from discussing them, though rumors abounded.

Reaching the spirit classroom had been difficult, and since he had been able to use his connection to the furios, he had succeeded, though he wasn't sure whether he had cheated—or if it even mattered.

The next step in his progression through the Academy would be more difficult. It was designed that way, intending for only the most capable to progress through each level, but Tolan didn't view himself as one of these.

He had passed the Selection, which meant some part of him was able to be a shaper of the Academy. Which element should he focus on first? That seemed to be what Marcella wanted from him, but he wasn't sure exactly how to describe the elements. He was aware of them in a vague sort of sense, and while he, like most, had a connection to the element bonds and could sense them, anything more than that wasn't usually within his capabilities. Most of the time, it was outside his grasp.

Fire.

Through his use of the furios, he had a connection to fire, though it was a different sort of connection than he possessed with the other elements. Was there anything he could detect about fire?

He touched the furios in his pocket. As he focused on fire, as he felt for the warmth of it within the air, the stirring through the furios called to him.

There were strange eddies flowing through everything. Heat comprised all living things, connecting them. As he focused on that, he was aware of it in a way he hadn't been otherwise. Those connections flowed through him. It was what he focused on first of all, but they also flowed through Marcella, and as he shifted his awareness away from himself and over to the master shaper, he could feel the way she was the one using the heat, and that it was radiating from some place deep within her. The longer he focused on it, the more he could practically see the way it was a part of her, but also separate from her.

When he had connected to the furios before, he had detected similar currents of shapings. Recognizing it came from Marcella wasn't anything new, but it was how it was connected to her that he found himself taken by. Her shaping came from a place deep within her, drawn out and connecting to the air, her power channeled outward, creating that connection between the element bond and the heat in the air.

Tolan could practically see it. There was enough power there that he focused upon it, but even that left him feeling different. Anything he might do would be very different from the way Marcella shaped.

Without turning to her, he connected to his shaping, drawing upon the power through the furios; he attempted to subtly add to what she had done. He wasn't certain he would even be able to do much, and it was unlikely he would be able to match the way she held a warmth within the air. Mostly, Tolan was curious about whether or not he could add to her shaping and whether it would resemble the way she pulled power.

"You've been silent long enough," Marcella said.

"I can sense how there is shaped heat in the air. I can sense how that heat comes from deep within you, and that your shaping is what has turned the air, making it warmer." A flicker of movement behind her caught his attention and his breath caught. He made a point of not looking beyond her, not wanting to bring her attention to the fact there was an elemental now prowling at her rear, but how could she not know?

And it was his fault.

Anytime he used the furios, he somehow pulled elementals from the element bond. It was dangerous to do so, but it was also dangerous for those elementals to be allowed to roam freely. Even after everything he'd been through, he still believed that, believing the elementals were dangerous.

Worse, he wasn't sure it *was* an elemental. It might only be his shaping.

"Shaper Ethar?"

Tolan blinked, keeping his gaze on her rather than looking beyond. He didn't need to look in order to know and feel the elemental. More than even his connection to the heat in the air from her shaping, the connection to the elemental was potent, and that power filled him.

He could draw upon it. Now the elemental had been freed or summoned—Tolan didn't know which it was, and a part of him hoped it was only that he'd summoned the elemental rather than freeing it—he had a much greater connection to power.

Not just a connection to power, but an awareness of fire and the nature of it. Mostly, he could feel the elemental nearby, a small creature resembling a fox, though made entirely of flame. The elemental remained hidden, as if a creature of fire like that could hide. Tolan could practically feel the elemental watching him, as if waiting, trying to determine what Tolan might do, but there was nothing he could do. He didn't have the necessary power to push the elemental back into the bond, and wasn't certain he had the desire, either.

"Ethar!"

He blinked, focusing on her again.

"I can sense the way you're working your shaping. You have twisted it in such a way you intend only the air around the two of us to be shaped," Tolan said. As he used the elemental, as he focused on that bond, he realized that was true. It was a localized effect, nothing more, and it wasn't as if Marcella was trying to shape extensively. It was almost as if she intended to shape only so that he and she were aware of it.

"Keep going," she said.

"I don't know what else to say."

"You're focusing on fire, so focus on what effect you can sense of the shaping."

"I can detect the way you hold it." Tolan could practically see the shaping as it influenced the air around them. There wasn't any reason he should be able to see something like that. Detecting a shaping, sensing it, was something very different, but being able to actually see the shaping?

That shouldn't be something he could do.

"I don't know anything more," he said.

Marcella watched him, her lips still pressed tightly in a frown, and she shook her head. "That's unfortunate," she said, turning away. She released her shaping and the heat extinguished, but so too did the wind, along with the steady flowing of the water and even the pressure upon him coming from the earth. All of her shaping suddenly relaxed.

She started away from him, but stopped, freezing in place.

"Shaper Ethar, you need to stay back."

"Why?"

"There's something dangerous here," she said.

"What?" His body tensed, and he knew she must have detected the elemental. Now she did, what would she do with it?

Ever since they had found the Convergence, Tolan had been aware that some elementals at least were helpful. It was possible not all were, and he acknowledged some were even dangerous. He had seen the destruction caused by certain elementals, but others were clearly helpful. At least to him.

More than that, it meant this wasn't just a shaping but a true elemental.

He didn't know whether this foxlike elemental was helpful or not but had a sense it wasn't dangerous. If it were, it would have attacked, or would have attempted to destroy, but there'd been nothing other than his sense that the elemental was there, practically watching them.

"There's a rogue elemental," she said. "I can feel it, but I'm not entirely certain where to find it. I don't want it to spring out on you before you have a chance to get away."

Tolan swallowed, trying to force moisture down his throat. She couldn't see the elemental? It was there, barely only ten paces away from her, though hidden behind the tree. Even as the elemental hid, he knew it didn't do so all that well. The tree concealed part of the elemental but did nothing to hide the heat flowing from it, nor did it do anything to prevent Tolan seeing it.

Why could Marcella not see it?

"What do you intend to do with it?" he asked.

She glanced over her shoulder at him, her frown deepening. "You've been at the Academy long enough to know the answer to that, Shaper Ethar. The elementals are dangerous, which is why they must stay a part of the bond. When they go rogue, they are incredibly destructive. Entire cities have been ravaged by them."

As much as Tolan had the sense that the elementals weren't dangerous—at least, not all of them—he had seen the destruction they caused. Even when there were master shapers around, men and women capable of containing the elementals and confining them back within the bond, they had caused significant damage.

This creature seemed timid, almost shy, yet curious. The elemental had approached and remained hidden despite the fact Marcella had an enormous shaping of heat washing over her.

"What's involved in replacing the elementals within the bond?"

"For the most part, we wrap the bond energy around them," she said, taking a step forward.

Tolan waved at the elemental, trying to encourage the creature to move on, even to disappear, but it didn't. It stayed, watching, and the longer it did, the more likely it was that something was going to happen to it.

"Does it hurt the elemental when you do that?"

"Hurt?"

Tolan nodded. "These are creatures, aren't they?"

"They aren't creatures in the same sense of the word as others, Shaper Ethar. They don't have any way of hurting, not like you or I."

"Can they die?"

She paused and spun toward him. "What?"

Tolan shrugged. "Can they die? I'm just trying to understand more about the elementals."

"They have a long lifespan, if that's what you fear. And while we don't know whether they are immortal or not, they are unlikely to feel pain when we place them back within the bond."

"*Unlikely* doesn't mean they don't," he said.

He needed to be careful with this line of questioning. It was possible he would anger Marcella. He had enough issues at the Academy as it was and didn't need to have another master shaper upset with him. He needed her willingness to work with him, to help him, so he could continue to progress. He was tired of lagging behind.

"Do you think we should be more tolerant to the elementals?" Marcella asked softly.

"I don't know. I've been studying some of the ancient history, looking back at the time when it seems the elementals were freed, and it didn't seem as if they were dangerous then."

"The elementals were freed, but we didn't have the same control over our power as we do now. Think of everything we've done with shaping. You can see it with the Academy and everything within Terndahl, Shaper Ethar. Without our connection to shaping, without our ability to have done what we have, the city wouldn't ever have become the place that it is, and it is a place of power. We owe all of that to the element bonds and the way we can draw power from them."

Tolan studied her, considering debating, but he wondered how many of the master shapers understood it was more than the element bonds that kept Terndahl safe. It had just as much to do with the place of Convergence as with the element bonds. Were it not for that convergence, a place that drew considerable power, he doubted Terndahl would have flourished.

"Is it still here?"

Marcella looked around, still frowning. "I can't detect it. Perhaps it has disappeared."

Tolan made a show of spinning around, but as he did, he could still see the elemental nearby. He could still feel the power coming off it. He almost smiled to himself. At least the elemental had realized it needed to hide, if nothing else, so she didn't harm it.

"The Trackers must be alerted," Marcella said.

"*We* could track it," he said.

"That is not our responsibility. And the others have more skill at such things, not to mention after what happened at the waste..."

"What about what happened at the waste?"

"It's nothing."

"I was there. I know it's not nothing."

She scanned the forest before turning back to him. "The grand master suspects it was an attempt to release more rogue elementals within Terndahl."

"Why would they do that?" He glanced at the elemental, which still hid. Perhaps it had nothing to do with him and everything to do with the Draasin Lord.

She frowned at him. "They seek to upset the balance of power, Shaper Ethar. The easiest way for them to do that is in releasing elementals that distract our focus away from Amitan. As it is, we are spread thin chasing them."

Tolan hadn't heard that. "The Trackers are spread thin?"

"All of us. With as many rogue elementals as we've discovered, even master shapers have been drawn after them."

The Trackers would be brutal when it came to the elementals. He'd seen the way they combated rogue elementals before and how quickly they took care of them, dispatching them in a way that seemed almost brutal. The idea of the Trackers doing the same thing to the smallish elemental he'd seen, one that seemed nothing but curious, bothered him.

If only he had a greater control over his connection to the elements, and a better understanding of how to use the furios, he might be able to make it seem as if the elemental had returned to the bond. Far safer still would be for him just to encourage the elemental to disappear. If the Trackers couldn't find the elemental, they wouldn't be able to force it back into the bond and then there would be nothing they would do that would harm the creature. Regardless of what Marcella said, he had a sense that forcing the elemental into the bond did cause harm.

"It's time to return, Shaper Ethar."

With a shaping, she streaked upward.

Tolan hesitated. She expected him to follow, but first he wanted to check on something.

He started toward the tree where the elemental hid, pulling the furios from his pocket and moving quickly but carefully. He needed to get this over with before Marcella realized something was amiss and returned. The moment she did, he would run the risk of her realizing he had some connection to the elementals. Other questions would arise. They were the kind of questions he intended to avoid. They were the kind of questions he had avoided asking himself.

"I'm not going to hurt you, but you need to get moving," he whispered.

The elemental crawled forward. Hyza looked much like a fox but larger, and made entirely of flame, and heat radiated off it, but not unpleasantly so. That heat stretched from the elemental to Tolan, swirling, and probed him almost tentatively.

"She's gone, but I don't know how long she'll be gone," he said, glancing toward the sky overhead. Already, Marcella would have questions about why he had taken so long to return. And he could deflect those questions by pretending to be unable to follow, but he worried that wouldn't be enough. She was a master shaper, and she was clever. "You need to get moving before others come. She intends to alert the Trackers, and—"

The elemental began to shake.

Heat shimmered around it and when it shook, Tolan couldn't help but feel the same agitation the elemental must be feeling. It was as if the elemental wanted him to know, and as he focused on it, he realized what it was that troubled it.

The Trackers.

"You fear them?"

The elemental continued to shake and took a step back.

It was even more reason to believe the Trackers were brutal. More than that, it suggested the elementals were aware of the Trackers and what they did. Did that mean the Trackers harmed them? From everything he had seen, the elementals had wanted to come out of the bond, which was why forcing them back left him troubled.

"You need to hide. Or return to your bond." Tolan didn't know whether that was possible.

He turned his attention upward and could feel the heat from Marcella's shaping.

"I need to go, but you need to keep yourself safe."

He pushed off with a shaping of fire, launching himself toward the distant Shapers Path. As he went, he watched as the elemental remained frozen in place. It might only be his imagination, but the creature seemed as if it still trembled.

Tolan wished there was something different that he could do, and wished there was some way he could ensure the Trackers didn't harm the elemental, but what was there? He was not powerful enough, not by a long shot, and even if he were, what would he do?

When he reached the Shapers Path, Marcella watched him. "What took you so long?"

"I had a little trouble with my shaping," Tolan said.

She pressed her lips together again in a deep frown. "I'm glad you managed to get it together. I don't have any interest in carrying you back to Terndahl."

He forced a smile and she started off, leaving Tolan to follow. He glanced back down to the ground, and though he couldn't see the small elemental, he had an awareness of the creature and worried he was leaving it there to die.

4

THE GROUNDS OF THE ACADEMY WERE WELL KEPT, NEATLY groomed, with all of the shrubbery shaped to look like various animals. The greenery lining the central courtyard always astounded Tolan, especially when he returned after being outside the city and experiencing what it was like in other places. Amitan was unique within Terndahl, a place that possessed dozens and dozens of shapers of various capacities. It was so different than what it had been like in Ephra, a relatively large city on the border of Terndahl with only a few master shapers. There were shapers within Ephra, though only four Tolan knew about who had trained at the Academy.

"You have the afternoon to yourself," Marcella said.

She strode away, heading into the Academy, leaving Tolan alone. He debated following her. He could return to his quarters in the Academy, perhaps go to the library and continue his studies, but there weren't too many days on which he had complete freedom, and he liked the idea of being able to spend it outside. Besides, in the months he'd been in Amitan, he had yet to fully explore the city.

He didn't really want to do it alone, which meant looking for one of his friends. Jonas was working with his mentor, which meant he would be unavailable, especially as Master Yael could be quite demanding. Ferrah should still be around, and rather than going off on his own, Tolan decided to go and see if he could find her.

He paused at the wide double door leading into the Academy. The markings upon the door were powerful, runes representing each of the various elementals, but he only recognized a few. He wondered if he would ever understand them all, though that was something for more advanced shapers, which he most definitely was not. Until he managed to reach the other elements more effectively, learning about things such as the runes would be beyond him. Anything he'd learned so far had been on his own, and almost accidental rather than intentional.

He paused in front of the door, tracing one of the marks he recognized. It was a triangle with a single shape at the center, one he had come to realize represented spirit. Ever since stopping Jory at the Convergence, Tolan had realized he must have some other connection to spirit than he had ever known. Having seen this rune at the place of Convergence, Tolan had realized he'd seen the same shape before. Those memories were faint, difficult to reach, but they were there, buried within him.

The door opened and Tolan tore his gaze away and

glanced up at Master Sartan as he emerged, his flowing robes fluttering behind him.

He cast a sharp glance at Tolan before pausing. "Shaper Ethar. What are you doing out here? Aren't you supposed to be in your studies?"

"Marcella released me for the day," he said.

As Master Sartan pressed his lips together in a frown, Tolan realized he had been far too familiar with the other shaper. Marcella allowed him to call her by her first name, but few other shapers did. They preferred to be referred to by their honorific, and though it didn't matter quite as much to Tolan, there were some to whom it mattered quite a bit.

"Even if you have some time off, you should still spend it wisely."

"I intend to go to the library," he said. At least that wasn't a lie. He figured he would find Ferrah in the library, if he found her anywhere. She would be unlikely to be in the students' quarters, and if she were still in the Academy buildings, the library would be the place where she spent most of her time. Though she had been shaped, memories of their time in the Convergence wiped away, she still chased knowledge of power similar to what would be found in Par.

"Then don't let me keep you."

Tolan was tempted to find out what he was up to, but questioning a master shaper, especially one who instructed and led one of his classes, wasn't a good idea. Master Sartan might have tolerated him, but there would be limits to his tolerance, and Tolan anticipated there would come a time when he would exceed those limits. He had very nearly done that already with his failure to improve as rapidly as some of the master shapers would've preferred.

Hurrying inside, he discovered the Academy was far more active than it often was at this time of day. A few other first-year students made their way through the hallways, talking quietly, though none was someone he was altogether close to, other than Wallace, who roomed with him. A few older students wandered the halls, but he didn't know them, either.

He veered off the main entrance and headed toward the library. The Academy library was enormous, several stories high, and seemed to be half of the main part of the Academy itself. Tables filled most of the open space, and an elevated dais at the far end of the room provided seating for two of the master librarians. Neither looked up as he entered, though Tolan wondered if they were aware of him. A tingling washed across his skin as he entered the library, a sensation that could be from whatever wards had been placed along the library to prevent others from shaping within it, or it could be from Master Minden, the master librarian whom Tolan still suspected of having the ability to shape within the library.

As he paused and scanned the students, his gaze fell upon Ferrah. Her bright red hair had been braided down the back of her flat gray student robe. Her head was bowed as she leaned over a book flopped open on the table.

As he approached her, Master Minden glanced in his direction. He flashed a smile, though doubted his smiling would do anything to influence her. Most viewed her the way his friend Jonas did, as nothing more than a senile shaper. Tolan knew better.

Master Minden was incredibly knowledgeable, particularly when it came to the elementals. It was because of her that his knowledge and understanding of the elementals had continued to grow, and it was because of her that he had books on the elementals stored in his room, ones he had been allowed to borrow, something very few students would normally be allowed.

He took a seat across from Ferrah but she didn't look up. "Don't bother me today."

"And why would you think I would bother you?"

"You're done with your studying with Marcella already, so I know you want a distraction. I'm trying to find what I can about the waste." She looked up. "You know, you *could* help like you promised."

"How could you know I'm done studying already?"

"Because you're here."

"Just because I'm here doesn't mean I want a distraction, and it certainly doesn't mean you should ignore me like that."

Irritation flashed in her green eyes. She normally smiled easily, but today her face was drawn, the lines around her mouth tight.

"What is it?"

"It's something Master Jensen provided to me." She pushed the book over to him.

Tolan looked down at the page. It was a flowing script, written in a language he didn't know, but knowing her it was probably Par, though he had no idea what it might say. He frowned at it before looking up at her and shaking his head. "I don't really know what you're trying to show me."

"Don't you remember what I've been researching?"

"Par?" She frowned and he leaned forward. "I know what you've been researching, but I don't think there's any way of finding what you think you will."

To keep up appearances, Tolan hadn't shared with her or Jonas that they had found a Convergence. Presumably, they all had been spirit-shaped, which meant none should recall anything about the Convergence, though when Master Irina had shaped him, he had somehow retained his memories. Either she had intended for him to do so, or her spirit shaping had failed for some reason. He still hadn't figured out why or what that might mean, but a nagging part of him wondered if perhaps he didn't have some capacity to use spirit. If he did, how—and *when*— would he ever reach it?

"According to this volume, there are references to the power I've been telling you exists in Par."

"And I assume this is written in Par?"

"Why?"

"Because I can't read it. I don't know what it says or what you're trying to show me."

"You really should work a little harder at your studies. There are things you can learn in the language of others. You don't need to be so focused on what you might find in Terndahl."

"Just tell me what you are getting at, Ferrah."

"I'm getting at the fact that everything I've been suspecting all leads me to the same truth."

He tried to keep his face neutral but didn't know if he succeeded. He couldn't have her knowing that he already had experience with the Convergence, the power she searched for. If she knew, would she go looking for it? It wouldn't be safe for her to do so, but at the same time, Tolan didn't want to betray her. Already, it felt like a betrayal keeping from her his knowledge of the Convergence.

"You don't believe me."

"It's not that I don't believe you, it's just—"

"Shaper Ethar," Master Minden said, sliding soundlessly up to the table. She leaned forward, resting her wrinkled and crooked hands on the surface of the table. "Do you still have those volumes I have lent you?"

When he looked up at her face, noticing her milky eyes, he understood how easy it would be for people to mistake her for old and confused, but that would be an error. Master Minden still had an incredibly sharp mind, and with that came knowledge he hadn't experienced from anyone else, not even from the Grand Master himself.

"Do you need them back?"

"They must be returned to the library eventually."

She studied him for a moment, seeming to still somehow see him through those milky eyes, though he wasn't sure how that was possible, or if it even was. Maybe all of that was nothing more than imagined, rather than real.

When she was gone, Ferrah leaned forward and studied him. "What was that about?"

"You saw what that was about."

"No. How many books has she allowed you to borrow?"

"She's been helping me understand the elementals. You know that." Tolan lowered his voice and leaned close to her, not wanting any others in the library to overhear what he was about to say next and thankful the library was a place where very few would have any ability to shape wind and listen. "I need to use the elementals in my shaping. I'm trying to find whatever edge I can when it comes to reaching for that power."

"So, you're looking for more than what the masters can teach?" Tolan arched a brow at her, amused at this side of her. "Do you really think that's a good idea with the rumors out there about you already?"

Tolan tore his gaze away from Master Minden, who was weaving along the rows of shelves. He looked over at Ferrah. "What rumors?"

"It's not all that much of a surprise that people talk, Tolan. You're the first student to have seen an elemental prior to coming to the Academy in a long time. People talk about that."

"And now many people have seen elementals," he said.

"There haven't been any in weeks."

"Marcella told me there have been more recently. Enough that it spreads the Trackers thin and is now drawing other shapers out of the city."

"I suppose you want to go after them."

She couldn't know he had gone after Jory. "I don't think so."

She glanced around the library. "I know the Grand Master reported the person responsible was captured, but you were a whole lot more eager to go after this a few weeks ago than you have been lately. Why the sudden change?"

It was the reason he wanted to share with her the fact they had been involved in stopping Jory, but how could he? If Ferrah made a mistake, and if Master Irina realized he hadn't been spirit-shaped, he had no idea what would come of it. It was possible nothing would come from it, but it was equally possible she would attempt to shape him again.

There were rumors about people who had been spirit-shaped, only to lose everything. Most of those rumors came from people unskilled with spirit, but Tolan wasn't comfortable with the idea of losing any part of his memories, especially as he had only begun to have any shaping ability over the last few months. Even that ability was still tenuous at best. While he could focus on the elementals, and use that to reach for shapings, it was different than other shapers, so if he forgot, he feared how long it would take him to reach that connection again.

"I think I've been distracted by our studies, and worried more about what the Grand Master might say if he learns we've been chasing after the rogue elementals."

Ferrah stared at him before looking back down at the book. "Which is even more reason for me to understand this."

"I don't really get why."

"Because if there's anything that ties to the elementals in the element bonds as we've been trying to understand, it's this power I know exists. We just have to find it."

Would it come down to needing to mislead Ferrah? If it did, how long would he be willing to do so? She was his friend, but more than that, she had helped him when he had no idea about how to shape. Ferrah had not judged him and had been willing to accept the fact he wasn't the same kind of shaper as others. He appreciated that about her, and she deserved for him to tell her, but fear of Master Irina kept him silent.

"I was just going to see if you wanted to spend some time out in the city."

"You can go without me," she said without looking back up from her book.

"You know, it would be good for you to get out of the Academy, too."

"Why? This is how I want to spend my free time, much like you enjoy spending your free time with your head buried in books about elementals."

"I don't know I would say that my head is buried in those books."

She looked up at him, arching a brow. "Maybe not buried, but you certainly have a significant interest in the elementals, enough that you are becoming something of an expert in them. The other masters haven't said anything, but you need to be careful about how often you're identifying the elemental they're depicting in class."

If nothing else, his time spent studying the elementals had revealed knowledge he hadn't had before, and also discrepancies between what the masters taught and what was depicted in some of the books Master Minden had shown him. Considering how old some of those volumes were, he could almost believe they were inaccurate. But at the same time, there was the distinct possibility—and probability, if he got down to it—that whoever had written the books on the elementals had understood them better than the more recent masters.

"Are you going to come with me, or not?"

"I really don't want to," she said. "You can go and ask Jonas."

"Jonas is still off with Master Yael."

"And I have to go meet with Master Kralil later."

"You sound almost as if you're disappointed."

"It's not who I would've chosen to study with, and I'm

hoping I can move past him and make a different selection."

"How often do they allow that?"

"Not often," she said, closing the book. She breathed out, glancing over at the dais where the master librarians sat, and shook her head. "Maybe I *should* get out with you. If nothing else, you can let me clear my head before I have to go to my afternoon session."

"It can't be that bad," he said.

"Are you so sure? How much have you enjoyed your sessions with Master Olive?"

"Marcella is—"

"Marcella? You're on a first name basis?"

"She doesn't mind the informality while we're outside the Academy."

She chuckled and shook her head. "I forget she's still pretty young. She's not that much older than us, is she?"

"I haven't asked her age."

Ferrah waved her hand. "I doubt Master Olive cares all that much about propriety."

"You might be surprised," Tolan said.

The door opened and he glanced up to see Marcella enter the library with two other master shapers. One was a Selector, a man in his thirties with high cheekbones and deep black hair. He had a muscular build and exuded a sense of authority. Had a Selector like him come to Ephra, Tolan wasn't sure he would have risked barging into the selection process. The other person with Marcella was one of the older students, a compact woman who looked as if she might have been made from one of the earth elements.

"Is that why you're here?" Ferrah asked, following the direction of his gaze. "Did you know she was going to be here? She is quite lovely, but I didn't figure you for the type to swoon over your instructor."

Tolan turned away, trying to hide the heat rising in his cheeks. "I'm not swooning over anything, and certainly not over Marcella."

He kept his voice low, and yet Marcella looked in his direction, meeting his eyes for a moment. When she turned away, he looked down.

"See? Like I said, you're swooning over her."

"That's not swooning. That's avoiding her."

"According to Jonas, there aren't too many men who would avoid Master Olive—excuse me, *Marcella*."

"Would you stop?"

Ferrah shuffled her books, stacking them, and she nodded at him. "Are we going to get out of here, or was that all for show?"

"I really would like to go out into the city."

"Good. Because I need to get away from here now."

Tolan grunted. It was odd to see this side of Ferrah. She was usually the rational one, the kind who didn't get caught up in things like jealousy, especially with one of the masters. He was still a first-level student, having not yet passed the test to move on to the second level. He still wasn't sure what would be involved in that test and was in no hurry to discover it. Reaching the spirit tower, passing that test, had been enough of a victory for him. And he had discovered a connection to shaping. If nothing else, he could use that and wouldn't be confined to Amitan and serving in the Academy. If he was able to shape, he would always be able to serve Terndahl in some way. Though now he was here, he wanted more than just to serve in some way. He wanted to understand, especially as he thought there was something different about him and his ability.

They headed out, hurrying into the courtyard once again. The sun shone down, warm and inviting, sending his skin tingling. He glanced over and realized the tingling came from Ferrah shaping near him.

"How long do you think we can be gone?" he asked.

"I have a few hours before I need to be back," she said.

"I've been wondering," he said as they neared the gate leading out into the street, "when is the next Selection?"

"We've only been here a few months, Tolan. The Selection usually happens once a year."

"That's what we've been led to believe, but partly because those who don't pass are spirit-shaped so they don't remember the Selection process. What happens if it's more often than that?"

"We know there are classes of students at the Academy, Tolan. The Selection is only once a year. Don't worry; you still have time to master more shapings before the testing."

He hoped so. Fire had become not necessarily easy, but certainly easier. It had only been fire, though. Eventually, he would need to do the same with another element, and if he couldn't, he might be sent away from the Academy.

"What do you think is involved in the testing?"

"To hear the second-year students talk about it, it's something horrible, but I'm not sure what to believe."

"Why?"

"I suspect most of them have been shaped to forget it, similar to the Selection."

"What would the purpose in that be? Why even make the Selection so mysterious?"

Ferrah's face darkened. They stepped out onto a street, and a carriage shaped to move on its own rolled past them, the three people inside looking around. Their eyes widened when they saw Tolan and Ferrah, pointing at them and murmuring something about Academy students.

"I thought about that for a while, but more so since we've been here. Things don't completely add up."

"What sort of things?"

"It feels as if I'm missing something, and I've been nothing if not meticulous in how I approach my studies."

"I've seen that."

"And yet, I can't shake the sense there are gaps. It makes me wonder if the spirit shapers are using various shapings on us from time to time."

A cold sweat beaded his forehead. "Why would the Inquisitors do something like that?"

"I'm not saying they would but think about the Selection. Knowledge of that is secretive, hidden from others within the shaper schools, as if they're afraid that knowing what might come would somehow allow the shaper to pass. Having been through it, I don't see how that's even possible. Without knowing the key to getting through it, I don't know that it would be any easier. And it's the same thing with passing from year to year. There's no point in hiding what's involved, unless there's some other ulterior motive."

"What sort of motive?" Tolan asked. They were heading toward the center of the city where a massive market existed, though he'd never visited. There hadn't been time, and he hadn't had the inclination to go alone.

"Finding Inquisitors," she said.

"Why do you say that?"

"The more you get to know about your shaping ability, the more you'll be able to protect your mind from spirit shapers. Eventually, I suspect they will reveal the trick to us, though there are some like Draln who might already know, especially as his parents came through here. But spirit shapers have a natural protection. They don't have to learn how to protect their mind, and all they need to do is simply be. They can push back against that shaping, regardless of what's used on them."

He wanted to say something to Ferrah. In that moment, he thought he *needed* to say something to her, to tell her about what he'd experienced and to reveal the presence of the Convergence, but more than that, to reassure her she had only been shaped one time—but what if that wasn't true?

Did he have gaps? He hadn't put much consideration into it, not knowing whether he was missing memories. It was entirely possible spirit shapers had worked on him before.

It wasn't as if he hadn't succumbed to a spirit shaping before. The Selection was all about a spirit shaping, so there had to be some way of using that on those who did have the potential to spirit-shape.

"How about we don't worry about it for today?" Tolan asked.

"That's not how my mind works," she said.

"I know that's not how your mind works, but sometimes it's nice to just to get away, to ignore the presence of shaping, and to—"

Tolan didn't get a chance to finish. A sudden buildup of pressure struck him, overflowing him. It came from the far western edge of the city. It was a shaping, and an enormous one.

He and Ferrah shared a glance, and without saying a word, they each shaped, streaking into the sky to the Shapers Path.

5

WHILE THE SHAPERS PATH WAS USUALLY A METHOD FOR fast travel across Terndahl, Tolan had a sudden and different understanding of how he could use it. Within Amitan, the path was one of accessibility, and it was designed for all within the city to be able to use, to navigate above the city; it was still primarily used by those with some shaping ability, though.

The Path was mostly empty, and he and Ferrah raced along it, following the road as it wound above the city. It was easier to travel this way, and though he might be able to shape himself into the air, he didn't yet have the strength necessary to do so for very long or for much distance, not the same as some shapers. Master shapers would be able to hold themselves in the air for long periods of time, and there were stories of incredibly powerful shapers who didn't need the Shapers Path to travel by. Eventually, Tolan hoped he would reach that point, something that seemed impossible to consider even a year ago.

"What do you think it was?" Ferrah asked as they ran.

"I felt the pressure, and—"

"Felt?"

He nodded. "Why? Didn't you feel it?"

"I heard it, Tolan. There wasn't anything I could feel."

"What did you hear?"

"An explosion. It was thunderous, the sound something like a building crumbling or a tree falling in the forest."

He hadn't heard anything, but then, the sudden buildup of shaped power had drawn his attention, making it difficult to hear anything. When he felt shaped power in such a way, it was the only thing he was able to focus on, and so with that, he had paid attention only to the building power.

"When the masters find out we came this way…"

"I'll take the blame," Tolan said.

"Right. Because they'll believe you forced me to come with you."

"I think they blame me enough the way it is," he said. "I've asked enough questions about the elementals to drive most of them mad, and those who still bother to answer are annoyed by the fact they have to."

"They're only annoyed because they don't have the answers."

They veered off the main Shapers Path and took a narrower side route that led in the direction from which he'd felt the explosion of power. Power built again and he skidded to a stop, raising his hand as he glanced over at Ferrah.

"Do you feel that?"

"Like I said, I don't feel anything. If you're feeling something, it's different from my ability, Tolan."

He closed his eyes, letting his awareness of the shaping roll through him. It was a mixture of element bonds, that much he could tell, but not the intent.

Something was different.

He snapped his eyes open and pointed to the south. "They've moved."

He reversed direction, hurrying along the Shapers Path. When he reached a different side pathway, he made his way along it, pausing long enough to glance back and see whether Ferrah was keeping pace with him. She could probably shape herself along the Path, something Tolan couldn't do. He required the Shapers Path even in the city.

An explosion of power thundered, the elements' magic washing over him. He paused, waiting to see if he would detect anything else, but there wasn't anything.

It would come again, he was certain of it, but from what direction? If it came from the east and the south already, would there be another similar attack from the other directions?

"You head north and I'll go west," he said.

"What are you talking about?"

"We need to figure out what's going on, and so far,

we've had two directions, so what if they attack from the others?"

"We don't even need to be the ones who solve this, Tolan. There are master shapers who will be up here, and they will likely reach this before we get to do anything."

"But what if they don't?"

"Tolan…"

Another buildup of power began, and he was certain it was coming from the north. Rather than wait, he grabbed Ferrah by the wrist and dragged her with him. "I need you to shape us."

"Shape us where?"

"To the north. Get us across the city before this next attack strikes."

"And what if there's not another attack?"

"Trust me."

Ferrah met his eyes and nodded. A shaping built, a tingling sensation causing his skin to feel tight and pressure to build behind his ears, and wind whipped around them, mixed with heat from a fire shaping. They exploded, launching across the city, streaking with a controlled arc he would never have been able to accomplish. They crossed the distance, landing on another Shapers Path on the far side of the city.

"I'm not sure what this was about, and I don't even know if we should be—"

He squeezed her hand as power accrued, rising quickly.

Where was it coming from?

It was near, that much he could tell now they were close to it. They had managed to find it, but now they had, what could be done about it?

As he scanned the ground, he realized he might be looking in the wrong direction.

He turned his attention upward.

Three people stood high over the city on another Shapers Path. One held a shaping of considerable power. Tolan pointed up and Ferrah followed the direction of his gaze and frowned.

"What are they doing?"

"I don't know, but whatever they're doing is building."

He focused on a shaping, thinking of the hyza elemental and drawing strength from it as he often did, but he wasn't going to be fast enough. The shaping building above them was far more powerful than he could compensate for, and the shaper far faster than him.

"Ferrah—"

She grabbed his arm and quickly shaped them up.

Power washed over him as they streaked into the air, and Tolan tried not to think about what it meant. He focused on hyza, the elemental giving him both strength from the earth component as well as the heat and power from fire, and when they landed, he pushed outward, sending a sheet of heat and flames rolling away.

The flame was incompletely controlled, more a nature of his connection to the elemental component, and within that flame, hyza raced away, leaving the flames as it streaked toward the three shapers.

Another shaping built, but this time directed at his flames, and surprisingly, the shaping failed, washing past his flames, unable to stop them.

Power exploded near him and it took a sudden wind shaping from Ferrah to keep them on the Shapers Path.

"This was stupid," Ferrah muttered.

"They're attacking us," he said.

"Because you attacked them," she said.

"Because they're attacking Amitan."

Ferrah swirled wind and sent it streaking away, but her shaping disappeared. Her mouth tightened into a frown as she started shaping again, but another buildup of power was coming from the three shapers opposite them.

Tolan realized he couldn't see them easily, and he wondered how they were able to disguise themselves. It must be some other shaping. Knowing something like that would be incredibly useful.

Their shaping continued to build, likely targeted at him and Ferrah. Tolan needed something with which to defend them, but the fire elemental hadn't been enough. It had been incompletely directed, and he wished he had used the furios in order to summon it, but he had done it without the help.

Reaching into his pocket, running his finger along the runes, Tolan quickly attempted to summon another fire shaping, focusing once again on the form of hyza. He'd seen firsthand the destruction caused by the elemental, and using his furios, he thought he should be able to call upon that kind of power for an attack of his own. He held it out, squeezing it as the nearest figure approached.

They wore a hood, masking their features, and power crackled from them, continuing to rise with more shaping strength than he had felt anywhere other than the Convergence.

Could they be drawing from the Convergence?

The elemental sprang out of the end of the furios, growing larger and larger, taking on the size of a massive fox. Rather than an uncontrolled flame, it was a focused form, a figure that looked just like the elemental he had seen. Tolan continued to hold onto that image, continuing to focus on the elemental, and it powered through the figure, knocking them back.

Two others came close, their cloaked forms the only part of them visible, and he whispered softly within his mind a silent command. *Keep us safe.*

Would the elemental—or whatever this form was— know what he wanted?

He still wasn't convinced he had actually summoned a real elemental, or whether this represented his mind's manifestation of an elemental as he shaped power, but the more often he did it, the more he questioned whether he was somehow separating an elemental from the element bond, however briefly.

The elemental turned, heading toward the nearest figure, and slammed into them, knocking them off the Shapers Path. The third figure turned toward the elemental, as if finally realizing there was a real threat to it.

Flames burst, but it wasn't enough. The figure held their hands out, compressing power, and the elemental started to shrink, collapsing downward. Tolan had seen something similar before, when the masters had confined the elementals he had summoned while in the Convergence and realized the same sort of magic had to have been used.

Wind gusted, swirling around the figure, and power radiated from Ferrah, though he wondered how long she'd be able to hold onto it.

The figure turned to her, and with the flick of his wrist, the wind suddenly died, collapsing into nothingness.

If she wasn't able to hold onto the shaping, there might not be any way of stopping this figure. Tolan strained against it, trying to come up with some sort of shaping that would allow him to push back. The shaper turned toward him, power beginning to rise again, enough that he felt as if he would be overwhelmed.

He held out the furios, pointing it at the figure, trying to summon another elemental, but either he was unable to do so or the shaper standing before him had some way of overpowering him and his ability.

"They send untrained shapers to war?"

The voice was rough and dangerous and Tolan trembled, trying to ignore it. There was something frightening about the sound, and as much as he wanted to ignore it, he felt compelled to move forward, as if he was being shaped.

Could that be why this man had such an easy time

dismissing the elemental? Was he a spirit shaper? Tolan was convinced he had some connection to spirit, and even if that connection was faint, it had to be real. That was how he had his memories.

The shaper took another step toward him. Where was Ferrah?

He wanted to look behind him, to see if something had happened to her, but didn't dare risk that until he knew for sure that this man had been slowed.

It was a mistake coming here. He should have waited, remaining back at the Academy, avoiding coming here and having to face someone who had significantly more power, but he'd let his pride draw him here. Pride, and a belief he was somehow more capable than he truly was.

He focused, thinking of the fire elemental, but there was no sense of it.

What about another elemental?

Earth. He had to be able to call on an earth elemental. It might not be nearly as powerful as anything he could summon through the furios, but he had an affinity to earth through his sensing. It was why he had apprenticed to a woodsmith in the first place.

There was one elemental he thought could be helpful, but up here, far above the city itself, far above a place where an elemental might appear, it would be unlikely to work.

Which was why he had to try it.

Jinnar's appearance was something like a man and Tolan focused on it, thinking about what he remembered when the elemental had attacked, both in his vision and in the clearing near the Academy. If he could somehow call upon that power, and could use it, maybe he would be able to stop this attack, if only for a moment or two.

The Shapers Path trembled.

Tolan took a step back, trying to maintain his focus, trying to hold onto that connection to earth and his vision of jinnar. As the path continued to tremble, the other shaper stood, hands apart, focusing on the Shapers Path. The trembling started to ease, but Tolan pushed, forcing more energy into his connection, praying to the Great Mother he could somehow summon the earth elemental.

As the path trembled, the shaper looked past Tolan. With a swirl of wind, he leapt into the air and, on a crack of lightning, disappeared.

The path continued to tremble and with the shaper gone, Tolan turned, looking for Ferrah. She was there and she stared, eyes wide.

"Ferrah?"

"I. Can't. Move." She spoke through gritted teeth.

He hurried toward her, reaching for her arm.

The trembling continued and Tolan hesitated, focusing on the shaping he had started to create, thinking that if nothing else, he needed to ease it back. They couldn't have the earth elemental bursting forth from the Shapers Path, but at the same time, he didn't know if he had enough control to suppress it.

He had to try. This was *his* shaping.

And it was a shaping, not a summons.

I don't need you.

The trembling continued and Tolan tried to focus on stabilizing the sense that he felt, but couldn't. He glanced over at Ferrah. She was looking past him, and he spun around to see the Shapers Path bulging upward.

The earth elemental.

He swallowed, backing up, sliding his feet along the Shapers Path as he retreated away from the earth elemental. Maybe this was only a shaping, but it reminded him far too much of an actual elemental.

The pressure of other shapings suddenly sprang around him, and Tolan looked around as three master shapers appeared. One was Master Sartan. Tolan was pleased to see him, and even more pleased when his fire shaping began, pressing down on the Shapers Path, suppressing whatever it was Tolan had done.

The other two were shapers Tolan didn't know. They worked with Master Sartan as they suppressed the elemental, squeezing it back into the path. When they were done, one glanced down at the fallen form, the figure Tolan had attacked with his fire elemental shaping. He grabbed one and the other shaper grabbed the other, nodding at Master Sartan before shaping themselves away, disappearing on a flutter of wind mixed with flames.

Master Sartan turned to Tolan. Anger raged on his face and he twisted his hand as he shaped, and Ferrah let out a heavy sigh.

"What do you think you're doing?" he asked.

"We were following the—"

"I know what you were following. What do you think you were doing, chasing power like that? You are still first-year students in the Academy. You are far too untrained for anything like that."

"Anything like what?" All Tolan knew was they had been attacked by some incredibly powerful shapers, but not who they were or why they had attacked.

Master Sartan motioned for them to follow him. He stalked along the Shapers Path, and as he went, shaping spread before him, smoothing out the Shapers Path in areas Tolan hadn't realized were damaged. Parts of it were gouged, as if the fire shaping had significantly damaged it, but after Master Sartan was done, it was completely smooth, leaving the path once again intact. He guided them quickly through the city, circling around the upper level. Every so often, Tolan would glance over at Ferrah, who shook her head, almost as if afraid to say anything. From above, the city looked no different than it did at any other time. There was activity throughout, with shaped wagons and merchants carting things through the city. Thousands of people made their way through the streets, looking so small from this high up. Buildings protruded, pointing toward the Shapers Path, and only the Academy came close to reaching it. Even the central capital building was not nearly as massive or impressive as the Academy.

When they neared the Academy, Master Sartan shaped himself down, and he wrapped both Tolan and Ferrah with a band of wind, pulling them down with him. They landed in the courtyard more roughly than Tolan thought was appropriate or necessary, but he didn't say anything, not wanting to further anger the master. They hurried into the Academy, sweeping past students, and Tolan caught sight of Draln, who eyed them with amusement.

They followed the hallway before reaching a small staircase along the back of the Academy, a place Tolan had never visited. Master Sartan hurried up the stairs, a band of a wind shaping still wrapped around Tolan and Ferrah. He could do nothing against it.

He didn't want to argue, and didn't dare resist without knowing what Master Sartan intended. A part of him feared Master Sartan had realized what Tolan had done, that he had released an elemental, but if he did, he expected the master would've said something more. Instead, he reached a small doorway and knocked.

After a moment, the door opened and Grand Master Erich Normandale stood on the other side.

The Grand Master was smaller than most, and the hallway made him appear even more diminutive. Behind thick spectacles, he had a gaze filled with so much power, that when he looked at Tolan and that power rested on him, it left Tolan unsettled.

"What is this?" the Grand Master asked.

"There was an attack," Master Sartan said.

"Who?"

"Disciples of the Draasin Lord."

Tolan and Ferrah looked at each other, sharing a glance. Those had been disciples of the Draasin Lord?

He had only a little experience with people who followed the Draasin Lord. All he knew was that they chased the elementals for power, seeking to control them, pulling them from the element bonds so they could lord over them and rule both elementals and shapers. The Draasin Lord was the worst of them all, wanting the kind of power he shouldn't be able to obtain, but supposedly far more powerful than nearly any other living shaper.

"Are you sure?" the Grand Master asked.

"You can ask these two. They raced off to confront them."

The Grand Master turned his attention to both Tolan and Ferrah, studying them intently. He had seen the way the Grand Master had disarmed Jory when they had faced him in the Convergence, leaving Tolan wondering just how powerful he was.

"Close the door," he said, nodding to Master Sartan.

Tolan trailed after the Grand Master, looking around what presumably was his office. It was enormous, with rows and rows of shelves around the room, books Tolan suspected were either too valuable or too dangerous to be held in the library stacked on the shelves. A table in the center of the room held strange-looking devices, some reminding him of bondars. Two plants were situated either side of the table, planted in enormous ceramic pots, their leaves twisting as the branches strained toward imagined light. Near the back of the room was a chalice that stood nearly as tall as Tolan. He couldn't see it clearly, but a silvery liquid seemed to reflect outward, a liquid remindeing him of what he'd seen at the Convergence.

"What did you experience?" the Grand Master asked.

Tolan turned his attention back to the Grand Master. He had taken a seat behind an enormous desk and rested his hands on the surface, holding Tolan and Ferrah with that heavy gaze of his, his eyes demanding an answer.

"There was a shaped explosion," Tolan started. There was no point in denying what he had sensed, especially as he suspected the Grand Master knew quite a bit more about him than he had wanted known. Could he even know about Tolan's connection to the elementals? It was possible he did, especially if he had been speaking to Master Minden. "I wasn't sure what it was, but I—"

"You detected an explosion and chased after it. A shaped explosion at that." The Grand Master stared at Tolan.

Sweat beaded on Tolan's brow and he wanted to shrink away, to disappear and be anywhere but here. He had survived the attack and had stopped them with Ferrah's help. Shouldn't they be treated with a little bit more respect than this?

But then, Master Sartan was right in that neither had thought it out. Mostly, it had been Tolan. He hadn't given it the necessary thought, and shouldn't have run after the explosion of power, especially without any real shaping to fall back on.

"I wasn't sure what it was, and before we said anything, I thought we should—"

The Grand Master leaned forward. "You thought you would chase after a shaped explosion. The same way you chased after an elemental both here and in your homeland." The words lingered in the air and the Grand Master leaned back, flicking his gaze to Ferrah. "And you brought another with you. Shaper Changen has considerable talent, and I would hate to see it wasted sacrificing herself against a disciple before she was ready."

"She didn't—"

"I went with him willingly," Ferrah said, glaring briefly at Tolan. "He needed help, and as he's my friend, I thought it was best I helped to ensure he didn't get into too much trouble."

"And did you get into too much trouble?" the Grand Master asked.

"They were powerful shapers," Tolan said. "They were able to dismiss every shaping we had."

"I'm not surprised they would be able to do so, Shaper Ethar. And while Shaper Changen is quite talented, even she doesn't have the same talent as the disciples, at least not yet. Perhaps in time and with training, she might develop it. So might you, Shaper Ethar."

"There were three attacks," Master Sartan said. "Each of them was targeting the Shapers Path, and had they not intervened, the path might have been destroyed."

The Grand Master looked past Tolan to Master Sartan, and Tolan shifted in his seat, wanting nothing more than to turn and look back at the master fire shaper, but decided against it. He was already in enough trouble as it was, and the idea of angering the Grand Master was not something he wanted to do. He had already upset him, so needed to be careful.

"Were you able to restore it?"

"I restored most of the section where they were. There will need to be quite a bit of work done on the other two sections, but they were able to prevent the entire structure from collapsing."

"Good."

"They were using elementals to attack," Master Sartan said.

"Are you sure?"

"I saw one. An earth elemental."

"An earth elemental on the Shapers Path?" the Grand Master asked.

"From what it appeared. We suppressed the elemental, but it was not easy. It was incredibly powerful, even there." Master Sartan took a step forward, positioning himself between Ferrah and Tolan, who were sitting on two hard wooden chairs. Tolan glanced up but couldn't read Master Sartan's face. "There was another elemental, though we didn't see it. There was evidence of fire that could only come from a fire elemental."

"Did they unleash it?" the Grand Master asked.

"I will search, myself," Master Sartan said.

"There was no fire elemental released," Tolan said.

He didn't want Master Sartan wandering out and searching for the elemental, and most certainly didn't want Master Sartan to come across the elemental Tolan had seen when out with Marcella. He still didn't know what his connection to the elementals might be, but it wasn't one where he was in danger from them. They had power, but then again, he seemed to have some connection to them. Maybe not control. That seemed to be too much to believe, but definitely a connection.

"How certain are you of this?" the Grand Master asked.

"They had a fire elemental, but it disappeared. They made it disappear." Tolan tried to clarify it at the end, worried it would sound almost as if the elemental had run off.

"Do what you must," the Grand Master said, nodding to Master Sartan.

"What of them?"

"Leave them with me. I have a few more things I will talk to them about."

Master Sartan glanced at Tolan and then at Ferrah before striding out of the room, leaving them sitting there, watching the Grand Master.

Moments passed before the Grand Master spoke again. "I can't decide if that was incredibly brave or incredibly stupid," he said.

"Stupid," Ferrah said softly.

"I was just trying to—"

"I know what you were trying to do, but as you are untrained, and with intermittent connection to your shapings, from what I hear, I'm not sure you were the best person to approach this situation. Then again, had you not intervened, it's possible the disciples would have succeeded. They planned this well. First drawing our most talented shapers away from the city and now focusing here."

The Grand Master leaned back, steepling his fingers together.

Tolan shifted in his chair under the weight of the Grand Master's gaze. There was almost a sense of a shaping, but he wasn't sure what kind of shaping it would be. If he was shaping him with spirit, would it work against him?

"Why is it important for the Shapers Path to be intact?" Ferrah asked.

The Grand Master glanced over at her. "That's what you'd like to focus on?"

"Marcella told me there have been more elemental attacks since we were out in the waste, so I understand that part. Why attack the way they did?" Tolan could feel Ferrah's gaze on him, almost trying to silence him. "The attack was focused on the Shapers Path. Why is that important? It seems as if Master Sartan intended to repair it quickly. Aren't the paths for people who can't shape?"

The Grand Master leaned back and took a deep breath, letting it out slowly. "The Shapers Path is mostly for those who cannot shape, and it allows others to navigate through our city more effectively than they would be able if we didn't have the Shapers Path, but it serves another purpose, one few who aren't elevated through the Academy know about."

"What purpose is that?" Tolan asked.

"It's one that provides protection."

"What kind of protection?" Ferrah asked.

"The Shapers Path is designed to create a barrier over Amitan. It does several things, but what's applicable in this sense is that it helps protect those who live within it, and it allows us to train here without the risk of attack we might face otherwise."

"There has to be more reason than that for the disciples of the Draasin Lord to have attacked it," Ferrah said.

"Ferrah," Tolan hissed.

She glanced over at him. "There has to be, Tolan. The Grand Master is saying something, but there has to be some reason behind it."

He thought she was right. If the barrier the Shapers Path formed created a protection within the city, could it not also serve another role that had to do with the Convergence?

The Grand Master watched him, seemingly ignoring Ferrah.

Was this some sort of test? Did the Grand Master know he hadn't been spirit-shaped?

"Is this about Jory?" he asked softly. It was a nonspecific way of broaching the subject, and if nothing else, it would allow the Grand Master to acknowledge what might have been taking place without needing to inform Ferrah. The only problem was that by asking, he suspected Ferrah would realize there was more to what was taking place than she knew.

The Grand Master stared at him for a long moment.

Something in his gaze shifted, and Tolan felt a stirring within him that he pushed back against.

That had to be a spirit shaping.

"Selector Harris probably managed to get word out about what he discovered," the Grand Master said.

"And if that's why the disciples attack?"

"Possibly, though we have dealt with attacks from the disciples of the Draasin Lord in the past. It wouldn't be the first time, though rarely do they manage to get so close to Amitan. For the most part, we have other ways of preventing them from reaching us, so we are quite protected here in the city. If they have somehow found a way of getting past those barriers, we need to be even more cautious."

"Why would they increase their attacks?" Ferrah asked.

Tolan looked over, hating that he had kept from her what he knew of the Convergence, but the same time, maybe the Grand Master would reveal its presence, and he would no longer have to keep things from her.

"And who is this Selector Harris?"

"He's someone who has betrayed us," the Grand Master said.

"And how was Tolan involved?"

"Selector Harris is the Selector who brought Shaper Ethar to the city. They are connected, and because of that connection, we investigated all other connections Selector Harris was involved in."

Tolan's heart sank. It would've been so much easier had the Grand Master been willing to admit what had taken place, but it seemed as if he was going to keep that to himself. This meant Tolan would have to keep from Ferrah the truth of the Convergence.

"Does it have anything to do with the memories I'm missing?" Ferrah asked.

The Grand Master shifted his gaze to Ferrah, staring at her. "Interesting." He chuckled. "Rarely do we have so many with such potential."

"What is this about?" Ferrah asked.

"I believe, Shaper Changen, you already know."

Her eyes widened and she leaned forward. "The Convergence?" she whispered.

The Grand Master nodded. "Unfortunately, it seems as if word of the Convergence has managed to escape, and now the disciples of the Draasin Lord are after it."

6

IN THE WEEK SINCE THE APPEARANCE OF THE DISCIPLES OF the Draasin Lord, Tolan hadn't seen Ferrah very often. She was present in class and would return to the room late at night, but typically well after everyone else had gone to bed and been asleep. He didn't try to find her after the first few days, realizing she wanted her space. What he wanted was an opportunity to explain, but she wasn't interested in that, and Tolan couldn't blame her, as he had kept things from her.

"Are you going to tell me what's going on?" Jonas asked on the evening of the fifth day following the events on the Shapers Path. He sat perched on the edge of his bed, chewing on a hunk of bread, glancing at Ferrah's empty bunk. Wallace wasn't in the room, either, and Tolan was thankful Jonas had waited until it was just the two of them to ask.

"Ferrah is upset with me about something."

Jonas grunted and tossed the remains of his roll at Tolan. "You think? I was hoping for something more specific than that, but if you're going to be an ass about it, then maybe I'll go ask her."

Tolan glanced at the door, but there was no movement on the other side. "It has to do with the attack the other day."

"You mean the one you once again ran toward and had another opportunity to see an elemental?"

"That one," Tolan said. He wanted to argue, but there wasn't any point in it, as he had done exactly as Jonas said. What was it with him running toward danger? It wasn't that he felt particularly brave, but at the same time, he always felt as if he needed to respond, even if there were others who could do as good a job. "There were disciples of the Draasin Lord attacking."

Jonas tensed. "Why didn't you tell me before?"

"Because I was told not to," he said.

"And why are you telling me now?"

"I didn't realize Ferrah would be so angry with me and wouldn't talk to me for the next week."

"This all has to do with you dragging her in with you?"

"Partly." He flicked his gaze to the door again, but there was still no activity. "But it has more to do with the reason behind the attack."

"Why do I get the sense you're not going to tell me?"

"Because the Grand Master doesn't want me to," Tolan said.

"He doesn't want you to tell me in particular?"

"He doesn't want anyone to know."

"Then why do you know?"

"I suspect if it were up to him, I wouldn't. I just happened to have been able to resist a spirit shaping."

Jonas frowned. "When were you spirit-shaped?"

What did it matter if Jonas knew? Now Ferrah knew, it was bound to get out. "Do you remember what we were doing when we were investigating the rogue elemental?"

"I remember being told there wasn't anything to worry about when it came to the rogue elemental. The Grand Master said it was taken care of."

"It was taken care of. By us."

"Us? As in you and me?"

"As in you, me, and Ferrah."

"And you still remember what happened?"

"Apparently I have some resistance to a spirit shaping."

"What did we do?"

He flicked his gaze once again over to the door, watching for signs of movement. There were none, but what if someone was wind shaping? A powerful wind shaper would be able to use a shaping to listen in, and with the right person behind the shaping, they might not even be aware of what was happening.

"Can you seal the room?"

"Do you really think someone is paying attention to us?"

"I'd feel better if you did."

Jonas shrugged and a shaping built, and he glanced over at Tolan before nodding.

"It's done."

Tolan breathed out in a heavy sigh. "We stopped one of the Selectors from going to a place of power deep beneath the Academy and attempting to free a draasin."

Jonas blinked before whistling softly. "We did *what?*"

"I know. It was pretty stupid of us to do that ourselves, but—"

"Stupid of *us?* That sounds like the kind of thing you would do. And why didn't you tell me?"

Tolan shook his head. "I wasn't supposed to."

"But we're your friends. If you were spirit-shaped and didn't remember it, wouldn't you want us to tell you?"

"I would want that, and I feel terrible, but I was only doing what I thought I needed to do, and what I thought I was supposed to do."

He feared Jonas getting angry with him too, just like Ferrah had. If he did, it would be completely deserved. He had withheld things from Jonas, more than once. When it came down to explaining to Jonas what he was capable of doing, and the way he shaped—or didn't, as the case had been—he had not been forthcoming.

"You know you can trust us, right?"

"I do know that."

"You say you know it, but you need to act like it, too. We're your friends, and we won't be able to help you if we don't know what's going on."

"I had issues when I was younger in Ephra," he said.

"What sort of issues?"

"It had to do with my parents and their disappearance.

Other people accused me of sympathizing with the Draasin Lord, and I closed myself off."

"You know that's no real excuse, right?"

Tolan frowned for a moment before nodding. It wasn't really an excuse, not when it came to his friends. They deserved more than that, and his own struggles with what he'd gone through as a kid didn't have the same bearing. What he needed to do was to work with his friends, and that meant he needed to search out Ferrah and mend things between them.

"You're not mad?"

"I'm a little mad," Jonas said. "But mostly, I'm upset at the fact I was spirit-shaped. How often do you think they've done that?"

"Spirit-shaped students?"

Jonas nodded. "If they were so willing to do that to us, it seems like it's something they've done before, and probably often."

"I'm not really sure," Tolan said. And he had no interest in going to Master Irina and asking. But Jonas was right that it was odd how willing they had been to spirit-shape the students. Was the Convergence that important they needed to protect it?

And they hadn't even protected the Convergence. If Jory had managed to get word out to the disciples of the Draasin Lord, then whatever they really wanted to do, whatever safety they thought they were providing by shaping them, had failed.

Tolan climbed off the bed and glanced down at the

books stacked on it before heading toward the door. When he reached it, he paused, aware of the barrier Jonas had shaped and knowing he wouldn't be able to pass through to the other side with the barrier in place. "Can you lower it?"

"Only if you tell me what you intend to do."

"I'm going to see if I can find Ferrah."

Jonas's shaping faded, and as it did, the tension on his skin eased and Tolan hurried out of the first-year rooms and down the steps. It was later in the day, and there weren't that many people out. Most were up in their rooms, studying or preparing for the next day, and only he was out. The thudding of feet behind him caught his attention and he spun to see Jonas racing to catch him.

His friend shrugged when he frowned. "I'm not going let you do this on your own."

"I think I have to."

"You only want to believe you have to. But I'm going to stay with you," Jonas said.

"I'm not sure if that's going to make things better or worse."

"What part?"

"The fact I've now told you."

"Well, you should've told us in the first place, so that's all on you."

Tolan sighed. "I'm going to start with the library and see if she's there."

"And if she's not?"

"I'm not sure where else we can look," he said.

When they reached the library, they found it as empty as the halls. One table had two older students sitting at it, and they glanced up when Tolan and Jonas entered, but for the most part, there was no activity here. Master Havern sat upon the elevated dais, the only librarian in here at this time of day.

"She's not here," Jonas whispered.

"I can see that."

Tolan hurried toward the master librarian and paused in front of the dais. "Master Havern?"

He was an older man with gray hair and a wrinkled face. Thick glasses hung down on his nose, and he pushed them up as he peered at Tolan. His lips were pressed into a tight frown.

"Have you seen Ferrah Changen?"

"I'm not familiar with that book," the librarian said.

Tolan shook his head. "She's a friend of ours, a student shaper. We are looking for her."

"I am a librarian, not a finder of students. Now, if you have some volume you'd like me to look for, I'm more than happy to do so, but if this was all about finding your friend, then you may leave."

Tolan glanced at Jonas, who flashed a wide smile. "I would like you to help me find something about the Inquisitors."

Master Havern considered Jonas for a moment. "And what is it about the Inquisitors you would like to learn about today?"

"I was curious about their history."

"Do you have an interest in joining? You should know the Inquisitors are quite careful with who they choose, and not just anyone is allowed to join their ranks."

Jonas shrugged. "I'm not really sure if I'm interested in joining or not. That's why I wanted to read more about them."

"Have you shown potential with spirit?"

Jonas nodded. "Oh, yes. So much potential."

Tolan wanted to grab his friend and drag him away, but Master Havern smiled.

"There aren't many who show such potential. In each year, there's only one or two, rarely more than that, though often it's not any at all. From what I've heard, there are already two within your year that are showing some potential," he said. "Perhaps you are one of them."

"I hope so," Jonas said.

Tolan knew him well enough to recognize Jonas was trying to bite back a smile. He didn't like the idea of taunting the master librarian in such a way and could imagine he would get angry at them if he knew Jonas was not being completely honest with him.

When the master librarian headed off to the shelves to begin looking for a few books, Tolan glanced at Jonas. "What are you doing?"

"I've been spirit-shaped. That's what you said, right? And if I've been spirit-shaped, then I want to understand why and if there's any way I can defend myself."

"You think studying the Inquisitors is a way to do it?"

"Studying the Inquisitors is part of it, mostly because

they're the only ones who can spirit shape. I figured if there's anything in the library to help us understand, it would be on the Inquisitors."

Tolan worried that perhaps Jonas was pushing things a little bit with the master librarian, but he wasn't going to be the one to say anything, not when it came to Jonas, and not when it had to do with that. He didn't want to anger his friend any more than he already had.

"Finding things about the Inquisitors doesn't get any closer to finding her," Tolan said.

"It doesn't, but it gives us an excuse to be in the library."

"I don't need an excuse to be in the library." Tolan looked around, wishing Master Minden were here. If she were, he could ask what she might know, and he felt fairly confident that she would be open with him about where and when she'd last seen Ferrah. The other master librarians weren't quite as accommodating, though he suspected Master Jensen might be willing to share, if only because he and Ferrah had such a connection with their research.

"I forget. You've been studying the elementals, and the more you do, the closer you get to that strange master."

"I'd be careful calling her strange. She knows things."

"If I were her age, I'd know things, too. She makes me uncomfortable."

"Why?"

"It's the way she looks at you. Or maybe I should say it's the way she seems to look at you. It's unsettling."

"Can I help you with anything?"

Tolan spun and saw Master Minden standing before them. She kept her milky-eyed gaze locked on Jonas, and Tolan had the unsettling sensation she knew exactly what they had been talking about.

"Master Minden. I was just saying that—"

"I know what you were saying, Shaper Ethar. Now, if there's anything I can help you find, you have only to ask. If not, then you can move away from the master's desk. We both know what happened the last time you decided to get too close to this desk."

Tolan frowned, meeting her gaze. Did Master Minden know what they'd done?

She would have to be aware of the Convergence. It wasn't as if it could be hidden from the librarians, especially with the door to it behind them, but they had distracted the librarians, and should have been able to sneak down without anyone being aware of them.

Only Master Minden seemed completely aware of what they had done. It was in her gaze, the way she looked at Jonas, and even the way she looked over at Tolan, though he couldn't tell how much she saw of him. It had to be enough for her to find books, as she seemed to have no difficulty with that, despite the fact he had a difficult time knowing how she could see anything.

And why was there no way for Master Wassa to heal her? With his connection to water, she should be healed, at least so much as to make it so she didn't have to deal with the difficulty of trying to see through the film over her eyes.

"What did we do the last time we were near the master's desk?" Jonas asked.

Tolan grabbed his friend's arm, trying to pull him away, but Jonas wouldn't budge. "Come on."

"I don't remember it. Is this what you were talking to me about earlier?" Jonas whispered.

"We can talk about it later."

Jonas glanced from Tolan to Master Minden before spinning and storming away in a huff. He threw himself down at one of the tables and leaned back, propping his legs out in front of him, and he waited until Master Havern came to him, carrying several books. How many of them would be useful for understanding what had taken place with the Inquisitors? Would any help him understand Master Irina?

"He doesn't recall," Master Minden said.

"I'm sorry. I didn't mean for—"

She turned her gaze to him, and there was the strange sensation of a shaping. It built slowly, washing over him, and then passed. As he often did, he wondered how she should be able to shape here. It shouldn't be possible, not in a place like this that had been protected, shielded from shapers for just this purpose.

"You didn't mean to what, Shaper Ethar? Did you think I wasn't aware you found the Convergence? We protect many things, knowledge foremost among them, but we have another role as master librarians."

"You protect the Convergence?" He kept his voice low, worried that others in the library might hear, but there weren't that many others here and he wasn't convinced Master Minden hadn't shaped them, concealing them in some manner.

"The power that lives within this place has been here a long time. There have been many who have protected it over the years, and we are the current caretakers. We offer as much protection as we can, recognizing the need to keep the power deep beneath the city safe."

Tolan looked around, surprised Master Minden was so willing to share with him. But then, she had been equally willing to provide him information about the elementals. Did she know he had some connection to the elementals?

"You're probably wondering why I'm sharing with you?"

He tensed. Could she be spirit-shaping him?

If she were, he didn't feel a thing, which meant she was either incredibly powerful—something he would not put past her, especially now he'd gotten to know her somewhat—or the question was simply plain upon his face.

"The thought did come to me," he said.

"As it should. There hasn't been a student come through the Academy in many years who uncovered the secret of the Convergence. And not only did you uncover it, you worked to protect it."

"Is that why you're sharing?"

She made her way to the stairs leading up to the dais,

and she took a place at the desk and leaned forward. "Do you think I should not?"

"I have questions."

"In this place, there are answers. That's the beauty of the library. You can look to the past for understanding, but only in looking to the future can you know."

"What do you mean by that?" When she didn't answer, Tolan glanced back at Jonas. He had begun flipping through the pages of one of the books, and Tolan wondered if he would actually put real attention into trying to understand the Inquisitors. Having lost memories, he could understand why he might be interested in doing so. Tolan shared the same unsettled feeling about the Inquisitors and their ability to shape memories away. More than that, the Selection had shaped into his mind and forced him to see something he didn't remember, visions of his parents that were different than his memories.

Unless they *were* his memories, only ones that had been unlocked. Could that be true? If so, why would he have had his mind spirit-shaped before?

"There've been others who found the Convergence?" Tolan asked, turning his attention back to Master Minden.

She bowed her head forward in a slight nod. "There have been others, but they came searching for a different purpose."

"What purpose?"

"They came searching for power. You, on the other hand, came for a different reason."

"I would take power," he said.

She chuckled and reached beneath the desk to pull out a book and flipped through it. The cover was made of a thick leather, and the pages she flipped through were coarse parchment crinkling beneath her hand as she went from page to page. "Most men would chase power if it were in front of them, but you didn't chase it for the sake of power."

"I just want to know…"

She looked up at him, waiting, as if expecting him to say something more, maybe something profound, but Tolan didn't have it in him. There was nothing profound that he could say. What *did* he want to know?

He wanted to know what he was able to do. He wanted to understand why his connection seemed to be to the elementals, or at least somehow tied to them, whether or not he actually pulled upon elemental power. And yet, he also wanted to understand why he seemed able to resist a spirit shaping.

"What is it you want to know, Shaper Ethar?"

"Did you know about the attack on the city?"

She studied him for a moment, her lips pressed into a tight line. "I have heard about it. What do you know about it?"

"I… I was there. I made the mistake of following what I sensed of power building." Why was he admitting this to her? He had shared with the Grand Master, but why was he admitting to Master Minden what he had done? She had no role in protecting the city. There was nothing she could do that would offer anything more than what the Grand Master had already done.

Yet he felt compelled, as if she wanted him to share.

Was it a shaping?

If so, it was subtle enough that he was aware of it, and aware of the fact something didn't feel quite right.

"What sort of power did you detect building?"

"A shaping," he said. "It was all around the city, and they targeted the Shapers Path. The Grand Master said the Shapers Path was used to provide protection."

"It is."

"Does it protect the Convergence?"

"It does. There are layers of protection that shapers over the years have used to help shield the Convergence. The power here would draw others who seek it. Shapers connected to the element bonds would be aware of that power, and those with less than respectable desires would come for it. As you have seen, Shaper Ethar."

"They were disciples of the Draasin Lord."

"And you survived?"

"I had help."

"Shaper Golud or Shaper Changen?"

"Shaper Changen."

She smiled. "Now I understand. She didn't know she had been spirit-shaped, and following the attack, began to piece things together. That one has quite the bright mind, so I can't say I'm altogether surprised, but knowing

Master Irina, I would not put anything past her. She would want to protect the secrets of the Academy as much as she can."

"Does hiding it offer any protection?"

"As I've told you, others would come for it if they knew of its existence."

"But is it really only meant for the Academy?"

She frowned. "That's an interesting question, but one that has been considered before. There have been many shapers over the years who have not trained at the Academy and who have claimed a right to the knowledge and power that could be found here. And who is to say they don't? We recognize the Academy isn't all-encompassing when it comes to shaping. How can it be, when there are other places that exist in the world that share significant power?"

Tolan shifted, feeling a little unsettled about what he wanted to ask, but if she was a spirit shaper, she likely already knew what he was thinking. The way she watched him suggested she was aware, even if she didn't say anything. "What about the elementals?"

"What about them?"

"Did they deserve to have access to the Convergence?"

"There aren't many who question what the elementals should have."

Tolan flushed. He shouldn't be asking about such things, and he knew it would draw the wrong kind of attention, especially since he had already been associated with the elementals. But something about Master Minden seemed to draw out such honesty.

"What if the elementals shouldn't be forced into the bonds?"

Her eyes narrowed and Tolan realized he had said too much.

"You've seen the destruction caused by elementals," she said.

"I've seen it, but—"

"The bond protects us from the elementals, but it also protects the elementals from us. There are benefits. And we are stronger for their presence in the bond." She sat up, clasping her hands on top of the table, resting them on the book. "Perhaps I made a mistake in allowing you such access to the books about the elementals."

"You haven't made a mistake. All I'm trying to do is understand."

Would she view his attempt at understanding as a way to power—which in Tolan's case, it could possibly be viewed as—or would she view it as simply trying to understand? Understanding was his reason for asking, and all he wanted was to try and learn about the elementals, if only to understand more about them.

"As a librarian, I recognize the need to understand. As a shaper, I warn you against trying to do anything that would involve the elementals. That way is a way to danger. That way is a way to the Draasin Lord."

A shaping built, and he couldn't help but back up. He wasn't sure if it came from her or from somewhere else, but in the library, a place where there should be no shaping, there seemed only one person capable of doing so.

"If you seek understanding, perhaps this might help," Master Minden said, sliding the book across the table to him. He took it and stuffed it into his pocket without looking down at it, his heart racing. "Search for understanding but avoid the Draasin Lord."

He nodded and turned away. When he reached the table, taking a seat across from Jonas, his friend stared at him. But Tolan ignored him, focusing on Master Minden. She never glanced up again, but he had the sense that a shaping continued to build from her.

What sort of shaping would she be attempting, and why did it seem targeted at him?

7

Tolan followed Master Marcella, joining her near the edge of the forest. From here, the sense of the elements continued to build, though he wasn't entirely certain whether that sense should be building for only him or whether he merely imagined it. When it came to working with Master Marcella, all he wanted was success in reaching the elements. He had a sense she grew disappointed in his failings.

"Today, we are going to focus on wind," she said.

Tolan looked around. Each time he came with Master Marcella, he felt as if he disappointed her. Today would be no different. They were near the edge of the forest, and so far, there wasn't much of a breeze. Typically, he had heard from the wind shapers, such as Master Rorn, there was benefit in working where there was an abundance of the element. Then again, when it came to wind, wasn't it in all places?

"I haven't had much success in reaching wind," he said.

"As far as I've been able to determine, you haven't had much success in reaching any of the elements other than fire."

He swallowed, licking his lips, resisting the temptation to reach into his pocket and feel for the bondar.

"In order for you to pass on to the next level, you will need to be able to control more than just a single element."

"What happens if I can't?"

She shot him a hard look. "I will not have one of the first students I mentor fail."

"I don't want to fail, but what happens to me?"

"Students in the second level must be able to command more than one element."

"That's it?"

She shook her head. "I'm not allowed to discuss anything more when it comes to your testing."

The testing was all many of the students could talk about. Everyone knew it was coming eventually, and when it did, everyone wanted to be ready, though Tolan, like everyone else, had no idea what was going to be involved. Everyone agreed it involved shaping more than one element bond, even more reason to continue to find a way to connect reliably to earth. Without access to a bondar, he wouldn't be able to do so.

"Is it just reaching more than one element bond?"

"In order to pass, you must have control of the elements. Which is why we're here. I'm determined to help you reach each of the elements. Wind is no different from fire, and I will have you find your way to the wind bond."

As she said it, the wind began to swirl around her, gusting and sending her dark hair fluttering.

He didn't know enough about the various element bonds to be able to argue effectively with her, but he felt certain wind was different from fire. For that matter, earth was different from fire. When he'd reached earth, he had been clear about how his connection to that element was different than it was when he reached for fire.

Somehow, he needed a way of reaching for the elements reliably without the bondar, and yet there remained the possibility he wouldn't.

He didn't like to think about it, but if he failed to reach another element bond consistently, it likely meant he was going to fail out of the Academy. He could imagine people like Draln taunting him. Even in that, he shouldn't feel terribly disappointed. His position had changed dramatically from where he was even a few months ago. When he hadn't been able to shape anything, his prospects had been limited. Now he could reach fire—regardless of whether it took a furios or not —he would always have some employment. It might not be what he wanted, and the longer he spent at the Academy, the more certain he was that he wanted some role with shaping that he had yet to discover, but it was something.

"Breathe in the wind. Focus on it. As you do, you can know it's there, the power exists, and as you allow it to flow through you, you can find your connection to the bond."

It sounded far easier than he knew it to be.

Without a bondar, Tolan had no chance of really connecting to the wind. Part of the challenge in working with mentors like this was that they had different ways of teaching than the primary master shapers. Then again, that was also considered an advantage. Learning from someone else who had their own methods was meant to provide others with a way of shaping they wouldn't otherwise have.

"I'm trying," he said.

She stared at him. "Again, Shaper Ethar, I get the sense you aren't trying nearly as much as you should be. If you don't take this seriously—"

"I'm taking it seriously, Master Marcella. It's just that I haven't even mastered wind with a bondar."

"The witherings are fickle."

Tolan hadn't the sense the withering was the issue. When it came to using the wind bondar, it was more about the shaper.

"You have several hours before your next class. I would encourage you to use that time."

"You're not going to stay with me?"

She cocked a brow at him. "Do you feel my presence will provide you with greater motivation?"

A warm flush worked up his neck and Tolan shook his head. "I just thought that was the point of us meeting out here."

"The point of us meeting out here was for you to connect to the elements. Today, I would like you to focus on wind. When you discover it, we will celebrate."

With that, she started off, leaving him at the edge of the forest on the border of Amitan.

Tolan focused on the wind. There was a gentle breeze, and as it brushed past his cheeks, he focused upon it, straining to see if there was anything he might be able to uncover within it, but as before, there was nothing. He breathed out, knowing there was supposed to be a connection to his breath, but even when he focused on that, he wasn't able to reach the wind bond.

He started wandering, heading into the forest, simply moving aimlessly. He focused on everything around him: the earth, the warmth of the sun, even the wind as Master Marcella wanted him to. He understood the desire to connect to the elements, but they didn't come to him well enough.

Resisting the urge to pull out the furios and shape was difficult. If he was going to practice, he might as well use the one element he could connect to, but in this place, she wanted something else from him.

As he wandered between the trees, he lost track of time. Eventually, he turned back toward Amitan, and when he did, a sense of movement caught his attention.

Tolan froze, pressing his back up against one of the nearby trees, looking around. There wasn't anything he could find. He focused on the earth, using his earth sensing to discover whether there was anything out there, but as before, he detected nothing.

He started forward and walked a few steps before he thought he caught another flutter of movement.

His heart set off hammering.

Was it an elemental?

He didn't think so, but there were the rumors Master Marcella had mentioned that the disciples of the Draasin Lord had released the elementals at the edge of the waste to draw off the Trackers or perhaps distract the master shapers from Amitan.

Worse, he had to worry it might actually be one of the disciples of the Draasin Lord.

As he neared another enormous tree, there came a flutter of movement.

This time, he was certain of what he saw.

Tolan started running.

He tried to focus on a distant sense of Amitan and the Academy, and as he went, something pulled on him.

That had to be the Academy, didn't it?

He wound through the forest and had lost track of where he was when the forest opened up.

A grassy plain was set into the middle of the forest, surrounded by an old stone wall. He approached slowly, carefully, looking around for any signs of movement, but there was nothing. He steadied his breathing, trying to relax, fearing one of the disciples was after him.

As he looked back toward the forest, he decided to climb the wall. On the other side, he found a sculpture rising in the center of the park. He'd never seen anything like it. It was tall, angular, and came to a point at the peak, the four sides tapering as they reached the top.

He jumped down, looking around, thinking that if nothing else, he could hide from whatever had been following him. A sense of shaping energy built, but he saw nothing around.

There was no one inside the park, which made the sense of shaping even stranger. He approached the wall and looked inside, focusing on whether he could see anything, but there wasn't anything here to notice. It was all long and overgrown grass. Some flowers managed to overtake sections of the lawn, and in the center of it was the enormous sculpture.

It was like a finger of rock, all solid, suggesting to Tolan that it had been shaped straight from the ground. From here, he could see how the stone had weathered over time, the surface rough, and parts of it almost seeming to be crumbling. If it had been shaped, it surprised him that it would be crumbling at all.

The sense of shaping came from within here.

Tolan looked for an entrance to the park, but there wasn't one. There was only the low wall all around it.

He scrambled up the wall, pausing on top. It was only two feet wide, easily wide enough for him to stand, and he stared around. From here, the hillside overlooked much of the city. The Academy was in the distance, the five towers representing each of the elements making it easy to observe from a distance.

He couldn't shake the sense there was a shaping near him. It continued to build, an overwhelming sense of power, and he was drawn toward it. Fire and wind, and as he focused on it, he sensed a hint of water within it. Would there be earth, too?

He jumped off the wall and into the grass. It was nearly knee-high, and he trudged through it, wishing he had boots rather than his soft-soled shoes. Then again, this wasn't how he had anticipated spending the time he had after working with Master Marcella. He had intended to study the runes, looking to see if there was any connection to the various elementals that he could come up with.

The area inside the park felt strangely peaceful. All around in the city was activity, but here there was almost a sense of silence. Other than the shaping he detected, nothing else drew him. There were no distractions, and he didn't fear students coming here and discovering him. This would be a good place to practice.

At the base of the structure, he paused. For some reason, it seemed as if the shaping emanated from here. He tapped on the stone, and when he did, the sense of shaping suddenly stopped.

Tolan staggered back, fear filling him.

Was there someone inside?

He didn't know if it was hollow or not, but the fact that the shaping would suddenly abate the moment he approached and tapped on it suggested something like that.

Tolan circled the tower, running his hand along it,

feeling for any sense of shaping, but none came. As he circled, his gaze drifted upward, looking toward the top of the tower. As he did, he realized there was a shape on this side. He continued to make a circle and found another shape. And then another. Four shapes in all, but none easy to make out.

He hurried back to the wall, trudging through the grasses, and when he reached it and jumped up onto it, he looked at the sculpture at the center of the park. From here, he couldn't make out anything. It was only when he was close to it that he was able to see it.

Tolan headed back, sensing whether there was any shaping taking place, but as far as he could tell, there was none.

As he neared the tower, he paused once again, looking upward.

He wished for Jonas's ability to shape wind and make it so he could visualize what might be up there. If he could enhance his eyesight with that sort of shaping, then he might be able to see just what it was.

And it was probably nothing. This park was abandoned, a place that had been here for centuries, a memorial to a time long past. If it were important, the Academy would have surrounded it, or they would have made some way to prevent others from coming here.

He took a seat, leaning against the tower, figuring that this was as good a spot to practice as any. If Master Marcella wanted him to practice, he would do as she wanted, though perhaps not in the location she had wanted.

He pulled the furios out, rolling it along his legs. He started to shape, feeling the energy of fire flowing through him. It was subtle, and for whatever reason, he felt better connected to it than he usually did. Perhaps it was the bright sun shining down on him, or perhaps the racing of his heart. He had learned that heightened emotion made him better attuned to the elements.

Maybe he could use that to help him recapture earth. He had shaped earth on his own without a bondar once, and had to believe he could do so again.

Master Marcella might want him to work on wind, but if he was going to pass the test, he was going to have to work on what his strengths might be. In the case of what he could reach, that meant fire and earth. Wind and water seemed almost impossible to even think about reaching.

Tolan worked through the various shapings he could recall, drawing upon fire, and then he focused on earth.

He tried to think of what Master Shorav had taught in class, the lessons coming slowly to mind, but as he attempted to reach for an earth shaping, nothing worked.

There had to be some way to do it. And he had to find some way where he wasn't under duress in order to reach it.

It might come down to having a bondar. If nothing else, that would allow him to reach the elements and feel the connection he needed. He had resisted the temptation to take one from the classroom, but with as much as he needed to still master, maybe that was what he needed to do.

He could easily imagine what his friends would say if they learned he'd taken a bondar. If he were caught, it was almost a guarantee such action would lead to repercussions—possibly expulsion. He didn't want to be expelled from the Academy, but if he didn't reach another element bond, that might not matter.

Tolan leaned his head back upon the tower. It was strangely cool and almost damp despite the warm sun shining overhead. Wind gusted all around him, and the pressure of the ground pushed up on him. He took a deep breath, letting the sense of this place fill him. It was peaceful.

Better yet, there was no one else here. He could come here, work on shaping, and not have to fear other students would watch. That was always his challenge, and his shame. If he had a place like this where he could practice unobserved, and a place that seemed close to the Academy grounds, he would take advantage of it. Perhaps some of the older students knew about it, but from what he could tell, the ground hadn't been trampled, and no one had been here in quite some time.

This would be his place.

Maybe it would be his secret.

Tolan started to shape again, focusing on earth. He would start there and work onto the other elements.

8

THE NEXT DAY, TOLAN FOLLOWED JONAS INTO A SEPARATE section of the Academy for their first spirit class. From here, there was nothing other than emptiness until reaching the spirit tower high overhead. It required a shaping to reach, proof that a shaper had at least mastered one element enough they could be trusted to visit this part of the Academy. Runes were worked along the walls, symbols that carried power but were hidden.

Tolan wondered how many of the students saw them the way he did. Maybe it was only because he had become sensitized to them that he noticed them, but it was in the way the runes were formed within the bricks making up the walls. It was subtle, the shape difficult to see, but he was convinced the power was real.

"What are you staring at?" Jonas asked from behind.

Tolan glanced over to see his friend holding onto a wind shaping. It was the default shaping that Jonas reached for when he wanted to reach the spirit tower. Jonas had control over other elements, with increasing strength of fire and earth, but wind was what he had mastered first, and it was wind he reached for first.

It was similar to how Tolan pulled on fire, though fire wasn't the only element he could use. Ever since the day he'd faced the disciples of the Draasin Lord, he had realized he now had a connection to earth. It had worked during a time of significant distress, and he was convinced the earth elemental had been real—and had been his fault.

"I'm looking at the walls," he whispered. He didn't want to bring too much attention to what he was doing or what he'd seen because he wasn't sure how anyone else within the Academy would react to his interest in the runes.

"I didn't know you were starting to study architecture, too. Pretty soon, you're going to end up in the library all of the time and ignore what's out in the rest of the city."

"The architecture of the Academy is quite impressive," Master Aela said, coming up behind them.

Tolan tipped his head respectfully to her. She was younger than most of the master instructors, and had black hair that hung to her shoulders and her skin was deeply tanned, almost olive. Brown eyes studied them, glancing from Jonas to Tolan, and a part of him worried she was using a spirit shaping on him as she studied him.

"Tolan was remarking on the architecture within the tower," Jonas said with a smirk. "I think he'd like to study it."

Master Aela regarded Tolan for a long moment, and there was a fluttering within him, a stirring. He ignored it for a moment but wouldn't be able to ignore it for long. He could feel the way she watched him and could practically feel her shaping crawling within his mind.

"I find the architecture quite impressive, particularly the spirit tower," Draln said, coming up behind them.

Tolan glanced over, barely hiding the disgust in his eyes. It didn't surprise him that Draln would try to convince Master Aela he was somehow superior. Considering how skilled a shaper he already had become, it might even be convincing.

"I'm surprised so many in the first year have begun to appreciate the architecture of the Academy. Most take until their second or third year before they begin to appreciate it, and even then, it's not often we have any who really understand how magnificent the construction of the Academy is. The ancient shapers who created it, the first of the Academy, were far more skilled than most give credit to."

Draln made a show of nodding, and Tolan wondered just how much he actually cared. Knowing what he did about the other man, it was likely all for appearances. More likely than not, he did it mostly to antagonize Tolan and Jonas.

"Now, if you all don't mind, it is time for class to begin." With a burst of shaping, either wind or water—Tolan couldn't quite tell which—Master Aela made her way to the spirit tower.

Draln smirked at him before turning his attention to Jonas. "I'm surprised you recognize architecture, Golud, especially considering that slum you called home."

"Your sister didn't think it was much of a slum when she visited," Jonas said, glaring at Draln.

Draln tensed and Tolan stepped between them, afraid a fight might break out. It wouldn't surprise him to see either man deciding to instigate. Jonas was proud, and Draln too stubborn to realize when he had someone else riled up.

"I'm surprised the two of you are able to even reach this tower," Draln said, glancing from Jonas to Tolan. His gaze lingered on Tolan the longest, and he pressed his lips together in a tight frown. "Though, it is too bad you only have a connection to a single element. How much longer do you think they'll allow you to remain in the Academy studying when you can't reach any others? True shapers don't use bondars," he said.

He leapt to the air on a shaping of wind and fire, swirling toward the spirit tower. Tolan glared after him before focusing, thinking about the fire elemental and drawing on the power of the furios. He feared trying to shape without it, but holding onto the furios, drawing on the strength it granted him, gave him a better opportunity to reach the spirit tower, and it didn't take quite as many attempts. The longer he remained below, the more attention he drew. He had no interest in continuing to draw attention from people like Draln.

"Do you have it?" Jonas whispered.

Tolan nodded.

Jonas spun up into the air, following a funnel of wind, and Tolan focused, preparing to explode upward. The shaping came easier to him, though still not as easily as he would like it to. He needed it to be faster. He needed for it to be second nature, but summoning the power as he did, focusing on an elemental as he did, made it so no power came all that quickly.

He exploded, and as he drifted toward the spirit tower, he glanced over to see Ferrah rising past him. He tried to catch her, but she was too quick.

How long would she stay angry with him?

When he reached an enormous archway marking the entrance to the spirit tower, he landed and staggered forward. He still didn't have the necessary control over the shaping to allow him to land with any sort of grace and dignity. He was thankful he was able to reach it at all, so landing was something that would come later.

He looked around. The others were all focused toward the front of the classroom, looking toward Master Aela. Swirls of letters had been shaped into the air, words written for them to take notes on.

As he hurried to his spot next to Jonas, he glanced over at Ferrah, hoping to catch her eye, but she ignored him, just as she had over the last few days.

"Did I miss anything?" he whispered.

"Nothing terribly important. She's mostly droning on about the need to reach deep within yourself to understand spirit. I don't have much hope that I will be able to do so."

"Even after your studies on the Inquisitors?"

Jonas raised a finger to his lips. "Don't talk about that here. If Master Aela learned about that, I can imagine her giving me more assignments."

"You don't want more assignments? I thought you loved the idea of learning all about them."

"Shaper Ethar, is there something you would like to share with us about your knowledge of spirit?"

He flushed. Warmth rolled through him and a bead of sweat started along his brow, running down his face. "I'm sorry, Master Aela."

"Please share if you have something. Each of us has our own unique experience, and if your experience has granted you insight to spirit, I would be thrilled if you were so inclined to pass on what you know."

"I don't know anything worth sharing," he said.

She frowned, and he wished he could disappear or shrink in on himself. She turned back to the space at the front of the room, continuing to create her shaped letters, and Tolan stared straight ahead. Draln snickered behind him, and he forced himself to ignore it. There'd be no good in paying any attention to that, especially knowing that was exactly what Draln wanted.

"As we've been learning, spirit is a connection we all share. There are some who believe each of us is born with the ability to reach for spirit. While I don't know if that is true or not, it seems as likely as any other answer."

"Does that mean anyone has the potential to be an Inquisitor?" Jessica asked from the side of the room.

Master Aela glanced over at her, and a smile spread across her face. "Do you think you'd like to be an Inquisitor?"

"I—"

Master Aela laughed softly, her voice light, reminding Tolan of a shaping. Was she using spirit even now? He couldn't tell, and he doubted any of the others could tell, either, which was somewhat troubling. What if she was shaping them?

It was unlikely anything could be done. All he could hope for was the possibility he would be able to resist her shaping, but he didn't know if he would be able to or not. He might have avoided a shaping from Master Irina, but that had been a single shaping, and he wondered if the spirit shaping done within their classroom would be a continuous and ongoing sort of thing.

"The Inquisitors will find any with the potential to join them. There are only a few roles for those with the necessary potential."

"Everyone who has the power to reach spirit is asked to serve as an Inquisitor?" Ferrah asked.

"The Inquisitors have an important role within Terndahl. If you have the necessary ability, then you will be asked to serve. You should consider that a great honor."

She held her gaze on Ferrah for a moment before smiling and turning her attention back to the front of the room.

If he did have some connection to spirit—and he wasn't sure, but it seemed possible—what did that mean for him? He didn't know many of the Inquisitors, really only Master Irina, but what he knew about them was enough to make him uncertain about whether or not he wanted anything to do with that sort of shaping. It seemed to him that there could be a much better use of spirit shaping, though he didn't know what else it could be used for.

"Once again, as we were saying, there has long been a belief that each of us has within us the ability to shape spirit. There is no question we are all connected, and that the ancient element bonds bind us together, though not all of us can reach them anymore. There was a time when everyone was said to have been able to reach the element bonds, though time or desire has waned, making it so such things aren't as possible as they once were. Perhaps in enough years, the ability to shape will be even more restricted, and we will eventually fade into nothingness."

"I didn't expect her to get so dark," Jonas murmured.

"Yet, spirit binds us together, and it's because of spirit that we know we belong to something greater. We are shapers, connected to the element bonds, to an ancient power that binds us. Those who reach spirit gain a greater understanding than those who don't, but even without that connection, most understand how they are unique."

Tolan was surprised at the direction she was taking and hadn't expected her to talk to them about the nature of the various element bonds. The other instructors had not started quite so basic, though in his case, speaking about the element bonds wasn't basic at all.

"For those of you who have the ability to connect to more than one element, I would have you practice binding them together. Doing so is one way you might be able to reach spirit, though in truth, those spirit shapers who require such access to the most blessed of elements aren't ever nearly as powerful as those who have a natural affinity for it."

"What do you mean by binding the elements together?"

"Focus on shaping more than one element at a time," she said, her voice musical and low. Seeing as how he had the ability of only reaching fire—and maybe earth—he wasn't going to be binding anything together, which meant maybe his belief that he could reach spirit—or somehow prevent spirit from being used on him— might've been wrong. "Those of you who have the ability of only reaching a single element," she said, sweeping her gaze around the room before it settled on Tolan, "must wait, though perhaps in hearing these lectures, and being taught about the most sacred of the elements, you might gain insight when—and if—you ever are able to reach it."

She turned away and took a seat at a table in the corner.

Tolan glanced at Jonas, sharing a look. "Is that it?" he asked.

"I think she intends for us to practice, though I'm not entirely sure. I would've expected her to share a little bit more if that's what she wanted from us, but maybe she thought we should know without her telling us."

"I guess I get to sit back and watch," Tolan said.

"Sorry."

"Don't be sorry. I'm the one who can only reach a single element. Maybe I should grab a bondar from the other classrooms and see if I can use each of them to combine together and somehow reach for spirit."

"That's not a bad idea," Jonas said.

"I was kidding."

"I know you were, but it still not a bad idea. Think about what you might be able to do if you could shape through a bondar for each of the elements. It would have to bring you pretty close to reaching spirit."

"It might bring you close, but it won't bring you the same closeness to the element as you would have if you reached it naturally," Tolan said, mimicking the singsong way Master Aela spoke. He glanced at the front of the room to make sure she wasn't watching and was thankful she seemed lost in whatever she was studying.

Power built from everyone all around him. Shapings burst into being, everybody attempting to call upon their power, combining it and using it so they could try to mix their shapings, reaching for spirit in a way Tolan could not.

But maybe he could.

Hadn't he reached for earth and mixed it with fire? That was the same as what happened with the elementals, the way hyza was earth and fire.

What if he started with one, and from there called upon the other?

He looked around at the others in the room and decided that here—and now—was not the place he wanted to do it. If he did manage to call an elemental, it would likely terrify others, and Tolan wasn't sure he had enough control over his shaping—or summoning—to do so in a way that wouldn't cause chaos. It would be better to do this in the park.

He got to his feet and started to make his way around the room. Others looked at him, and Draln glared at him and made a point of holding his hand out, a flame burning in his palm, wind swirling around it, and Tolan couldn't tell, but it seemed as if water caused the flame to hiss and spit. Whatever he was doing involved at least three elements, and if he were somehow able to add earth to it, he would be able to make spirit, wouldn't he?

And here Tolan had believed it was much rarer to do.

"Master Aela?" Ferrah said.

The master glanced over, and she smiled brightly when she looked at Ferrah. "What is it?"

"When we mix the four elements, how is it that we know if we have managed to combine them effectively?"

Tolan looked over at her and frowned. Could she really have managed to shape four elements at the same time? He knew Ferrah had skill—she had come to the Academy with significant shaping ability—but had the few months they'd been here already taught her how to reach all of the elements?

He glanced over at Draln and didn't think even he had managed that, not without a bondar. Draln flicked his gaze from Ferrah to his palm and clenched his jaw, focusing on his shaping.

"You will know if you are successful. You will feel it deep within you, and with it will come a sense of awareness you do not find otherwise. I don't know that I can describe it in any other way, but I do know that when that power comes, you will feel it."

Ferrah turned her attention back to staring at her hand, and Tolan wondered if she had already managed to reach spirit. What if she had some way of doing so?

And if she did, then he wondered if he could figure out some way of his own, but it would involve somehow managing to pull on the connection to more than one elemental at a time. Even if he could manage to, something that he still didn't know if it were possible, Tolan didn't think he could draw upon the power of more than two.

He made his way around the room, glancing from place to place, and noticed a bookshelf. What kind of books would she have here? Would they be the kind that would speak about spirit and reaching that sort of power? If there were books like that here, why here rather than in the library?

"Shaper Ethar, the instruction is for everyone to focus on shaping various elements together."

Tolan turned to Master Aela. She stood only a few steps away from him and smelled of perfume, but it seemed to cover something else, a hidden odor he couldn't quite make out. "I would, but I'm one of those shapers you mentioned who can't shape more than one element."

"Then you can use the time to work on reaching another element," she said.

"It's not quite as effective for me without having access to a bondar," he said. Tolan hesitated, looking in her direction. "Is there a bondar for spirit?"

She fixed him with a heavy gaze. "There are no shortcuts when it comes to spirit."

"I'm not looking for a shortcut. I'm just wondering—"

"You wouldn't be the first who has wondered if there might be an easy way to reach for spirit, but unfortunately—or perhaps, fortunately—there is no simple method of accessing spirit. It takes practice and patience and more than a little skill. It's why spirit is so revered. Spirit shapers are among the most powerful shapers Terndahl has, and we use the power of those shapers, and we have remained safe, a unified people for many years."

He wondered what the master shapers who couldn't reach spirit might say about hearing her speak in such terms about their elements. Most of the master shapers had the ability to reach more than one element bond, but as far as he knew, only the Inquisitors were able to reach spirit.

"What is involved in serving as an Inquisitor?"

"If you are interested in serving as an Inquisitor, I must

warn you it is difficult, and only those most capable are granted that opportunity."

"I'm not sure I want to serve as an Inquisitor, but I am curious what goes into the training."

"The Inquisitors are very secretive about what they require of their trainees."

"You're a spirit shaper. Does that mean you are an Inquisitor?"

"We all serve spirit," she said.

She turned away, heading back to the front of the room, and Tolan studied her, realizing she hadn't really answered his question. What did it mean that they served spirit? For all he knew, that meant nothing more than a denial that she was with the Inquisitors.

He returned to his seat next to Jonas, watching as his friend continued to work on mixing his shapings. He focused primarily on wind, and Tolan could see how he would add other elements to it, occasionally trying to swirl in fire, but he had seen a combination of shapings before, and this wasn't the way to combine the element bonds.

And maybe Master Aela was right and it was only those with the most skill who were able to shape spirit by combining the elements.

The class was a frustrating one for him, not least because it felt as if he could do nothing. He spent the entire time focusing on reaching earth, but there was no other response, nothing suggesting he was even close.

When class was over, most of the first-year students

shuffled out, and with a burst of shaped power, they descended back out of the tower itself. Tolan lingered, and because of that, Jonas did, too.

"What are you trying to do?"

"I'm trying to get her to talk to me."

"Master Aela? What more do you want her to say?"

Tolan shook his head. "Not Master Aela, but Ferrah. I want her to at least acknowledge me."

He stood off in the corner of the room, watching and waiting, but Ferrah sat at her table, continuing to shape, trying to mix the elements together, and never once looking up at him. After a while, Master Aela made her way toward Ferrah, and she leaned over the table and they began to speak softly to each other.

"How long do you intend to wait?"

"I guess we can go," Tolan said.

"You don't have to sound so excited about it."

"It's just, I was hoping to come away from this with a few more answers than I have."

"What? You mean you don't have any answers about shaping spirit after being asked to mix your elements together? I'm completely surprised, Tolan."

He chuckled, and they stepped to the platform. Tolan focused on fire, using his ability to imagine an elemental but focusing through the furios. It was a crutch, but the kind of crutch he still needed. Hopefully, there would come a time when he could get away from using it.

When they landed on the ground, Tolan paused and studied the walls again. There was something here he didn't quite grasp, tied to the runes worked into the walls themselves. Were they found in other towers, as well? He hadn't noticed them before, but the other towers were different, with stairs sweeping around through them, giving access to the upper levels, nothing like the spirit tower designed to stand apart.

And because it was designed to stand apart, maybe Master Aela was right about spirit. Could it be that it was the most important element?

"Are you going to continue admiring the architecture?"

"I..."

He trailed off as they started out of the spirit tower, realizing Draln and several other first year students were there. He glanced over at Tolan, a wide smirk spreading across his face. "Ethar. I think you're the kind of shaper I might need to hire when I am promoted through the Academy. You know, they do still make some who fail serve the others."

Jonas started forward, but Tolan grabbed him by the arm, pulling back. "It's not worth it."

"Oh, look. Now we have two of them who think that with their weak shaping, they can impress us."

"I seem to remember seeing Tolan beat you at Imaginarium."

"It's about the only thing Ethar can beat me with."

"Would you rather challenge him to a shaper's duel?" Jonas asked.

"Jonas!"

Jonas glanced over. There was heat in his gaze, but

Tolan wasn't quite sure why. Usually Jonas could be brash and impulsive, but for some reason, he was letting Draln bait him far more than he usually did.

The two of them had some history together when they were in their home city, though Jonas never really spoke of it. Tolan had some idea, though not enough to know just how much the two hated each other.

"I don't think Ethar would be interested in a shaper's duel. And I doubt Ethar has enough skill to pose much of a challenge if he were willing."

The four students around Draln all chuckled, and Tolan resisted the urge to flush. Even here, where he had begun to show some skill, he felt something like an outsider. He knew he shouldn't—he had passed the Selection the same as everyone else—but he couldn't shake the fact he did feel somehow different.

That was much the same way he had felt in Ephra. He had felt different there, too.

"I don't know what a shaper's duel is, but I'm happy to oblige you, Draln," he said.

If it was the only way he would gain a certain measure of respect, shouldn't he be willing to do it? And it wasn't as if he feared Draln. He recognized the other man had skill, but he had limits to his knowledge. He would have to. And Tolan had squared off against one of the disciples of the Draasin Lord. If he could do that and survive, surely, he could face off against someone like Draln.

"I'm sure your friend Golud can explain the intricacies

of it. I'll give you some time to practice, not that it'll matter, and I'll let you know when we'll duel."

"Fine," Tolan said.

Draln turned away, grinning and laughing with the others. It made him dislike the man even more, but there wasn't anything he could do about it other than figure out what was going to be required with this shaper's duel, and what that meant for him.

"What did you do?" Jonas asked.

"You're the one who wanted that me to do this," Tolan said.

"I didn't want you to do that. I just thought we could scare him a little, maybe convince him you would be willing to do it."

"What is a shaper's duel?"

"It's just like it sounds. Two shapers face off against each other, and the best shaper wins."

"I don't see what the issue is then."

"Well, typically a shaper's duel is to the death, though I doubt he'd intend that here. When we were in Velminth, he used duels as a way to abuse other shapers, not kill them."

"What?"

"Right. That's my point. You don't need to be facing off to the death."

Tolan wouldn't have agreed to anything had he known it was to the death, especially not with Draln. The other man was a more powerful shaper, and he had a connection to multiple elements, which gave him a significant advantage.

"Come on. We can go train."

"I'm not going to do it," Tolan said.

"But you agreed."

"I might've agreed, but I agreed to something I didn't have any idea what it meant. There's no way he expects me to fight him to the death."

"I don't know. This is Draln we're talking about. He has weird ideas about things. Part of that comes from the fact he believes himself as powerful as the shapers of old, something I imagine his parents helped instill in him, but part of that is the fact he actually is a skilled shaper."

As they made their way down the Hall, Tolan glanced back and caught a glimpse of Ferrah. Had she been listening? Before he had a chance to find out, she hurried off down one of the side halls, away from the students' quarters, and disappeared.

He wanted to know what she was up to but doubted she would let him.

And he had other things to think about. If he was expected to face Draln in a shaper's duel, he needed to prepare, even if he didn't intend to really face him.

But if he did, would he be able to use his connection to the elementals? It might be too risky to do so, but if he didn't, he couldn't help but fear Draln might use it as an excuse to hurt him.

9

FOR WHATEVER REASON, EACH TIME TOLAN CAME TO THE park to practice shaping, he felt as if he improved, almost as if the park had a calming effect on him, enhancing his ability. He was able to shape more effectively, at least when it came to fire. He still hadn't managed to reach any of the other elements, though there seemed to be some part of him that thought he got closer to reaching earth.

It was time for him to return. How long had he been sitting here, practicing all by himself? Possibly hours.

Crawling over the wall, he looked around but saw no signs of movement. He hurried back, taking a different path than he had out here, knowing now how to find his way easily. He didn't want to leave any sort of trampled path for others to follow.

A strange sound caught his attention, and he paused.

Whenever he came out here, he remained nervous he might encounter one of the disciples of the Draasin Lord, but other than the first time he'd come here, he had come across nothing suggesting the disciples were out in the forest.

This time, he came across movement.

Only there was something familiar about it.

He trailed after it, using his connection to earth sensing, and realized it was Ferrah he tracked.

He followed her until he reached the edge of the city. Stepping out of the forest, he stopped to admire the trees. They were much larger than those near his home in Ephra and they climbed toward the sky, making almost a perfect separation between the forest and the city. Many of the trunks took him a dozen paces to make his way around, but they stopped abruptly, as if the city prevented them coming any closer, and if there were secrets hiding in the depth of the forest that defined its edges.

Tolan crept back to the city, still trailing after Ferrah.

He stayed near one of the outer buildings. These were run down, not nearly as nice as some of the buildings deeper within the city, and some were abandoned, the stone having crumbled and the entire thing falling into disrepair.

Tolan remained hidden against the edge of the building, trying to stay concealed in shadows but not thinking he did that great a job. He wouldn't be surprised if Ferrah realized he was here, but so far, she hadn't turned to him.

He needed to talk with her. He needed to apologize. She had continued to avoid him, staying out of their room until late at night, and Tolan had had enough of it. He was determined to reconnect with his friend, to force her to at least acknowledge him and give him a chance to apologize.

More than that, he wanted to show her the park he'd discovered and see if there might be anything she could help him understand about it. He'd only been there a few times, but each time he went, he felt convinced he was getting closer to understanding its purpose.

She spun suddenly toward him. Wind swirled around and whipped at his cloak. He tried to pull it closer around him but wasn't quick enough.

"You can stop following me at any time." Her voice carried on a shaping of wind.

The control she had over it impressed him. She was able to focus the wind in such a way that it amplified her voice, or maybe that wasn't it at all. Maybe she sent it on a whisper of wind, carrying it to his ears only.

Tolan stepped forward, out of the shadows of the crumbling building, and jogged toward her. At first, it looked as if she intended to bolt, but she stayed frozen in place, watching him. A mixture of emotions flickered across her eyes as he neared, that of irritation and anger, but maybe there was some relief? Tolan hoped for the last.

"I wouldn't have to follow you if you wouldn't avoid me."

"I'm not avoiding you."

She started to turn, and Tolan ran to get in front of her. "You've been staying out of the room, and you've been avoiding the library."

"I haven't been—"

"I know you've been avoiding the library. I asked both Master Jensen and Master Minden. Neither of them has seen you in the library nearly as much as before." The only times Tolan had seen her had been in their classes, and even those had been fleeting, with her sitting toward the front of the class, alongside other students and not saving room for him or Jonas as she normally would. When class was over, she always hurried out, racing ahead of them.

"I have a right to be angry, Tolan. Besides, I'm not the only who's been avoiding things. You've been gone too."

Now wasn't the time to tell her about the park—not when she was this angry. "I'm not saying you don't have that right. I'm just saying... I'm trying to say sorry."

She frowned as she stared at him and finally shook her head. "I need more than an apology. With what happened to me, I deserved to know."

He nodded. She did deserve to know, and he should have shared it with her. He shouldn't have kept from her the fact a spirit shaping had been used on her, hiding her memories.

"You deserve more than an apology. You deserve an explanation."

"I don't need an explanation. I know exactly why you did it."

"You don't know exactly why I did it," Tolan said. He looked around, and was thankful they were still outside the city, at the edge of the forest. At least here, there wasn't anyone around to overhear him as he talked to her. "When you see my shaping, what is it you notice?"

"What do you mean?"

"I mean that when you see me performing a shaping, what do you observe?"

"I see a shaping, Tolan."

"My shaping is different."

"You said that before, and I'm not sure it really is. It might be different in the fact you are coming to it later than the rest of us, but that doesn't mean your shaping is any less impressive."

He smiled. "That's almost a compliment."

"It *is* a compliment, you dolt." She pushed on him with the shaping of wind, and even with something as simple as that, Tolan was made aware of the difference between the two of them. While he could shape—or whatever it was he did—it didn't happen quickly, not like hers.

"When I shape, I've told you how I use the image of elementals."

"You said that," she said.

He took a deep breath. She needed to know this. "There are times when it seems the elementals actually appear. It's like when we were facing the disciples of the Draasin Lord. There was a sense, to me at least, that I had used an elemental for power."

"I didn't see an elemental. All I saw was a potent shaping."

"You saw fire?"

"That's what I said."

"And with that fire shaping, did you see anything within it?" He glanced around. He had a sense there was movement near him, but maybe it was only his imagination.

"There wasn't anything within the flames, if that's what you were asking."

Could she not have seen it? He was quite certain there had been a fire elemental within the flames, but maybe it *had* been only his imagination. Could it be that he had been so focused on performing the shaping, visualizing the power of the elemental, that he had believed he had formed one?

"What about the earth elemental?" he asked.

That one, he knew he hadn't imagined. Master Sartan had been needed to tamp it down, suppressing it.

"The disciples freed the earth elemental, Tolan. They were trying to destroy the Shapers Path. They freed the elemental in order to do so."

"That was me."

"You freed an earth elemental?" She started laughing, shaking her head. "I'm sorry, Tolan, but you aren't a skilled enough shaper to do that. I don't mean that in a way to hurt your feelings, but if you had that kind of potential, you wouldn't struggle to reach your shapings."

"It was the first time I ever freed earth," he said.

"What if you only believe you did it? What if they were the ones who freed the earth elemental, and what if they were using a spirit shaping on you to convince you otherwise?"

"Listen to what you're saying. For them to have done that would be far more steps than what should have been possible while attacking us. I just don't see how that was possible."

"We didn't pose any real threat to them. It wouldn't have taken many steps for them to have shaped you in a way to convince you that you were the one responsible for freeing the earth elemental. I'd love it if you had that power, Tolan, but it's just not you."

"There was another time, but…" As he said it, he realized she wouldn't remember. And maybe that was why she didn't believe him. "When we were at the place of Convergence, I used the furios and managed to summon an enormous fire elemental. It helped hold Jory off for a while, but even then, he was able to dismiss it."

"How certain are you it was a fire elemental?"

"Pretty sure. He also tried summoning a draasin and had the Grand Master and Master Irina not appeared, he would have succeeded."

She stared at him. "You're not making this any easier."

"Making what any easier?"

"Making it any easier for me to get over being angry with you. With everything you've been through, all these things you've seen, I can't help but feel as if I've missed out on them. And it was only a short period of time, but it was an incredibly important time that I'm now missing."

"It's not missing the time that's upsetting you. It's not seeing the Convergence, isn't it?"

She sighed. "You can't understand how long I've looked."

"I know how hard you've researched since you came to the Academy."

"I've been researching information about Par," she said.

"I know you have," he said. "And I should have known how much it meant to you to find that out." It wasn't something he had even considered, and now he realized why she was so angry, he thought he had a better sense of what he could do to make up for it. "How about the two of us go and break into the Convergence?"

Would that be any better use of his time than trying to understand what he'd discovered in the park? To Ferrah, it would be, which was why he needed to help her.

"If we do that, then we risk the anger of the Grand Master."

"He already knows I'm aware of the Convergence, so I'm not sure he would be any angrier."

She studied him for a moment. "I'll think about it."

It wasn't the expected response. Tolan had expected she would have jumped at the chance, especially knowing how eager she was to get a better understanding about the Convergence, but maybe that was tempered by her desire to maintain her place at the Academy. And didn't he feel a similar desire? He didn't want to lose his position here, especially now he had begun to fully understand how much he wanted to be here. It was surprising to realize that, especially because he had never once considered a life where he would be a part of the Academy.

And now he understood shaping, now he had it within him, he didn't want to be told he couldn't use it.

"What are you doing out here, anyway?" he asked.

"I told you I was working on my studies."

"What of your studies have taken you out here?"

"I…" She turned away from him, focusing out into the forest. A shaping built from her, though he couldn't tell what the intent behind it was. Why would she conceal her shaping from him?

"Ferrah?"

"I'm searching for elementals," she said.

Tolan wondered if she would even find anything about the elementals, or would knowledge of them be hidden from her? "On your own?"

"Not all of us chases the elementals when they appear," she said.

"I don't always chase the elementals." When she arched a brow, he shrugged. "Well, I don't usually. I don't know why I feel compelled to go after them."

"I thought it had something to do with you being from Ephra."

"My being from Ephra doesn't give me an affinity to the elementals." At least, he didn't think it did. He did have some connection to them, but was that from the fact he'd grown up so close to the waste, or because of who he was?

There were still memories buried within him that he didn't have the answers to, and those memories needed him to search for answers, though Tolan wondered if they would ever come, or would he forever feel as if he didn't know some deep part of himself?

"Why would you chase elementals?" She didn't answer at first and he frowned, looking at Ferrah. "What is it you don't want to tell me?"

"You don't get to do that," she said.

"Do what?"

"Accuse me of withholding things from you."

"I didn't accuse you of anything."

"You didn't need to. It was in the way you looked at me. And I'm not holding anything back from you."

He chuckled. That she didn't see it amused him a little bit, though perhaps it shouldn't. It would probably upset her to know he was amused by that. "I could help."

"What if I don't want your help?"

"Why wouldn't you want me to come with you? I've been studying the elementals. So, if there is anything about them out here, I could help so you could understand them," he said.

"If I let you do this, you promise you won't tell anyone what I'm doing?"

"Who would I tell?"

"It seems you and the Grand Master have gotten close, so…"

Tolan shook his head. "I promise I won't share with anyone what you're up to. Including the Grand Master."

She nodded and reached into her pouch and pulled out a small length of stone. Etched into the stone were runes, and she palmed it, holding it out, and pulled on a shaping, using that to stretch outward as the shaping swept across the forest.

"What is that? It looks something like a bondar, but we've seen all of the bondars," he said.

"It looks like them, but it's not."

"What is it, then?"

"It helps find elementals."

"Like the Trackers?"

She looked away from him. "Where do you think I got it?"

He hoped she'd say more, but when she didn't, he stepped forward.

"Consider me curious. There have been reports of movement outside of the city," she said.

"Wait… are you looking to see if there are other disciples out here who might attack?"

"I'm not looking for that. What I'm looking into is why."

"To find the Convergence."

She turned away.

"Is that why you have that bondar, then?"

"I want to be safe in case I'm attacked," she said softly.

Tolan caught up to her, looking around her and into the forest. "I'm not so sure the elementals would attack."

"Why?"

He glanced at the bondar she held. If Ferrah had some way of reaching power that would help him with the elementals, it would be valuable to understanding more about what he could do.

"One of the things I've learned from what I've been reading is that the ancient shapers celebrated the elementals," he said.

"We know that. It's more than just celebrating the elementals. Something changed that made them push the elementals into the bond. What I want to know is why we keep finding elementals out of the bond."

"You think that will help you understand the Convergence?"

"I think it will help me find it."

"I've already told you I know how to find it."

"And the Grand Master doesn't want you to share."

He shook his head. "The Convergence can't be your only reason for doing this."

"I'm trying to understand the attacks, Tolan. No one gives us an answer and you're so focused on the elementals, but don't ask questions as to why. What do the disciples hope to gain?"

"We won't get the answers you want because we're first-level students."

"It's more than that. You said it yourself. There was something out in the waste. And now the waste shifted. That has to mean something." She glanced down at the item in her hand. "There was so much power."

He took a deep breath. "We've seen elementals we assume have broken free from the bond, but what if there are elementals all around us and we just don't see them?" That would be a better answer than him being the one to

release them. Maybe his shaping only summoned them—
but not from the bond.

She pulled on a shaping once again through the item
she gripped in her hand. As it swept out, he felt the way it
reverberated, echoing off the trees, drifting into the forest,
before fading.

Why should he be able to detect something like that?

"Why here?" he asked.

"The forest?"

Tolan nodded. "Why are you searching here rather
than somewhere else?"

"What makes you think I haven't been searching other
places?"

Knowing Ferrah, she probably had explored other
places before finally coming here.

He dipped his hand into his pocket and ran his fingers
along the furios. He focused on the runes and created an
image in his mind, using that to attempt a shaping. Heat
built slowly and Tolan pulled the furios out of his pocket
and pointed it into the trees. A streak of flame shot from
the end of the furios, and from there, it took the shape of
the hyza. As it did, the elemental began twisting, turning
back toward Tolan and Ferrah. Fire glowed where eyes
would be, and Tolan continued to hold onto the shaping.

"Why are you pulling on fire shaping?" she asked.

"You don't see it?"

"See what?"

"See the elemental. I've summoned hyza, mostly to
show you it could be done."

"You haven't summoned anything, Tolan. All I see is fire."

He glanced at the item in her hand. "Try that."

She frowned, but a shaping built, starting through the device before washing out. Where it struck the fire elemental, Tolan could feel an echoing, something of a reverberation that bounced off before drifting once again out into the forest.

Ferrah's eyes widened. "What was that?"

"That's the elemental."

"You can feel it?"

"I felt what you did, though I don't really know what it is."

"A shaping. The bondar uses the shaping, and it calls to the elementals."

"I thought you said it wasn't a bondar?"

"I never said what it was. It is a bondar, though not one we've used in our lessons before, mostly because it's incredibly dangerous."

"Why is it dangerous?"

"You really want to know?"

"I'm thinking I don't, but at the same time, I'm curious what you have and why you're using it."

"It's a bondar for spirit."

"Master Aela said there wasn't one for spirit."

She flushed. "It's not for spirit exactly. It lets the shaper hold onto each of elements more effectively. With that, we can summon spirit."

Tolan stared at her. Would he be able to use something

like that? He didn't see how he could. "How is it you have a bondar for spirit?"

"I came across it while we were studying in the spirit classroom," she said.

"Ferrah!"

"Our lessons there are different than they are for the other classes, and I was determined to see if I could uncover anything that might be of use. If this bondar can allow me to reach spirit, maybe I can uncover more about the elementals."

"I don't think that's what it's for."

"We don't know what it's for. Master Aela hasn't shared anything with us."

"Just because Master Aela hasn't shared anything with us isn't a reason to be stealing from the spirit classroom. If you get caught doing that, you run the risk of expulsion."

She stared at him, saying nothing for a long moment. "Are you going to help me, or not?"

"I'll help you, but…"

"But nothing. And I'm surprised you haven't taken a bondar from the other classes. With you having the furios, I sort of expected you to have one of each of the others."

Tolan wondered how easy it would've been to master reaching the other elements if he'd had a bondar to practice with.

As he stared at her, he realized he was still holding onto the shaping, and he released it. The elemental remained for a moment before turning and bounding off, leaving Tolan standing and watching Ferrah. She pushed on a shaping again, letting it move away from her, and it reached out into the forest, streaking away before dissipating.

"I don't detect anything else," she said.

"I'm not shaping anymore," he said.

"You shouldn't have to shape in order to detect something."

"Which means there's an elemental wandering."

"You don't know that. Besides, we don't know the mind of the elementals," she said.

"I'm surprised you think they have a mind."

"You forget, I'm from Par. We have paintings in some of the ruins that show the elementals mingling with our earliest and most powerful shapers. I can't think of anything other than the fact they have to be a part of our world."

"You have to be careful saying that or you'll have others accusing you of serving the Draasin Lord."

"I would never—"

Tolan smiled, shaking his head. "I know you wouldn't, but others wouldn't see it that way, would they? Others don't see me that way. In Ephra, there are too many who are happy to blame things happening on the Draasin Lord and his followers."

"What happened with you?"

"Nothing happened," he said.

"Something had to happen."

"I lost my parents. Everyone says they went to serve

the Draasin Lord, but that doesn't fit with memories I have of them."

"What if your memories were shaped so you only remember what they wanted you to remember?"

The question struck a chord, raising the same questions he'd been asking. "I don't know. When I was in the Selection, I had a memory of my parents I don't recall having. It makes me wonder if perhaps I had been shaped, but why? What were they trying to hide?"

"Maybe they were hiding the fact they wanted to serve the Draasin Lord," she said softly. "You may not want to believe it, but not all parents are good."

"Yours weren't?"

"My parents were fine, but I've seen enough people who have parents who push them or were abusive, and because of that, I know not everyone has the same experience."

Tolan swallowed. He didn't like to think his parents had gone off and chased the Draasin Lord, but what if they had? And worse, with him beginning to wonder about whether he had some connection to spirit, what if he were destined to go and serve the Draasin Lord? He had a connection to the elementals.

That seemed to him the way it would start. First, he would begin with abusing that connection to the elementals, feeling as if he wanted to free them from the bonds, and it wouldn't take long for him to move onto having a thirst for power that would only be satiated by abusing the elementals within the bond, forcing them to serve him.

Maybe Tolan was destined to *become* the Draasin Lord.

He shook away those thoughts and found Ferrah watching him, concern etched on her face. He forced a smile, though doubted he was very convincing.

"Come on," he said. "Let's see if we can't keep using your stolen bondar and uncover what might have happened." He would do this for her, fix the issues between them, and then ask if she could help him understand the park.

"Only if you want to," she said.

"I'll help you. Whatever you need, I'll help you."

10

BY THE TIME TOLAN HAD FOUND MARCELLA AND WAS prepared for his lessons for the next day, she was geared up to head out of the Academy. She had a traveling cloak and what looked to be a sword sheathed to her side beneath it, though her belt was cinched around her waist, making it difficult for him to tell—but it would also be difficult for her to unsheathe the sword if it were there. Her hair was pulled back and bound with a length of leather sash, and she wore a pouch slung over her shoulder.

"Are you ready for today?" she asked.

Tolan glanced down at himself. He was dressed for more classroom sessions, not for anything like the adventure she seemed prepared for. She seemed ready to leave Amitan. "I guess not. Where are we going?"

"I sent word that you needed to be prepared for our journey today."

Tolan shook his head. "I never got any word we were going anywhere."

"It doesn't matter. I don't expect us to be gone for long, so why don't you come as you are."

"If it's something I need to change for, I can hurry back to the student quarters."

They weren't that far away, and if changing would allow him to be better prepared for whatever they might do, he'd prefer to be dressed for what they might encounter. It surprised him that she thought she had a need for a weapon. Any Shaper's preferred weapon was their ability to shape, nothing more than that, and for her to be carrying a sword suggested either there was some ceremonial reason for it, or she actually thought she might need the protection.

Either way, he felt underprepared. Even if she allowed him to return to his quarters, what was he going to grab? He didn't have a traveling cloak—he'd come to the Academy without much other than a small collection of belongings—and he certainly didn't have a weapon, ceremonial or otherwise.

"Like I said, I don't think you are going to need it." She continued down the hallway.

Tolan hesitated only a moment before following her. They were in one of the eastern wings of the Academy, a place where they often met, and from here, it was easy to leave and head to the park near the Academy. Most students who trained with their assigned master shaper spent their time in the park, but that hadn't been Tolan's experience with Marcella.

They reached the courtyard and she shaped, sending herself straight up into the air.

He hurriedly reached for his furios and called upon a shaping, sending it through it to allow him to blast into the air. He hadn't expected to need it quite so soon, but he really hadn't expected to travel along the Shapers Path high over the city. He hadn't been here since the attack, and when he landed on it—not nearly as smoothly as he would like—he stared, looking to see if it was still damaged.

From what he could tell, the Shapers Path had been completely restored. It was a circle over the entirety of the city, a translucent shape that provided transportation, though there were crisscrossing paths that arced over the main part of the city. None appeared damaged.

"How far will we travel?" he asked.

"Not far, but I thought it would be easiest if we took the Shapers Path. Besides, from what I understand, you have some experience with this recently?"

She cocked her head, regarding him for a moment before smiling and starting away.

"You mean the disciples."

"The Grand Master doesn't want too many to know about it."

"I haven't shared with too many."

"That's not really what I meant. He keeps it even from the master shapers."

Tolan wondered why that would be. There was no reason really for the attack to be kept secret from the master shapers, especially as they were the ones responsible for ensuring the protection of Amitan, and he suspected master shapers had been involved in repairing the Shapers Path.

"Why isn't he telling the master shapers more about the attack?"

"I think he's concerned about why disciples of the Draasin Lord have managed to reach the city."

"If you know it's the disciples, then you know about as much as I do."

"I probably know more than you do, Shaper Ethar."

"That's not what I meant. I wasn't trying to—"

She raised a hand, silencing him. They reached the western edge of the city and from here, Tolan looked out, noticing the rolling plains heading away from the city. An enormous paved road led toward the city itself, and carts moved along it with people walking alongside. Most of the carts appeared to be shaped, though there were some pulled by animals.

Marcella paused, crouching on the Shapers Path, looking down as she did. A shaping built from her and she sent it toward the ground and the people far below.

"What was that for?"

She cocked her head to the side, looking up at him. "What was what for?"

"The shaping."

"There aren't too many who have such affinity for

shaping that they can detect it when others use it, Shaper Ethar."

"I've always been able to detect when shapings have been used," he said.

"You don't think that's unusual?"

Tolan shrugged. "I don't know if it's unusual or not, but especially since coming to the Academy, I've been able to detect it."

"It's an impressive ability. Is that why you were able to determine there was an attack taking place?"

"I could feel the buildup of a shaping, but not who it came from or what it was intended to do."

"Why did you chase after the disciples if you didn't know they were the disciples?"

Was this some sort of interrogation? Why Marcella and not the Grand Master? He would've expected it from the Grand Master, especially as he would have more reason to question Tolan after the attack but getting it from Marcella was surprising. It had been a week since the attack, more than that, and long enough that he shouldn't have to worry about master shapers quizzing him on what he might have seen.

"Stupidity."

"Stupidity?"

"I went after the sense of power. I shouldn't have. The Grand Master made that clear."

Marcella stared at him for a moment, and then she smiled, standing. "Good."

She continued on the Shapers Path but veered off,

heading toward the west. From here, the Shapers Path narrowed, and they were high enough over the ground that Tolan wondered if he would be able to even shape himself up to it. At least in Amitan, there was the hope of reaching the lower path, but out here, over the plains, there was no such hope. If anything happened and he crashed to the ground, would he be able to summon a shaping quickly enough to save himself?

He tried not to think like that. There was no point in it.

"Where are we going?"

"It's my responsibility to test your shaping ability, and to help draw out areas where you might be weakest. You have shown some strength with fire," she said, glancing back at him. Did her gaze go to his pocket where he kept the furios? He didn't think so, but it almost seemed as if she looked knowingly toward it. "And if you are to progress beyond the first level, you need to be able to master a second element."

"That's the test?"

"You know I can't share that with you, Shaper Ethar."

"I just meant—"

"I know what you meant. And I'm telling you I can't reveal what you want to know. There is more than just managing to shape a second element. If that were all it was, many of your classmates would be able to skip the first level. As you can see, none has done so, so there is more to it."

There had to have been more to it. Part of the test to

remain within the first level involved shaping in such a way he could reach the spirit tower, and regardless of how powerful many of the shapers were when they came to the Academy, having enough strength within shaping to lift themselves from the ground was something even those shapers had struggled with.

In the distance, the landscape shifted, changing from the rolling hillside to blue.

Tolan pointed, and Marcella only smiled. "That's where we're headed."

"The ocean?"

She glanced over at him. "You say that as if it's something to fear."

"Not fear, it's just..."

She ignored him, continuing onward. He'd never seen the ocean. That much water was so different than where he'd grown up near the forest and the waste. Traveling along the Shapers Path allowed increased speed, and they were able to make much better time than they would otherwise have been able to do. He knew Amitan was days away from the nearest ocean, but with the Shapers Path, it took barely more than an hour to reach it. And when they did, he stood over the Shapers Path, looking down at the water. Waves crashed along the shore. The sound, even from here, was impressive.

"What do you know of water shaping?"

Tolan stared down at the ocean. The shore was rocky, a cliff that seemed cut off, a sheer drop leading down to the ocean. The waves slammed into the rock, almost as if there were elementals within it trying to peel away stone, as if they were angry at the earth elemental.

"I don't have any ability to reach water. I've been trying to while using the nyamin, but even with that, I don't have much ability."

"Relying upon bondars for all your shaping is only one way of succeeding. In time, we all must become confident and competent on our own. Especially if we're going to be a shaper of any capability."

She had to know about his bondar, didn't she?

He resisted the urge to slip his hand into his pocket and use it. Even the Grand Master didn't know about his bondar—unless he had some way of shaping spirit and had stolen that knowledge from him.

"Which is why I brought you here. There is something to be said about standing near the ocean, to feel the power of water. Even the weakest shaper is able to connect here, and when they do, when they can feel the way that water flows around them, they often will begin to master a connection to it."

"I can see how powerful it is," he said.

"*See it*, certainly, but what I'm suggesting is that you consider feeling it."

"How?"

A shaping built, and a gust of wind slammed into him.

Tolan staggered back to the edge of the Shapers Path, fear coursing through his body, sending his heart hammering. The Shapers Path ended.

He fell.

He didn't fall quickly. It was as if wind itself resisted him, holding him, but it was still faster than he was able to reach for fire. He reached for his pocket, gripping the furios, afraid if he were to lose it as he fell that he would be without, and when he struck the water, cold suddenly slammed into him, coursing through him. His breath was knocked out of his lungs.

Tolan splashed, trying to keep above the surface of the water, but he was no swimmer. There was no reason for him to learn in Ephra. There were rivers, but none so deep as to need to swim across. There were no lakes, and certainly no ocean. This was something he'd never experienced.

The water began to pull him down.

He struggled against it, trying to stay afloat, but without knowing how to swim, Tolan wasn't sure he could.

Why had she done this to him?

There had to be an easier way of getting him close to the water, for him to know what it felt like for the water to surround him, something better than this.

Flailing his arms, kicking his legs, he attempted to do anything to stay above the surface of the water.

But it continued to pull him down.

As he sank, he took a gasping breath and was plunged deep beneath the water.

Waves crashed against him, washing him first one way and then another, swirling around him as if to shake him free. He continued to kick, struggling against the water, but he was pushed down and down.

Pressure of the water built, making his ears pop.

He wasn't going to die like this. Not without having a chance to fight.

Could he use a fire shaping? Surrounded by this much water, he doubted he would be able to summon the kind of elemental power he needed in order to free himself, but that didn't mean he wasn't about to try.

Gripping the furios, he squeezed it, letting the runes press into his palm. As they did, he focused, drawing forth an image of hyza, and he strained.

For a moment, he felt steam, and there was the crackle of water as it hissed from the rising heat, but then that faded. Anything he thought he might be able to do failed. His power was cut off.

He continued to sink, and his feet touched down on a soft bed of sand. His head felt heavy, pressure building within it, making his ears feel as if they wanted to burst. His eyes felt as if they might pop free from his skull.

Fire didn't work, but he had summoned earth once before.

Could he do it again? At least with earth, he had contact with it, and maybe…

Tolan focused on the elemental jinnar. It was a powerful earth elemental, and he hoped he could use that earth elemental and connect to it, somehow bringing him to the surface, but there was no response.

He thought about the other elementals he knew, those

that mixed more than one of the elements together, but there was no sense of a connection. He couldn't reach water or wind. Earth and fire had already failed.

Great Mother!

Why couldn't he reach it?

His vision gradually darkened, the pressure of the water making it difficult to see anything, and he had been holding his breath as long as he was able. With a gasping breath, he sucked in a mouthful of salty water.

He tried to cough, but there was no strength left in his body to do so. The sense of water filled him. Everything was turning black. All he was aware of was the washing movement of the waves.

Why would Marcella have done this to him?

The distant part of his mind, the dying part, started thinking about the various water elementals he'd read about, straining to remember. It was the only thing he could focus on. It was better to focus on the elemental and the power he could remember reading about rather than what was happening to him. It was soothing, much more soothing than the emptiness beginning to fill him.

Names of water elementals rolled through his mind, ending with the great water elemental udilm, one who had power over the ocean. If only the elemental would save him, but all elementals had been brought into the bond, and without any connection to the water bond, there wasn't anything Tolan was able to do to save himself.

Emptiness. Darkness. Pain.

All of it slowly subsided, disappearing.

A vague sense of movement stirred, and he wished for calm and peace, for nothing more than an opportunity to rest. At least if he rested, he...

No. Resting meant death. And he wasn't ready to die. He wanted to live. He wanted to know what it would mean to begin to shape. He wanted a connection to the element bonds. He wanted to stay at the Academy.

His mind began to clear and he realized he was moving, but more than that, he realized something had been shaped around him. For a moment, he thought it was the water elemental, but then he burst free from the surface of the ocean and Marcella hovered above the water, some shaping allowing her to simply stand there. With a surge of power that washed through him, he gasped.

He jerked forward. He took another breath. And then another. With each breath, his mind clarified a touch more. The darkness he'd been feeling and seeing was fading. His mind came back to him.

"You fool. You didn't even try to swim!"

"I don't. Know. How."

"How does anyone not learn how to swim?"

He looked up at her as water dripped from his hair, running down his face. Everything within him throbbed, but mostly his head, leaving him with a pulsing headache. "I've lived in Ephra. There's no water to swim in."

"Great Mother," Marcella swore, turning her back to him and lifting him with a shaping of wind.

They landed on the rocky shore and he sat there, looking out over the water. He wrapped his arms around his legs, pulling them close, each breath coming to him like a relief.

"You should have warned me you couldn't swim," she said.

Tolan sat for a moment, gathering his thoughts, struggling to clear his mind. "I didn't know you would push me in."

"You haven't reached water, and Master Wassa thought all you needed was an opportunity to get closer to it. This technique of his works for others, and—"

"Almost drowning someone has worked before?" He coughed, clearing more water from his lungs. "What kind of technique is that?"

"There have been many techniques employed over the years to help people reach their potential."

"And what does it mean if I nearly drowned?"

She met his gaze, and there was hardness in her eyes, enough that Tolan wondered if she had left him in the water for too long intentionally. Did she think she was somehow going to coax a connection to water out of him?

"It means water is not a potential element for you."

"What if I haven't managed to reach it yet?"

"You have failed with the bondar. That is the easiest way for us to help those with the right connection to water. The next—and least preferable for most—option is to do what we have just done. In your case, unfortunately it appears you have no real connection to water. While you may gain the ability to shape the other elements, water does not seem to be in your future."

"Have others ever reached an element bond they failed through this shock therapy?"

"Those who fail to reach the element bond in this manner are never destined to shape the element." She walked to the edge of the cliff and looked down. "I can't say none have, but in the years the Academy has kept records, none eventually developed that ability."

It shouldn't bother him. He had come to the Academy without the ability to shape at all, and the fact he was able to reach for fire was far more than he had ever hoped for himself. All he had wanted was to survive his days in the Academy, and so far, he had. Reaching for fire—even if it did require he used the furios—should be enough to be satisfied by.

Only, the longer he was at the Academy, the more he experienced, the less he was satisfied with reaching only a single element.

"What now?"

"We still have two other elements I need to coax from you," she said.

"And what sort of shock therapy do you intend with them?"

"Who said anything about there being a shock therapy?"

"You did it this time, so I have to imagine you have another attempt in mind."

She smiled. "Don't worry, Shaper Ethar. You have some time to recover."

He didn't like the sound of that, but he also didn't like that he had failed to reach water.

Maybe he could continue to work with the bondar, and if he did, maybe he'd finally find some way of connecting to the element. It was possible he was different, but how different did he think he would be? There were enough differences between him and other shapers that he'd like to be somewhat normal, if only for a little while.

She lifted into the air on a shaping of wind and hovered in place, waiting for him. Tolan took a deep breath, his lungs burning as he did, and focused on a shaping. He slipped his hand into his pocket, reaching for the furios, and with a burst of fire, launched into the air toward the Shapers Path.

11

"YOU HAVE TO FOCUS MORE," FERRAH SAID, SITTING ACROSS from Tolan in their room within the first-level student quarters.

He held his hands on his lap, looking across at her, trying to suppress the rising frustration within him. She was trying to help, and she was helping. It was just that he didn't have the necessary skillset to do what she was asking of him. She wanted him to use his shaping, create fire on command, and to do so without the furios.

Each time he tried, he had to focus on the elemental, and each time, he stayed with the same elemental he had been using before. It was hyza, but he didn't have the necessary power to call upon hyza without the furios. At least, that was what it felt like.

The one thing he did possess was knowledge of the elementals. He had spent countless hours reading through the various volumes about them, and his memory was good enough that he didn't struggle with recalling the things he'd seen and read. With that knowledge, he thought he could come up with perhaps a different elemental that might be a better fit. Wasn't that the key?

At least, it was his key.

There were other elementals he could try. Some were incredibly powerful, and Tolan had no misconceptions about his ability to summon things like the draasin, or even hyza without the help of the furios. What of something like saa? It was a smaller elemental, at least in his experience, like a flicker, a sparking flame.

He focused, thinking of saa, drawing forth the image and memory of everything that elemental took. As he did, he felt a stirring deep within him. It was there as it always was, the steady stirring that came as he spoke to the elemental, summoning it to the forefront of his mind.

There came a streamer of smoke, and after it, there was flame.

It danced across the floor, curling, twisting, and through the flame, he saw a shape.

Saa was very different from hyza. Whereas hyza reminded him mostly of a fox, a mixture of heat and power, saa was wispy, true flame, heat and fury. It was strong in a way hyza was not.

He thought about the characteristics, thought about what he was asking of it, and he pulled forth that image, directing it into the flame. It began to grow brighter and brighter, power flowing outward from it.

Ferrah smiled. "That's a good one. That's got some real

heat behind that shaping. Something like that might throw Draln off when you're having your contest with him."

Tolan had mostly forgotten about the duel, though he shouldn't. Draln wouldn't forget. A time would come when the other man would demand he duel—and Tolan had made the mistake of accepting. "According to Jonas, I need to do more than just throw him off."

"I don't really think Draln is going to try and kill you," she said.

"I don't know; we both know the kind of person Draln is. I wouldn't put it past him to use this as an opportunity to hurt me in some way."

"Of course, he's going to use it as an opportunity to hurt you. You're talking about shaping each other. Only one outcome can come from it."

"I thought you were determined to help keep me from dying here," he said.

"Fine, maybe there's two outcomes. But in one of them, you end up hurt, or he does. The other outcome involves one of you dying. Now, we can avoid the second, but I don't think we can avoid the first. I want you to be prepared for whatever he might throw at you. The key is remembering a way to counter things."

"And if I can't remember?"

"Then your best bet is to avoid getting attacked altogether."

"That's great advice."

"I'm being honest with you."

"He'll know I have a tendency to use fire."

"You have more than a tendency," she said, smiling. "He'll know that's the only element you can shape. He's seen how you reach into the bond and the power you can use, so either he will be prepared for what you might throw at him or he will simply use a different element that has some immunity to fire."

"Like earth."

She shrugged. "Watch."

She focused on the small flame shaping, and the ground rumbled, rolling forward, and it swallowed the flame, suffocating it. The strength of her earth shaping consumed his flame, cutting it off with little more effort than the tiniest of earth shapings.

"Great," Tolan said.

"You wanted to see the kind of thing he might throw at you."

"I did. I just didn't realize it was going to be so easy for you."

"I might be a stronger shaper than Draln," she said.

There was no boasting in it, and for his sake, he hoped she was a stronger shaper than Draln. Facing someone like her, who had the ability to challenge him and the kind of mind he knew her to have, would force him to continue to improve. The only problem was that he didn't have much time. Days rather than weeks. Even if he had weeks, Tolan wasn't sure it would be enough time to master the parts of shaping necessary to make this something of an even match.

Not without unleashing the elementals.

That was the part of this he worried about. It wasn't entirely that he worried about facing Draln—though he did—but it was more that he worried what might happen if he revealed he used elementals as part of his shaping. Would someone make the connection that each of his shapings seemed to take on the shape of one of the elementals? So far, no one had made that connection, and even the person he thought might had only believed he was wildly shaping power. If Ferrah couldn't see the elemental within his shaping, maybe it meant Draln wouldn't, either.

"You need to try it again," she said.

"What's the point? If I use fire, you're just going to counter it."

"I might, but you need to see if you can come up with a shaping that will allow you to ignore what I might do. That's all part of the duel. Not only is it a matter of strength, but it's a matter of creativity. Strong shapers don't necessarily always defeat weaker ones. Sometimes, a weaker shaper will outsmart a stronger one. And sometimes, you can use an element bond the other isn't expecting, or perhaps use it in a way they weren't expecting."

He focused on fire, once again thinking of saa. If he could use that elemental, he might be able to draw more power, but *how* would he use it? He knew the way saa existed, and having read through the various elemental books, he had an idea of what type of flame saa preferred, but nothing more than that.

In order to defeat Draln, he would need a greater understanding not only of himself, but of the elementals.

As the flame crackled into existence, a shaping built from Ferrah, and earth once again rumbled, starting to come out of the ground.

Tolan focused on his connection to saa, trying to feed more power into it. As he did, the elemental blazed more brightly, and as her earth started to curve around his shaping, he exploded outward, sending a surge of power that forced the stone back, shattering it.

Ferrah was thrown back.

"That was good," she said, leaning forward.

She twisted her shaping, taking it in a different direction, and with a combination of earth and water, she smothered the flames, starting to tamp them out. Tolan nudged saa. He wasn't sure exactly what it was he did, only that it seemed as if he coaxed the elemental to change directions. The flame shifted, crackling more brightly, burning through the water shaping that Ferrah attempted to use, and when she did, the elemental exploded outward against earth again.

Ferrah leaned forward, smiling. "You're better at this than you give yourself credit for."

He released his hold on saa, relinquishing it slowly. It took a moment, but the flames flickered, and then they disappeared.

"How did you do that last one?"

"I don't know. I changed the direction of the flame."

"I saw that, but that's an unusual shaping. Usually,

when you mix water and earth in such a way, there's no way for fire to overpower it."

"I told you how I perform a shaping."

"And I told you I don't think that's exactly what you're doing. You might be using your imagination to help you with those shapings, and that might be what grants you some connection, but I don't think you're having the effect you believe."

He shrugged. "Does it matter? If it works, then—"

She wiped her hands on her pants, leaning toward him. "It doesn't matter. That's what I've been trying to say to you. And if it does work, then use it. Be creative. You have strength in fire shaping, and maybe that's all you need to defeat Draln, but even if you don't, if you can be creative like that, you should be able to stop him."

Creative. What if he could call upon a mixed elemental? Hyza was earth and fire, but there were other mixed elementals. If he could reach one, then it might be enough to throw Draln off.

She leaned back, resting her head on the wall. "I feel like I've been trapped here for far too long," she said.

"You want to get out into the city?"

"The last time we did, there was a little more excitement than what I wanted."

"I doubt we're going to find more of the disciples."

"You might have just cursed us."

She smiled and he took her hands, helping her to her feet. They made their way down through the Academy building and out the main entrance. Once outside, he glanced up at the sky. Clouds streaked across it, heavy and dark, practically screaming of a coming rain. If he could reach for water, he might be able to detect how much rain was coming, but then, if he could reach for water, he might be able to push away the storm clouds and keep the city from getting soggy.

But then, there had to be shapers who did such things. The city rarely saw rain, only enough to refill rain barrels and provide water for the city, but even that might not actually be necessary. With water shapers and their ability to pull moisture from anything, it wouldn't take much for a simple shaping to replenish the city's stores.

"Where do you want to go?" Ferrah asked.

"Well, we were heading to the market before. And then there's something I want to show you." It was time for her to see the park.

"The market won't be active."

"Why not?"

"It's the wrong time of day, and the market when the attack came was on the Farthing Festival."

Tolan frowned. "I'm not familiar with that one."

"You probably wouldn't be, not from Ephra. It's a more easterly sort of festival, and celebrates a bountiful catch, something the sailors of old used to celebrate."

"Why would they recognize it in Amitan?"

"All festivals are recognized in the capital, Tolan. They want to make sure everyone feels welcome, and in order to do so, everyone's customs need to be appreciated."

"There are some customs that could be forgotten," he said.

"Such as?"

"There are some in Ephra I never really liked. One was the Sharven, a day where we traveled to the edge of the waste and the shapers would send their shapings out over it, as if to demonstrate our strength over it still."

"So, you *have* been to the waste before."

"Not like we did with the Academy. Most just watch from a distance. The Shapers get close. When I was younger, before I knew I had any ability to shape, I never really understood what the big deal was. The shapers always portrayed themselves as incredibly brave for even approaching the edge of the waste." Tolan could remember seeing Master Daniels as he approached, the faint streamer of his earth-shaping building, the ground trembling with each step, as if echoing in time with Master Daniels' fear of making his way toward the waste. At the time, Tolan hadn't really understood. He had thought the masters had been exaggerating, blowing their fears out of proportion, but the more he understood what they had done during the festival, he truly appreciated just what they had risked.

"I can't say I've ever heard of the Sharven celebrated in Amitan," Ferrah said. "Though now we've been to the waste, I wonder if that's the masters' way of celebrating it."

They wandered through the streets, the occasional shaped cart moving past them, and Tolan would have to step off to the side to avoid getting run over by it. He looked around, still marveling at the way shaping power was used within Amitan. So many simple things were shaped here, things that would never have been shaped in Ephra, but the use of shaping made sense. This was a place where shapers existed with much power, a place where they were able to exert their strength, to demonstrate the various exotic ways in which shaping power could be used. Why wouldn't everything be shaped here?

"You've been distracted," Ferrah said.

"I'm no more distracted than I usually am," he said.

"Is it Marcella? I've seen the way you look at her, and when you came back from your last training session, you were quiet."

He hadn't told anyone about how Marcella had tossed him into the ocean and preferred to keep that memory to himself. It wasn't so much that he was embarrassed, but it was the idea of failure that troubled him. If he had no hope of reaching water, what would the point be of attending classes with Master Wassa?

And maybe that would be what came next.

"Tolan?"

He forced a smile, shaking his head. "It's nothing."

"I can tell when it's more than nothing," she said.

"Fine. It's not nothing. I found something," he said.

"What did you find?"

"You'll have to come with me."

She frowned at him, tucking a strand of her red hair behind her ears. "This sounds interesting."

"I don't really know what it is. I thought you might be able to help."

"Why me?"

"Because of what you've described in Par." There had to be something similar to what she had discovered in Par. There were ancient artifacts and he believed what he had found was something like that.

They turned the corner, and he felt the building sense of a shaping. It wasn't uncommon to feel the slow building of shapings within Amitan. With as many shapers as were scattered throughout the city, it would be unusual not to find someone shaping, but this was the kind of power reminding him of the attack on the Shapers Path.

He glanced over at Ferrah. "Do you detect anything?"

"Why?" she asked carefully.

He breathed out, a part of him wishing he didn't pick up on this sense of shaping, wanting to have a moment to simply wander the city with Ferrah rather than to be worried about what might be coming their way. The last time had been a significant attack. If he ignored it, wouldn't he be contributing to the disciples if it were them again?

"It's just the sense of power building again."

"You don't think it's *them*."

He shook his head. "I don't know. It's not up above us like it was before."

"Come on, Tolan. Let's go see what you want to show me."

As much as he wanted her help, he was drawn toward the sense of power building, and turned down a few narrow paths before reaching a part of the city he'd never visited before. A wide park opened up, stretching out but leading toward the capitol building. The capitol was comprised of stone shaped smooth, and it had two arms angled off a main section, each of equal size and prominence. Tolan stared at it, feeling that power rising, and wondered if it came from within the building. There was no reason there wouldn't be shapers within it, especially as many of the rulers of Terndahl had been trained at the Academy.

"Here? This is where you detect the buildup of power?"

"You don't feel it?"

"I don't have the same connection as you when it comes to the rising sense of power. I wish I did. Then I wouldn't have to feel quite as helpless as I do when it comes to you and your ability to detect shapings, but—"

A sudden explosion cut her off.

One wing of the capital building exploded.

Stone was flung everywhere, streaking toward them, and Tolan reacted, swinging his arm, holding the furios and focusing on hyza. Flame erupted, streaking from the end of the furios, and he managed to prevent the explosion from catching him. Debris continued to rain down, and he could feel the shaping Ferrah held pulsing out from her.

"What was that?" she asked.

"I don't know. A powerful shaping."

Another shaping started building, once again coming from the capital. Tolan raced forward, and when he neared the building, he could feel the effect of the shaping as it began to grow ever more powerful.

Ferrah grabbed his arm, pulling him around to face her. "We can't be here, Tolan."

"But there's going to be another explosion."

"There might be, but you can't be here. You were present during the last attack, and if you're here for this one, what do you think the master shapers are going to say?"

He looked over at the capital. She was right, but that didn't make it any easier to turn away and abandon an attempt to help. He felt as if he needed to help, that he needed to do something.

Even if he stayed, there would not be anything he could do—not without finding who was responsible for causing these attacks. If they were powerful enough to destroy a building like this, it would be powerful enough to destroy him, too.

Ferrah dragged him backward.

He allowed her to pull him, and as he reached the street, another explosion thundered, the stone of the capital once more cracking, debris and fragments of stone raining down. Ferrah wrapped them in a shaping of wind, creating a buffer, but even that wasn't quite enough. She pressed her hand up and heat added to the wind, and the combination caused the stone falling all around them to explode back outward, away from them.

"We need to get back to the Academy," she said.

"Wait," he said.

"Wait for what? Another explosion? We were lucky the Grand Master didn't push us too much during the last attack."

"They won't blame us for this."

"Are you so sure? The two of us present at two attacks within the city? What are the odds of that?"

"They won't believe me capable of it, anyway."

"But they might believe *me* capable."

He let out a frustrated sigh as Ferrah dragged him down the street. As they went, he stared, wondering if there was going to be any evidence of another attack, but none came.

After a bit, he pried his arm free and turned back toward the capital. "I just want to see who was responsible. If this was the disciples of the Draasin Lord—"

"If this *was* them, then we need to keep moving."

As he considered resisting, there came a sense of building power, though from a different location. Movement from behind him caught his attention. Shapers from the Academy and throughout the city would be coming this way, and if he stayed here, if he remained where he was, it was possible someone would realize they were here.

"Come on!" Ferrah urged.

He had turned to follow her when he caught sight of a figure streaking away from the capitol building that turned along their street.

He glanced over at Ferrah before starting toward them. He held tightly to the furios, gripping it against his palm, letting the runes press into his skin. As he ran, he focused on an image of hyza. Depending on what he encountered, he wanted to be ready. It was possible the person he followed was nothing more than someone escaping from the attack, but the faint sense of a shaping suggested otherwise. He didn't want to get caught unprepared.

The other person rounded a corner, leading him along a busy street.

"Who were you chasing?" Ferrah asked.

Tolan looked around, searching for a sign of where the other person had gone, but he had lost them. They had to be along this street.

"There was someone who came this way. I think they were a part of what happened back there."

"Are you sure?"

"Not really, but I'm not willing to sit back and do nothing."

"Tolan… this isn't our fight."

"Aren't we a part of Terndahl? Doesn't that make it our fight?"

She studied him before shaking her head and sighing. "Fine. Where do you want to look?"

Tolan was thankful she was willing to come along with him. He would have gone on his own but having her here made it more likely they could find where the person had gone.

"See if you can detect any shaping," he said.

Power built from her, and Tolan didn't know what sort of shaping she used to detect others. He had some way of detecting a shaping that didn't involve focusing on it. Through that, he was able to focus on the presence of shaped power, and in this case, it was coming from far along the street. He grabbed Ferrah's arm and dragged her with him. They hurried past other people, and he murmured his apologies as they went.

At the end of the street, he finally caught a glimpse of the person they had been trailing. The dark cloak caught his attention, and he pointed. "Do you think you can hold them?"

"What if it's not the right person?" Ferrah asked.

"And we've made a mistake, but if it is..."

"Fine, Tolan. Let me just tell you I'm not thrilled you have me doing this."

"Your objection has been duly noted."

She growled at him, and her shaping stretched outward. As it did, it wrapped around the figure. They stopped suddenly, completely tense.

For a moment, Tolan thought that was all they would need to do. They could hold him and figure out who he was and what he was after. Academy shapers could come and they wouldn't have to hold them any more.

Then the shaping Ferrah held exploded.

There was no other way of describing it. It forced her back and Tolan lunged for her, grabbing her before she struck the ground. He looked up, half afraid the man would be coming in their direction.

Instead, he found him staring at them. The face buried in the folds of the cloak was difficult to see, but Tolan had seen it before. It was a face he recognized.

Why would Master Daniels be involved in the explosion?

12

TOLAN PACED IN FRONT OF THE OPENING TO THE GRAND Master's room. He was convinced he'd seen Master Daniels, but if that was true, why was he here? He was supposed to be getting his refresher, whatever that meant, and shouldn't have been seen out in the city. More than that, he shouldn't have been anywhere near the attack on the palace.

Ferrah had warned him against coming to the Grand Master, thinking he had imagined Master Daniels, but Tolan didn't think so. He was convinced that was who he had seen. If it was Master Daniels, he needed to understand more about why.

Summoning the courage to knock was the hardest part. He had been here once before, so he knew where to find the Grand Master, but then, he had been dragged here by Master Sartan and hadn't come of his own accord.

Coming this way meant no one else would be there with him for support.

Maybe he should have convinced Ferrah to accompany him. He didn't think he needed it but having her with him might have made this much easier. Before losing his nerve, Tolan quickly knocked on the door. He took a step back, waiting.

Voices came from behind him, and Tolan glanced back to see Draln walking with one of the other master shapers, someone Tolan didn't recognize. Draln smirked when he saw him, giving him a look that seemed far too knowing.

How much would Draln be able to piece together? The attack in the city had taken on a life of its own, and there was a flurry of conversation about what had happened. Even within the students' quarters, people were talking about it, most giving voice to various theories about who and how many had attacked. Considering Tolan and Ferrah had been there and only seen one person running, the idea that it might be more than one involved was possible, but not fitting with his experience.

When no one answered, he knocked again.

This time, the door opened quickly.

Master Wassa popped his head out, glancing at Tolan. "What is it, Shaper Ethar?"

"I was hoping to have a word with the Grand Master."

"The Grand Master is a busy man, Shaper Ethar. Surely you've heard about the attack in the city."

"I have, which is why I—"

Someone came up behind him, and he glanced over his shoulder to see Master Irina approaching. She regarded him for a long time, the vague sense of a shaping washing over him. As it did, he attempted to push against it, trying to resist whatever it was she was doing to him. The whole thing left him questioning whether she'd spirit-shaped him.

As the sense of the shaping passed over him, he attempted to push against it, trying to resist whatever it was she was doing to him.

Tolan had no idea whether it would even be effective, not knowing whether there was anything that he— someone not very skilled at shaping—would be able to do to oppose a master spirit shaper, but he wasn't willing to sit back and do nothing.

"Shaper Ethar. Are you once again embroiled in things you should not be?"

"I'm not embroiled in anything, Master Irina."

"Then why are you here?"

Tolan blinked and realized he had an opportunity. If Master Daniels was involved, then wouldn't the Grand Inquisitor know? "I have a question about one of the shapers from Ephra."

"What of it?" Master Irina said, glancing over his shoulder and toward the Grand Master's quarters. Master Wassa had left, returning to the meeting going on inside the Grand Master's room.

"You sent Master Daniels to the city for a refresher."

That drew her attention, and she looked at him, frowning. "I did. He neglected his understanding of the elementals. When the elemental attacked in Ephra, he wasn't able to properly identify it."

"Why him?"

She frowned and a shaping built, sweeping over him. What was it she was trying to do to him? Was that all about spirit? He pushed against it, not sure whether it made a difference or not. "What is your point, Shaper Ethar?"

"My point is, why did you send Master Daniels for refreshing rather than Master Salman?"

He hadn't given it much thought at the time. There had to be some reason she had chosen Master Daniels rather than Master Salman. Was it because Master Salman had identified hyza? As a fire shaper almost exclusively, it wouldn't be all that surprising, but then again, Master Daniels, as an earth shaper, should have known hyza was partially of earth.

"There are times when shapers prove they need an opportunity to reacquaint themselves with lessons gained during their time in the Academy."

"What's involved in it?"

"It involves study."

"What kind of study?"

Master Irina held him with a firm gaze. "What are you getting at, Shaper Ethar?"

"I don't mean any offense. I'm just trying to under-stand the nature of Master Daniels' assignment in the city. I was thinking of checking in with him."

Tolan wasn't sure why he felt the need to deceive her, but there was something about the fact she seemed dismissive of his question. And there was something uncomfortable in the way she looked at him.

"You would be best served leaving your Master Daniels to his studies."

"He should know I made it to the Academy."

"I can send word to him," she said.

"There's no need for that. I'm happy to go and let him know myself." Why was he pushing her like this? He knew better than to pressure one of the master shapers, espe-cially one who was the Grand Inquisitor, but here he was, finding himself antagonizing her in a way that would only lead to more trouble.

Another shaping built, and this time Tolan was more certain than ever that it washed over him. He had no idea what the intent was behind it, but he felt a certain residual effect as it left him, as if she had tried to do something to him with her shaping, but it had failed.

"You will leave Master Daniels to his studies," Master Irina said.

She stared at him, her dark eyes practically burning a hole into his mind, and Tolan nodded. He didn't need a shaping of spirit to let him know it would be a mistake to go against her wishes on this. Then again, he didn't know why she would have used such a shaping on him in the first place.

"Would you care to tell me why you had come to see the Grand Master?"

Tolan licked his lips and swallowed. "I just thought to inquire about the attack on the palace."

"There's no need for the students to be concerned. We have it completely controlled."

He stared at her for a moment, wondering why she had chosen to deceive him, but decided not to push the issue. Instead, he started away, and when he reached the end of the hall, he turned, attempting to look over his shoulder without getting noticed, and saw both the Grand Master and Master Irina looking his way. Tolan hurried off, and when he started up the stairs toward the student section, he shivered, shaking away the sense he had barely avoided something awful.

What was taking place? Why was Master Irina hiding something about Master Daniels?

When he reached his quarters, he found Jonas dressed in his loose pants and shirt, sitting on his bed. He was flipping through pages, looking at a note, and he looked up when Tolan entered.

"What is it?"

"What do you know about spirit shaping?" Tolan asked.

"You're asking that because I was questioning about the Inquisitors?"

"I just thought I would see what you knew about spirit."

"I know about the same as anyone else. It's the hardest element bond to reach, but when you do reach it, there's significant power to be found."

"How can you protect yourself from someone with significant power?"

"I don't think you can protect yourself." Jonas smiled. "I don't mean it in some way to offend you, it's just you don't have enough skill with shaping to do that. The Great Mother knows I don't even have enough skill with shaping. It's some way of securing it, using the power of the element in a mixture so the spirit shaping is deflected. At least, that's what I've always been told."

"Are there other ways of avoiding a spirit shaping?"

"You're asking the wrong person."

"Is there anything in the books you've been researching that would tell you otherwise?"

Jonas glanced down at the book. "I have to admit they are quite interesting, but the history of the Inquisitors is different than I expected. They were used as part of the advance force when Terndahl was first formed. They were soldiers. I never knew that before looking through these histories. Now they're something else."

"Terrifying," Tolan said.

"Only if you draw their attention. Now we're at the Academy, there's no reason the Inquisitors would even pay any attention to us. They want us trained the same way we want to be trained. There is a benefit to it."

"I'm not so sure they want us trained the same way," Tolan said.

"Why not? The Inquisitors are involved in the Selection. You had the Grand Inquisitor as part of your Selection, something no one else did. They want us to reach for that ability."

"I don't know. When I think about what Master Irina did during the Selection, I'm not so sure she is all that interested in me shaping."

"Why would you even say that? She allowed you to come here."

Tolan considered telling him about Master Daniels and what he had experienced with Ferrah but didn't know if that would only upset his friend. He didn't need to worry about what might happen to him.

Hadn't Ferrah's irritation with that been enough of a lesson? He didn't want to anger Jonas along with Ferrah. He deserved more than that.

"You remember how I told you about the master shaper I was apprenticed to."

"Yeah. You had that woodsmith you were working with. I still can't believe you were apprenticed rather than spending time in one of the shaping schools. Think about how much time I wasted in Velminth, only to realize I could have been Selected regardless."

"Anyway, the master shaper I worked with was sent to Amitan for a refresher."

"Whatever that is."

"Supposedly, he needed to be reminded of the

elementals."

"Supposedly?" Jonas grinned. "You don't agree with what Master Irina did?"

"It's not a matter of agreeing with it so much as it's a matter of whether or not it was necessary."

"And why wouldn't it be necessary?"

"How much do you think the master shapers in Velminth know about the elementals?"

"I don't know. We don't have too many elemental attacks, so they haven't really had to deal with it. I suspect if there were an attack, they might prove what they know. But then, they all trained here. All of them would have the same knowledge every shaper who comes in here has."

"What have we learned about the elementals so far?"

"What's this about, Tolan?"

"Just humor me. What can you say you've learned about the elementals in the first part of this year?"

"We've learned names of elementals. We learned what part of each element they tend to prefer."

"Some of that we've learned because of what we've researched on our own."

"That's still us learning," Jonas said.

"Think about it. If the master shapers are expected to remember all of the elementals they've encountered, wouldn't they all be at risk of needing a refresher the same way as Master Daniels? Master Salman didn't know anything more about the elemental than Master Daniels."

"Okay. So, let's say he didn't. Why does that matter?"

"I don't really know, only... When the palace was attacked, I think I saw Master Daniels."

Jonas sat motionless for a moment. "You were there? Tolan—this isn't a good look."

"Ferrah and I were there, but not intentionally. We didn't chase the attack this time."

"Are you sure?"

Tolan glared at him. "We didn't. There was the attack, and I could feel the power building, but we didn't know what was taking place."

"So, you *did* chase it."

"I didn't chase anything. Like you said, I just—"

"You just followed the sense of power that ultimately ended up being an explosion that leveled the entirety of the ruling palace, forcing the Council to move into Terenhall while the palace is rebuilt."

Tolan hadn't heard that. "The Council is moving into Terenhall?"

"Unfortunately. It means some of the master shapers are getting displaced, and from what I've heard, there has been more than a little grumbling about it."

Tolan could imagine there would be. Why here? There would be other places they could go. Unless they feared for their safety.

Terenhall would be safe. It would be a place not easily penetrated, not by any shaping attack, which meant it would be the kind of place the Council would come.

"I hadn't known that."

"What does this have to do with spirit?"

"I don't know. All I know is that when I saw Master Daniels, it didn't seem as if he recognized me."

"Maybe it wasn't him. That could be your explanation as to why he didn't recognize you."

"But if it was him, I still don't understand why he wouldn't have recognized me."

"I can help you look," he said.

"Thanks. I don't know if we'll find anything, but when I asked Master Irina about it, I—"

"Wait. You asked her about whether Master Daniels was involved in the attack on the city?"

"No. I wouldn't be as stupid as that. I just asked her about his refresher and whether I could visit him."

Jonas started laughing. There was a slightly hysterical note in his voice. "You need to be careful, Tolan. You're dealing with an Inquisitor! The Grand Inquisitor! Just think of what would happen if she were to decide to spirit-shape you."

"That's just it, I think she tried. Like she did after the last attack. It didn't work."

"Are you holding out on me, Tolan?"

"Holding out what?"

"Holding out knowledge of how to protect yourself from a spirit shaper."

"I'm not doing anything like that. I just felt the effect of the shaping."

"I would believe that if you were a master shaper. It wouldn't be terribly surprising for you to have some way of protecting your mind, but even then, you're talking about the Grand Inquisitor. That's way different than just a simple spirit shaping. If anyone would be able to overwhelm you, it would be her. And if she did that, there's no way for you to have been able to ignore it."

"When we went to the Convergence and came back, she shaped both you and Ferrah, but I wasn't shaped. She said I would be. I remember the conversation. But... I don't remember losing anything after that."

"If you were spirit-shaped—and let me tell you that I think you would have to have been—you wouldn't remember. That's the nature of the Grand Inquisitor. The Great Mother knows I didn't even remember being spirit-shaped until you said something."

"Do you remember it now?"

"No. All I remember is having conversations with you, and..." He closed his eyes and started shaking his head. "I remember hearing the person responsible for the elemental release was captured. Nothing else. And then we dropped it."

"We dropped it because the Grand Master wanted us to drop it."

"Then we should drop it."

"If I don't have the necessary shaping skill to protect myself, and let's assume I was able to ignore her shaping, then how was it possible?"

"I don't know. Maybe there's some sort of bondar. Or maybe someone else spirit-shaped you to protect you from another spirit shaping."

Tolan sat on his bed, leaning back. He didn't think it

was a bondar. Those had to be actively used, and if nothing else, he was certain he wasn't actively trying to shape to protect himself, though if he knew what she was attempting, he might have done so. And then, he had pushed against her shaping, though he didn't expect it to do anything. He had resisted, trying to fight off the possibility she would shape his mind and make him forget. If nothing else, he was determined not to forget.

But then, there were the memories of his parents. There were plenty of memories that he'd had before he had lost them, times when he had been happier, not worried about what others might accuse him of doing, times before he had gone to Master Daniels and apprenticed. More than that were the memories that had come to him during the Selection. He had never had those before, and in those memories, he had seen his father making something.

His father had always tinkered, but in this case, what he'd been tinkering with was something with meaning. If only he could step back into those memories some way, and if only he could recall what it was, but he couldn't.

"Is it possible someone could be spirit-shaped to protect another's mind?"

Jonas looked up from his book. In the silence that had passed, he had turned his attention back to his studies.

"I don't know much about spirit. Only the Inquisitors do, and other spirit shapers, and they don't really talk about it. There have been stories, though. When I was growing up, we would tease each other that we were spirit-shaped and try to make the others believe they weren't in control of their own choices."

"That's a terrible game."

Jonas shrugged. "What can I say? We were kids. We would try to convince others they were birds or sheep or sometimes even water. Those easily persuaded would be the most fun. As we connected with our shaping ability, we would sometimes add elements to it, making them believe."

"What's your point?"

"My point is, we don't know what a spirit shaping does. It allows the spirit shaper to know another person's thoughts, but it also supposedly lets them influence them. Can you imagine what would happen if the Grand Inquisitor used that on us, forcing us to do whatever she wanted?"

"How do you know that's not the purpose of the Selection?" Tolan asked.

"Because I wanted to be selected since I first learned to shape," Jonas said. "That's my choice. Coming to Amitan and to Terenhall has been my choice. I know that's not shaped. I know that's not something she placed in my mind. And I know that's not what one of the other Selectors did to me."

"What if there were other things they did place during the Selection?"

"We won't know until we keep training," Jonas said.

Tolan leaned back. He couldn't shake the sense that somehow, he was avoiding a spirit shaping. It had to be more than simply the fact he was connected to spirit, though he believed that was a part of it.

As much as he wanted answers, and as much as he hoped his friend would have them for him, he didn't think Jonas cared. He had wanted to come here, and nothing was going to convince him he hadn't. Not even the possibility some of this had been shaped.

TOLAN WHISTLED SOFTLY TO HIMSELF AS HE WOUND between the trees. His voice drifted off, carried by the wind, and he could almost feel as if he had some great connection to it. Sitting in the park had been relaxing, and as it was now time to return to the classroom, he was heading back. He had no interest in missing any of his classes. There might be something he could learn in them.

A strange sound caught his attention.

Was that the sound of a branch cracking?

He froze, listening. The wind seemed to whisper differently than it had before.

He looked around, unable to shake the sense something was off.

Glancing all around but not finding anything, he started forward again.

As he went, a strange sense grew. It came through his connection to earth, and as he picked up his pace heading through the forest, wandering away from the park and back to the city, he thought he detected something.

Every time he spun, looking behind him, he found nothing.

Just his imagination.

But then, the idea the disciples of the Draasin Lord were in the forest was enough for his imagination to fill him with fear.

The strange earth sense remained.

He started running. Even running, there was that feeling of pursuit.

Every so often, he glanced over his shoulder, seeing nothing, and when he plunged through the border of the forest and into the city, relief swept through him.

He ran the rest of the way back to the Academy, and all the way up to the water classroom. He sat there, breathing heavily, and as everyone filed in, taking their seats and the class began, he couldn't shake the strange fear that had filled him. It was anxiety mixed with the sense of what he'd seen during the last attack, and how he was convinced he had seen Master Daniels. Though he and Ferrah had searched through the entirety of the city as much as was safe to do, there had been no additional sign of him.

Tolan remained convinced it had been Master Daniels, except the man he knew and remembered hadn't had that kind of power.

Maybe he'd been wrong. Maybe that wasn't Master Daniels, but if not, it was someone who resembled him.

Jonas elbowed him and Tolan swiveled on his chair to look over at his friend.

"Aren't you going to pay attention?" he whispered.

Tolan flicked his gaze to the front of the classroom. Master Wassa was droning on about some technique of shaping, and it was one they were all expected to utilize, drawing on the power of the bondar.

"I am paying attention," he whispered.

"No, you're not. You're staring off, and I've seen that from you often enough to know there's something bothering you."

"What's the point?"

"What do you mean? The point is, you will attempt to shape through the bondar, and eventually you will master water. Isn't that the point of being here?"

Tolan considered telling Jonas he was never going to reach water, and regardless of how many times he might try to shape through the bondar, it simply wasn't going to work for him. And yet, if he did share that with Jonas, all he would do was admit he had failed.

"You're right," he said.

"I'm right about what?"

"About me needing to pay attention." At this point, it seemed he would be better served spending his time in the park. At least it was peaceful there.

"The nature of water is such that there are different flows within it," Master Wassa was saying. "Some of you will reach water in its gentler forms, while others of you will need to feel the full assault in order for you to be able to manage it. And even when you can reach it, some of you will require that water flow within you before you can use it in any sort of way."

Tolan certainly knew what it meant to have the power of water slamming into him, but what did he mean about allowing the sense of water to flow through him?

Maybe he wasn't expected to understand.

"Today, I would challenge all of you to search for the gentle form of water."

"How are we supposed to find the gentle form of water?" Tobias asked. He was younger than most and had quite a bit of potential, but unfortunately—at least for Tolan—he had a preference for Draln and was one of his frequent hangers-on.

"There are many ways of reaching the various types of water. When we are dealing with the gentle form, I would suggest we think about a burbling brook, or a soft waterfall, or even the mist sprayed up from the sea."

"All of those are different?" Tobias asked.

"All forms of water are different, and all take a different touch. When you begin to understand it, you can begin to understand water. Some of you may never reach water in its fullest form, but for those of you who can and do, you will be rewarded by the kind of strength other elements cannot easily match."

He pulled a tray out from one of the shelves along the wall and set it on his desk. He motioned for them to come forward and claim the bondar if they needed it. Only a handful within the class still required the bondar, Tolan being the only one needing it for all of his classes.

When Tolan had grabbed one of the bondars and taken a seat, he rolled it in his hand. Water was different from the others, but what was no different was the fact he had never managed to convince water to be effective for him, regardless of how much he could try.

"Did you hear they still don't know who attacked the capital?"

Tolan glanced over to see Draln leaning over his table. The other two sitting on either side of him had their focus on him. Only one had a bondar, and Tolan wondered why Draln tolerated Cassie and her inability to shape water without it. But then, Cassie had wavy black hair and a curvy figure, so maybe he understood a little bit. And it wasn't as if Cassie had no abilities. She was particularly powerful with earth, and he'd seen she could hold onto a significant wind shaping as well.

"I can't believe someone managed to destroy the entire palace," Lauren said. He was a little older and had a slight figure along with a sharp nose. His eyes seemed set almost a little bit too close together, but despite that, Lauren was an incredible shaper, rivaling Draln.

"It was the disciples again." Draln looked around the room and Tolan averted his gaze, not wanting to be seen looking and listening.

Jonas was caught up in his attempt at shaping, unmindful of the fact Tolan hadn't even tried to shape through his bondar. He hadn't heard anything from anyone else in the city, not enough to know how others had received the news of the attack. Most probably, they didn't even know anything about it, nothing other than that it had happened. With the Shapers Path, the master shapers would have been able to conceal the fact the city had been attacked, but when it came to the palace, there was no concealing it.

"Again? We don't know there was an attack before."

"I told you what I heard," Draln said.

"That's what you heard, but Master Gilbren said there was no damage to the Shapers Path. I even went—"

"You don't think the masters can restore the Shapers Path? Who do you think created it? It's invisible to anyone else, so it would be relatively easy for them to restore. What I'm talking about is something far more difficult to hide."

"Why do you think the disciples would attack the palace in the first place?" Lauren asked.

It was the same question Tolan had. There would be no reason to attack the palace. It didn't disrupt anything unless they thought that by attacking the palace, they would somehow disrupt the rule within Terndahl, but all it had done was shift part of the ruling of the country into the Academy.

"It's a show of strength." Draln raised his hand and water coalesced above it, forming a ball. He swirled it, rotating it slowly, and then with the flick of his wrist, it went streaking toward Tolan and exploded in a spray.

Tolan jerked his head toward Draln.

"What was that about?"

"A demonstration of what you have to look forward to."

"Is that right? Am I supposed to be impressed you will throw water at me?"

"Just wait till that water is scalding hot and scorches your skin off. It doesn't take much to take that little bit of water and mix it with a little heat..."

The moisture in his clothing began to burn and Tolan swore under his breath, focusing on the furios and drawing the heat out of the water and into the furios. At least he had enough control over fire shaping to do that. It had the added benefit in that it dried out his clothing, and he glanced over at Draln.

"Thanks. You should really try a little harder if you intend to throw me off."

"Don't worry, Ethar. I fully intend to take care of you when we have our duel."

"Are the two of you done?" Master Wassa asked.

Tolan glanced over, not having realized Master Wassa had been observing them from the side. Had Marcella told Master Wassa about Tolan's inability to reach for water? It wouldn't surprise him, and as much as he wished she wouldn't, maybe it would be a blessing. He could focus on other tasks during the class time. He had shown the ability to reach earth once, and though he hadn't managed to do it again, and certainly not in a time when he needed it, the fact of the matter was that he thought he could reach one of the other elements. If he could get wind to answer, then he would be still quite accomplished, and more so than most of the shapers living in Ephra.

"I'm sorry, Master Wassa."

"Save your experimenting for the student section. The classroom is for you to focus on the tasks I have assigned. And I would like you to focus on finding gentle water, Shaper Ethar."

A flush crawled up his neck and raced toward his face. Being called out like that left him wanting to do nothing more than disappear from the room, to go off and hide, but he couldn't. He was stuck here until the end of the class session.

He turned his attention back to the bondar, focusing on what he could think of that might be a gentle water shaping. Master Wassa had suggested a burbling brook or a stream, and now he had been thrown into the ocean, he had some idea of what mist spraying off the waves felt like.

He started to think about the elementals of water and tried to imagine which of them were gentle. None came to mind as such. Maybe water didn't have a gentle elemental, but Master Wassa believed there was some way of shaping in a gentle fashion.

"You should be more careful before your duel," Jonas said.

Tolan glared at him. "You do realize the only reason I'm forced to do this duel is because you set me up for it."

"I didn't make you do it. You agreed to it."

"You didn't tell me a shapers duel would involve fighting to the death."

"It's not going to go that far. Look at him. He's a skilled shaper, but he's still nowhere near as powerful as some of the master shapers. He can use each of the elements and reach into their bonds, but what you're suggesting is he somehow has the ability to harm you using that. That simply isn't possible."

"I think you're overlooking something important when it comes to Draln." Tolan kept his voice low, not wanting the other man to listen in, but if he were using a wind shaping, there might not be anything he could do to prevent Draln from being aware of what he was saying. "When it comes to him wanting to harm me, there might be an element of creativity that will do just as much."

Jonas gaped at him. "You've been talking to Ferrah, haven't you?"

"I asked Ferrah to help me."

"Figures."

"Why does that figure?"

"Because you didn't come to me."

"That upsets you?"

Jonas shrugged and pulled on a water shaping, letting it flow over him and across his hand before cupping it in his other hand. "I'm not upset. It's just that I grew up around him, you know? I've always been second best in Velminth. As much as I tried to develop my shaping, my talents never progressed nearly as quickly as his."

"Which is why you wanted me to have a duel with him?"

"He's already beaten me. I thought maybe you'd have a better chance."

Tolan set the bondar down, turning his attention to Jonas. "Is *that* what this is about? You'd lost to him, and now you want to see if I can do better? I don't have the same capacity with the element bonds as you do, Jonas."

"Maybe not the number of element bonds, but you have the ability to use fire in ways I don't think even Draln can do." Jonas looked over Tolan's shoulder and stared at Draln.

Tolan hadn't noticed how much Jonas actively hated Draln. He knew they'd never gotten along, and that there was an element of agitation between them but seeing this sort of hatred on his friend's face was unexpected.

"Ferrah said I need to have some creativity. If I can't overpower him, she thinks there might be other ways of beating him."

"I hope so." He took a deep breath and tore his gaze away from Draln and flashed a wide smile. "Either way, he's not going to do anything that can hurt you. Like I said, when I had a shapers duel with him, there wasn't anything he did that was more than painful."

"How painful?"

Jonas didn't answer, turning his focus back to shaping water.

"Jonas? How painful?"

"I did have to visit a water shaper, but I'm sure that won't happen to you."

Draln laughed, and Tolan couldn't help but feel as if he had heard Jonas talking. He forced thoughts of Draln out of his mind and focused on the bondar, trying to see what he could do with water. He went through the different elementals he could imagine, going from one to another, and with each one, there was no sense of the familiar fluttering he felt when he called upon hyza and the fire bond. Perhaps it was a matter of finding the right elemental, or maybe it was exactly as Marcella said and he truly had no ability with water.

But then, he once *had* created moisture along the bondar. That had to matter.

He and Jonas passed the rest of the class in silence. Every so often, Tolan would try to listen in to Draln, but he realized they had muted their conversation, likely shaped so he couldn't listen. It wouldn't take much to do so, a subtle shaping of wind that would wrap around them to prevent their voices from carrying. It was the kind of shaping he wished he was able to do.

When they were done, Tolan replaced the bondar on the tray at the front of the class. He lingered, others in the class heading out in front of him, and Jonas waited by the door. Ferrah had already disappeared, though that wasn't entirely unusual. She had her session with her master, and Tolan knew she liked to be on time, which meant getting there early.

"What is it, Shaper Ethar?"

He glanced over at Master Wassa. "Do you believe all shapers have it within them to reach each of the elements?"

"We have proven through the years that most shapers have the ability to reach each of the element bonds, but whether they do or not is a different matter altogether. Part of what we put each of the students through is the Selection, a process that helps us determine whether someone will have the potential."

"How does the Selection help determine someone's potential?"

"It's a complicated process," Master Wassa said. "And one that has been fine-tuned through the years. Over time, the Inquisitors have discovered various aspects of the Selection that are more insightful than others. The fact you're here, Shaper Ethar, is enough to know you have that potential within you. The real question is whether you have some way of unlocking it."

He looked around, but the classroom was empty. If he couldn't ask Master Wassa, who could he ask?

"The mentor I was assigned seems to think I won't reach water."

"And why is that?"

"Because I don't have much potential with the bondar, and her attempt at a sort of shock awakening of my ability didn't work."

Master Wassa set his hands on the desk, clasping them in front of him. He looked up at Tolan, frowning down his nose. "What sort of shock are we talking about, Shaper Ethar?"

"She brought me out to the ocean, and she—"

Master Wassa touched his hand and a wave of shaping washed over him. It was cool, and with it came a passing of the anxiety that had been filling him. All of that simply dissipated, disappearing.

"Did she have another with you?"

"There wasn't any other," he said.

"She brought you herself and tried immersion therapy?"

"That's what it's called?"

"It's an ancient way of awakening water. There are reports of some having found their connection to the bonds in such a way, but we don't practice it anymore. I'm surprised your mentor would even think to try it. I would have preferred she come to me with her concerns."

"It's okay. It didn't work."

"And now you think you have no potential to shape water."

"I struggle. Without the bondar, I can't do anything at all, and even with the bondar, all I managed to do was create moisture along the surface of it. That's not nearly enough to convince me I have any water shaping ability."

Master Wassa turned his gaze down to the bondars stacked along the tray. He organized them, sliding them along the surface of the metal tray, arranging them in a neat line. His lips moved as he counted, and when he was done, he looked up at Tolan. "You know the age of the oldest student known to reach water?"

"I don't. That's not something I spend much time looking into."

"Have you wondered why we have students of different ages?"

"It's part of the Selection, I suppose."

"It's all part of the Selection, and one thing we have learned about the Selection is that some shapers will be able to reach their potential earlier than others. But even those who fail to reach their potential are never fully excluded from the opportunity to be Selected. There are some who come to us barely able to shape, and with the proper training, we can draw out their potential. I haven't given up on you, Shaper Ethar, and so I don't want you to give up on you, either."

Tolan looked down at the stack of bondars. If only he could grab one, he could use it and finally practice, but he would need to do so in a way that Master Wassa wouldn't realize what he did. Now that he had come to him sharing his concern, any attempt to take a bondar and practice on his own time would be noticed.

Maybe there was a different approach.

"Who discovered the secret of the bondars?"

"Unfortunately, knowledge of the bondars has been lost," Master Wassa said. "Some of us who have a particular attachment to the bonds have attempted to re-create them, but..."

"But what?"

"But we have been unable to do so. The knowledge of constructing the bondar is twofold. Not only is it understanding the element bond, but it's also understanding the appropriate markings."

Tolan looked down at the water bondar, thinking about the runes that had been used in creation of it. "Wouldn't you just have to copy these?"

"Why do you think we have so many?"

Tolan thought he understood. "Someone copied the originals."

"They used those to create others, and yet, the original is still the most powerful and the most effective."

"Do you ever let students use the original?"

"The Academy has decided it would be unfortunate if something were to happen to those originals. We tried copies, and then copies of copies, but none was nearly as effective as the original bondars. And so, we keep them secure, tightly regulated and restricted, so as not to lose them. You understand, of course."

Tolan nodded. He wondered if he could even copy one of the bondars. He had used the water bondar often enough that he was familiar with the shape, so that wouldn't be the issue, and he had traced the runes enough times, going so far as to copy them on paper, so he could re-create them. Did that mean he could attempt to make his own bondar?

Maybe he didn't need to take one from the water tower and Master Wassa. He didn't need to risk angering him. It might be a copy of a copy, or even a poor replica, but it was more than what he had now. And if it worked, he could practice.

"Thank you, Master Wassa. You've given me something to think about."

"I hope you realized you shouldn't give up on yourself, Shaper Ethar."

"No. I haven't given up on myself. I will continue to do everything I can to learn from you."

"I would advise you to do everything you can to learn from each of your instructors, Shaper Ethar. Water is but one element, and when you're here, the intent is that all of our students will learn to master each of the elements."

"I thought there were some shapers who came to the Academy who never mastered all of the elements."

"They may never master all of the elements without the use of a bondar, but all students should be able to shape, to draw forth that power, even if it requires assistance."

When Tolan finally joined Jonas in the hallway, his friend looked over at him. "What was that about? Were you trying to get some extra tutoring from Master Wassa?"

"I was having a question answered, and I think I have an idea of how I can get a better handle on water." And if it worked with water, maybe it would work with earth and wind. How much better might he be if he had a bondar for each of the elements?

"Why do I get the sense I'm not going to like this?" Jonas asked.

"You don't have to be a part of it."

"If you're going to become some superpowered shaper, I'm definitely going to be a part of it. What do you intend to do?"

As they reached the end of the hallway, Tolan cast a glance back at the water classroom and smiled. "I'm going to make a nyamin. I'm going to make a water bondar."

14

IT WAS LATE AND TOLAN REMAINED HOLED UP IN HIS ROOM, lying on the bed with the length of wood under the covers with him, trying to carve the shape he remembered of the nyamin. Even as he worked at the wood, he wasn't able to draw out the shapes he thought he needed. He tried, carving slowly, drawing his knife along the surface, but it didn't work nearly as neatly as he had hoped.

And this was his tenth attempt.

The door to the room opened and Tolan glanced over to see Wallace flopping down on the bed. He carried a stack of books and the corners of his eyes were wrinkled, his face drawn and weary.

"What is it, Wallace? Where have you been?"

"With Master Heron. He's determined to make sure I can reach fire. It's the one element where I've managed nothing more than smoke, and only with the bondar."

"What's he doing?"

"He's had me working near enormous flames, out in the sun, anything that hot. It's like torture, Tolan."

"I can imagine. Marcella threw me in the ocean."

He sat up, leaning on one elbow. "She did *what?*"

Tolan nodded. He hadn't even told Jonas or Ferrah about it yet, so why was he telling Wallace? They weren't particularly close, though they roomed together. Yet there was something about shared misery that made him feel a little better. "She claimed it would awaken water shaping within me. She called it shock therapy."

"Did it work?" Wallace asked. He sat on the edge of his bed, leaning forward. Only then did Tolan realize the other man's shirt was completely stained, soaked with sweat, and there were certain marks all along it, but other places had been charred away. What exactly had Wallace been forced to do? Whatever shaping he'd been put through had clearly been brutal, and possibly as brutal as getting thrown into the ocean.

"I wish it had. I felt like I nearly died, though I suspect she was in control of the situation the entire time so I wasn't really going to. When I was lying there, drowning, I didn't feel any sort of stirring of water the way I think she intended."

"Why didn't you swim?"

"I don't know how to swim."

Wallace just stared at him and after a moment, he started laughing almost hysterically. "And here I thought Master Heron was bad. At least he didn't try to drown me."

"From the looks of it, he tried to burn you instead."

"Yeah. The last was one time in the kitchen. He had me near the oven, and it felt as if I was baking. When we were done, I felt like I needed to dump a bucket of water on my head. If I were any worse a water shaper, I might not have survived." He caught himself, his eyes widening. "Oh, Great Mother, Tolan. I didn't mean anything by that."

"I know you didn't."

"I think they're all agitated these days."

"Who?"

"The masters. They worry about the attacks."

Tolan squeezed his eyes shut. He didn't think Wallace knew he'd been there for them but wasn't certain. "Have there been any more?"

"Not from what I've heard, but they wouldn't tell us anyway. From what I can tell, they think the disciples are looking for something."

Tolan turned away. The Convergence.

"Which is why I think the masters are trying to push us along. They want us to be safe. Plus, testing for the next level has to be soon."

Tolan had been trying not to dwell on that. He hadn't progressed all that far from where he'd been when he'd passed the first test. What would happen when he was tested? More likely than not, he'd fail.

He sighed. "I'm not sure burning and drowning students is a way to keep us safe."

Wallace laughed softly. "What are you doing with those things?"

Tolan glanced down at the lengths of branches he had stacked on the end of his bed. Wallace was a skilled water shaper, so maybe he could help. And if the masters *were* concerned about the disciples, maybe they wouldn't care that he had been trying this.

"I've been trying to carve a bondar. I thought if I had my own, I'd be able to practice outside of class."

"You're doing what?"

Tolan held out the length of wood he had been carving. When Wallace stared at it, Tolan could only shrug. "I've been trying to carve my own bondar. I thought if I could create something out of it, then I might be able to shape some of the element bonds I struggle with a little bit easier."

"But bondars are tied to the element bonds in a specific way."

"Through these runes," Tolan said, holding up a sheet of paper. He had carefully written down the runes for each of the different bondars, making sure he had re-created the shape of the runes as closely as he could. If he could use that knowledge, and could use the runes, he thought he just might be able to create the same sort of shapes.

"I'd never considered trying to create a bondar," Wallace said.

"I don't know if it's even possible. Master Wassa said the ones we use in our classroom aren't even the originals. They're copies of much more effective originals. They don't let the students use the original bondars. They don't want us to damage them, fearing if we were to somehow damage them, they would lose access to them. If they did that, there would be no way of re-creating them."

"They don't know how to make them anymore?"

"I guess not. They can copy the ones already made, but it seems they can't make new ones."

Wallace reached for the sheet of paper and took it from him. He stared at the page, fixed on the various runes, and then handed it back to Tolan. "Even with this, I'm not sure there's any way of re-creating it."

"So far, I can't," he said.

"What have you tried?"

"Mostly, I've tried to use different types of wood, but that doesn't seem to be effective. I try to carve the shape, but I'm not sure I'm doing it all that well."

"Have you tried shaping it?"

"The only thing I can shape is fire, and even that's not all that effective."

"I wonder what would happen if someone did have some shaping talent," Wallace said.

Tolan tried not to take the slight as an insult. He knew Wallace didn't mean it in that way, but it was hard not to think of it as some sort of insult. He didn't need others reminding him.

"You're welcome to try," he said.

"I'm not sure I would be able to do it," he said. "I've seen the one for water. I've spent some time trying to use it, but…"

"But you didn't need it for very long," Tolan said.

Wallace shook his head. "I didn't. I still think it might involve you shaping some part of it."

If that was what it was, then Tolan might be out of luck. He knew the shape of the bondar, but didn't have anyone who could help him re-create it. And that was what was needed.

His idea of creating a bondar to help had failed before he even got a chance to get started. That left him with the options of once again attempting to take one of the bondars from the classrooms. If he did that—and got caught—the repercussions would be potentially significant.

Ferrah had taken a bondar. He'd have to see what she'd done. Maybe there was some way for her to help him.

"If you figure it out, let me know."

"I didn't think you needed the bondar to shape." Wallace was a skilled shaper with most of the elements. He wasn't the strongest shaper, but he had talent, and for the most part, he kept quiet about it, avoiding notice. There were times Tolan wished he would be able to avoid notice. He didn't want to draw the attention of so many others—and certainly not others like Draln.

"It's not so much I need the bondar to shape, but there is value in having access to something created by shapers with a significant connection to the element bonds."

Tolan stared at the page with his notes. "Why do you think that is?"

Wallace shrugged. "It was a time before the elementals

were forced into the bond. Maybe that somehow made them better connected."

Surprisingly, that made a strange sort of sense. Regardless of whether or not the elementals were dangerous, there was power that came from them, and having access to that power would probably make any shaper more talented. But then, Tolan had seen how the runes also made that power more impressive. There had to be some way to learn about the runes, to figure out how he could use them in a way to augment his weak abilities. Maybe that was going to be the key more so than trying to master shaping.

"You would think that with as long as the Academy has studied the element bonds, they would be talented at the intricacies involved within them," he said.

"With the bonds, and maybe with those markings," Wallace said, nodding to the page Tolan held. "But there are other aspects of shaping they simply abandoned."

"Are you suggesting it was a mistake to separate the elementals from the world?"

Wallace frowned, and his entire body went tense. Tolan realized too late he'd made a mistake. An accusation like that wouldn't go over well, and he wouldn't expect it to. He should have known better than to say something like that, considering his experience when he was younger.

"I didn't mean it like that, Wallace. I was just suggesting—"

Wallace gathered his things and stood. "You should be

careful, Ethar. Trying to make a shaping like that can be dangerous. Especially if the wrong person sees it."

Wallace walked from the room, his back rigid. Tolan glanced down at his notes, sighing. He should have known better than to speak so openly. What had he even thought about doing? There was no point in attempting to irritate his roommate, and though he wasn't necessarily close to Wallace, it wasn't that he disliked the man. He'd rather have a connection to him. He had few enough friends as it was.

Tolan took a moment to gather his belongings and headed out of the room. Voices near one end suggested there were students working in the hall, probably preferring to stay near the protected areas where shapings wouldn't impact anything. Tolan hadn't figured out how those areas were particularly safe, though he suspected runes were a part of it. Somehow, the runes were more of a factor than he had ever known.

Maybe there was one way to learn more about the bondars and the runes. He hadn't spent much time in the library since the attacks on the city, and had to wonder if there was anything in there he might be able to uncover. Master Minden might share with him, though she had certain things she preferred to keep secret. Like all of the master shapers, they knew certain teachings not meant for low-level students.

When he reached the library, he found it relatively busy. Most of the tables had students sitting at them, some by themselves, but others in groups of two or three. He scanned the room, wondering whether Ferrah might be here, but didn't find her. Maybe she was out with her private sessions, but he didn't know she was scheduled to have any today.

Master Jensen sat up on the dais, scratching notes in a binder resting next to him. Tolan doubted he was the only master librarian on duty; there were far too many students here for a single master librarian. Where were the others? It didn't have to be Master Minden. Master Stole could be here, or one of the others who weren't here nearly as frequently.

It was too busy to look for information about runes or bondars. That was something he should do when there weren't nearly so many students around. He'd learned that coming at slower times made it far more likely to get the information he wanted.

Tolan made a slow circuit of the library, looking for familiar faces. He recognized some of the second-level students but didn't know them very well. Other than the few students he had interacted with while playing Imaginarium, he didn't know the others. A couple of first-level students were clustered at one end of the room, and Tolan avoided them, not wanting to raise any more questions about him or his motivations.

At the back corner, where the shelves intersected, he paused near a ladder. Rails along the upper portion of the shelves allowed the ladders to be slid along the walls to reach the upper shelves and considering the massive scope of the library and how high the walls stretched, ladders like that were needed in order to maximize the space. A narrow winding staircase led to a second level over two stories above, and more shelves with more ladders ran along the walls there. The library was massive.

There had to be something in here that would help him learn more about the runes and about bondars. The librarians protected that knowledge, and in order to discover what he wanted to know, he would need to ask the right question. He couldn't simply go up to Master Minden and demand she shared what she knew about bondars and runes. She'd already made a point of telling him runes were reserved for older students.

As he meandered around, he found himself behind the elevated dais, a wall of stone with markings along it. There was no one back here.

Tolan hesitated near the door. All he had to do would be to open the door and sneak back down the stairs to look at the place of Convergence again.

Voices came from behind him.

Tolan hurried forward, away from the door. When he reached the end of the dais, he turned the corner and nearly ran into Master Minden.

Given her age and her stooped back, she still managed to come up to his nose. He suspected in her day and before age had bent her spine, she would have been quite a bit taller than him. Her eyes fixed on him, somehow seeing him despite the milky film coating them. It unsettled him, as it often did.

"Shaper Ethar," she said, clasping her hands in front of

her. She wore the dark gray robe of the master librarians and her sleeves hung down, covering her hands. A chain around her neck caught his attention. It was a dull gray, and if Tolan didn't know better, he would have suspected there were runes etched on the surface. It reminded him something of a bondar, but why would a master librarian need a bondar?

"Master Minden. I was just coming to see if you might be able to help me."

She held him with her gaze, and then looked past him, her flat stare taking in the emptiness behind. A hint of a smile spread on her face. "I'm not sure I can offer the kind of help you were considering."

Tolan glanced behind him and started shaking his head. "No. Nothing like that. I—"

"Shaper Ethar, this section of the library is generally reserved for those who have advanced further in their training."

Tolan looked around. It was dark back here, lacking the softly glowing orbs that lit the rest of the library. As he often noticed when he was near Master Minden, there was a sense of shaping.

"I didn't realize this section was closed. I thought more of the upper sections were restricted to older students."

"The older students aren't allowed in the upper sections, either. Those are restricted to master shapers and above."

"Other sections are restricted only to the master librarians?"

"Of course."

Tolan hadn't expected her to be so blunt with him. And he also hadn't seen any student in the upper stacks, though partly he thought that might be because the master librarians were still accommodating and came through here and offered their assistance frequently. There was no need for students to climb the ladders or even go up to the next level, not when the librarians were so willing to do that for them.

"What sort of things are restricted to the master librarians?"

"Do you have an interest in becoming a librarian?"

"I might." Ferrah was interested in serving as a librarian, and it suited her far more than it suited Tolan. He was interested in the knowledge, and it wasn't that he thought the librarians were something to look down upon, it was more that he preferred a more active role. But then, within the library, there was no judgment. No one questioned the master librarians and how they shaped. They were left to their studies, whatever they were.

"I think the Great Mother has another role for you, Shaper Ethar."

"And what role might that be?"

"You have to find it yourself, the same way we all have to find it ourselves."

"Did you always know you wanted to be a librarian?"

She smiled, and there was a hint of mystery to it. "I wasn't always a librarian, Shaper Ethar. There was a time when I served Terndahl in a different way."

"What did you do before?"

"My life has had many twists and turns. When you live as many years as I have, you come to find that you need to be prepared for the unexpected. You must embrace it, and when you do, only then can you find what you're meant to do."

"I'm just trying to understand my connection to the element bonds."

"As you should. You should take every opportunity while studying at Terenhall to master those connections. That's the purpose of your time here. If you would overlook that, you would be wasting that opportunity."

Tolan considered how much he should ask. If he didn't try, there would be no answers. The worst thing that could happen would be that Master Minden would simply refuse to answer him.

"I've been wondering about bondars," he said.

"The bondars are intriguing, I agree. Made by those with an understanding of the elements that surpasses what we often find today. One would think shapers of the Academy would have a greater understanding of the elements, but strangely, that's not always the case. Too often, we find we are connected to the element bonds, but we ignore our other connections to the elements."

"Such as the runes?"

"The runes are one other way of attaching to the elements. There are others, but they are perhaps the most notable, if only because they are so poorly understood."

"When do students begin to learn about the runes?"

"You will have an opportunity to begin your rune work when you have progressed far enough in your mastery of the elements. Very few reach that level."

"So, it's not until we've mastered shaping that we're allowed to work with runes?"

"Mastering shaping is the first step. Runes are a particularly difficult part of the element magic."

"Why?"

"Because they require you acknowledge there is more to the elements than simply the connection to the bond. You must acknowledge the elementals are a part of it. And more."

She smiled at him, and Tolan shivered. He hadn't expected her to share anything, and here she was, telling him far more than he had expected to know, so much that he wondered if perhaps it was a mistake to even consider trying to place a rune on a bondar. Would it be too dangerous?

"Is that why no one can make bondars?"

"Is that what you believe?"

"I was told that there are the original bondars and then the rest are merely copies."

"The bondars used by students at the Academy are merely copies, but there are some who remain with the talents to create original bondars. It's a dangerous process, and without fully understanding the element, you could end up harming yourself. Again, it's why knowledge of such things is restricted to master shapers."

Tolan didn't miss the implication. Master Minden was

telling him he shouldn't even try to make a bondar. He didn't have the necessary knowledge, which meant that if he were to try, he could get injured. He didn't want to destroy himself trying to create a connection to one of the element bonds he hadn't earned.

"If that's all, perhaps you should return to your studies."

Tolan nodded. He headed back around the dais but paused. Several of the tables had cleared, and now Ferrah sat at one of them, a stack of books piled around her. She kept her head down as she was reading.

He took a seat across from her.

"I didn't know you were here," she said.

"I was just having a chat with Master Minden."

"Don't tell me she was giving you more books on elementals."

"Why?"

"I think you've studied the elementals long enough. It's dangerous."

"No more dangerous than practicing shaping without any ability. Not like I have any way of reaching them."

"Aren't you the one who said—"

"I know what I said, but I think you're right. I think I don't really have any sort of connection. It's only in my head."

He flicked his gaze past her. Master Minden sat atop the dais, scanning the library before her gaze settled upon him again. How was she able to even see him from where she sat?

"I need your help with something."

"Why do I get the sense I'm not going to like it very much?"

"You don't have to do it if you don't want, but it would help me."

"What is it?"

"It's something Master Minden said to me. A way of helping me reach the other element bonds. One where I don't need to be in class to practice."

"You don't need to be in class in order to practice, Tolan. There are plenty of ways you can practice without sitting in the classroom."

"There might be, but there's one way that promises to be the most effective."

"No."

"You haven't even let me say it."

"I know what you're thinking," she said, her gaze drifting to his pocket. She knew he had the furios with him at all times, and the fact she glanced down to where he kept it told him that she knew exactly what he'd intended to ask.

"I don't intend to steal any, not like some people."

"You don't even know it was stolen," she whispered.

"Are you saying you were given it?"

"Borrowed. Nothing more than that."

Tolan frowned. Why would she have been allowed to borrow a bondar? Especially one for spirit? There would be a question for later.

"I need your knowledge of the element bonds and your connection to shaping."

"What for?"

"Because the masters are more concerned about these attacks than they're letting on." She looked up at him, and he lowered his voice. "If the disciples are searching for the Convergence, I want to be ready if they try something again." And he wanted to have another bondar that worked for him before their testing.

"How? The best way to be ready is to keep working in classes."

"I don't think that's going to help me, but there's something I think might."

"Why do I get the sense I'm not going to like this?"

"It's not that bad."

"Not *that* bad?"

Tolan glanced over to Master Minden, who still sat on the dais. "I can't shape on my own, but there's one way I can. Between the two of us, we might be able to make a bondar."

15

THE PARK BY THE ACADEMY WAS QUIET TODAY. HE'D BEEN tempted to head to the park outside the city, but with word of movement from the disciples, he had been afraid to do so. It was better to stay where it was safest, which meant close to the Academy.

The sun shone brightly overhead and a soft breeze blew through, fluttering the leaves, but it was comfortable, and the wind was not so much that it disrupted their work. Tolan glanced down at the sheet where he'd made the runes. Two pieces of heavy stone held the page down, keeping it from floating away in the breeze.

Ferrah sat across from him, her legs crossed, and she leaned over a piece of rock that she worked at shaping.

"This isn't working, Tolan."

"I don't expect it to be easy," he said.

"You're talking about somehow imbuing my shaping

with some connection to the elementals? Why do you even think that will work?"

He had to get this to work. For him to face Draln in the duel, he needed a greater connection to shaping. The only way he could do that would be with bondars. If he couldn't take one from the classrooms, then he'd have to make his own.

"Because of something Master Minden said. The bondars are connected to the elementals. Not necessarily the element bond, but the elementals. She said that in order to make them, one needs to have knowledge of both the element bond and the elementals, along with the necessary runes." He stared at the sheet with the runes marked on it. "We have the runes—at least those for making the bondars we've been working with. And Master Minden was the one who gave me what we needed to know about the elementals." He held out the book on the earth elementals, tapping the cover. It was made of stone and incredibly heavy, but he hoped that by searching through its pages, he might be able to come across some way of reaching earth. Especially if they worked together. Ferrah had the connection to the element bonds, and he had the knowledge of the elementals.

"What if we don't even have the right runes?"

"We know which ones work for the bondars we've been working with."

"But you're assuming the ones we know about are the same elemental you're choosing."

"I'm trying to choose an elemental that fits with what we know."

"What if it doesn't fit with what we know of the element bond and the runes?" Ferrah asked.

"I think it's tied to the shape more than anything," he said.

"The shape of the bondar?"

Tolan pointed to the drawing he'd made of the earth bondar. Over the last few days and classes, he had taken time to draw the shape of the bondar as carefully as he could, making certain he had as faithful a representation of the runes as possible, all preparing for the likelihood they would be able to make a bondar.

The challenge was understanding what shaping was needed. There had to be a link between the shaping of the element bond in the bondar and the elemental, didn't there? And then it was tied to the rune placed on it. If they could work backward, using the runes they already knew, figure out which elemental had been used, maybe they could add enough to it in order to create something similar.

Pulling open the book depicting the earth elemental, Tolan began flipping through the pages, going one by one. He had an idea of which ones fit with the shape of the golan, the earth bondar, but it depended upon the documentation within the guidebook on the elementals to be accurate. He wasn't entirely certain it was. What if some descriptions weren't quite right? He had seen differences between various books depicting the elementals and didn't know if that would make it difficult to determine the correct elemental.

Even when they did, would he be able to use what he knew about the earth elementals to make this work? He didn't have much of a connection to earth, and without that, might not be able to recreate it.

"I think we're going about this wrong," he whispered.

"Finally. I've been waiting for you to realize that. We should be practicing and preparing for our testing. That's going to come up sooner than we realize."

Tolan shook his head. He wasn't going to pass testing to the next level with what he knew at this point anyway.

He stared at the page, looking at the runes marking the fire bondar, though he didn't even need to study the page. He had the furios, and could use that and try to copy it.

Why had he thought he needed to start from scratch?

Once he figured out what the key was, he could apply it across the others. Making a fire bondar might not be as helpful as making one for water and wind, but it would prove the process was effective.

"What I'm thinking about is the fact I don't have much of a connection to earth, not the same way as I do with fire."

"That's kind of the point, isn't it? Don't you want to use what you can figure out and become better with the other elements?"

"But in order for us to ensure we know what we're doing, I think we need to take what we can uncover from the bondar I *can* use, and the one where I have the best connection to the elementals and copy it."

"Do you have anything in the book Master Minden let you borrow that might help?"

Tolan shuffled through his pack before pulling out the book on the fire elementals. He hadn't spent as much time looking through it as he had in the past. For the most part, Tolan had memorized much of it, taking time to study the various fire elementals, wanting to be ready for whatever he might be able to do while using it.

While he was flipping pages, Ferrah leaned close to him. "Have you gone looking for word of that earth shaper?"

Tolan glanced up, his hand resting on a page depicting saa. He didn't need to pause there. He had enough experience with that elemental, that he thought he could imagine it in his mind far more easily than any others except hyza. And that was only because his experience with hyza had made it so he could practically see it in his mind.

"I haven't gone after Master Daniels," he said.

"And you said the Grand Inquisitor sent him here?"

"She did. She was disappointed in his ability to identify an elemental."

When he flipped through a book as massive as the one Master Minden had lent him about the elementals, he wondered how anyone would be able to remember more than a couple.

Ferrah stared at the book he held open in his lap.

"Before coming to the Academy, I'd never seen a rogue elemental. We don't get reports of them in Par. There are depictions of the elementals. It's why I've been so curious about the Convergence, but we don't have the same. If I were honest, I would've said I never expected to encounter an elemental in Amitan. How could they escape when there are so many powerful shapers here?"

Tolan flipped through the pages of the book, pausing every so often to stare at the elementals. For some reason, he had used the furios to at least convince himself he was summoning more than one kind of elemental. Hyza came easiest, but it wasn't as if he couldn't use the furios to summon other elementals. He had used it in his classes to help with his presumed shaping, making it appear as if he had more talent than he did, all tied to his ability to imagine elementals.

What if the furios wasn't tied to a specific elemental at all?

He reached into his pocket and pulled the furios out, resting it on the surface of the book of elementals.

"Now what?" Ferrah asked.

"There's something I'm not getting."

"I think when it comes to this, there's quite a few things you're not getting. First and foremost is the fact there's no reason for you to even feel like you need to create bondars."

"Even if they do, won't we learn more about them by making our own?"

"You're talking about advanced shaping, Tolan. You

don't have that ability." She looked up at him. "*I* don't have that ability."

"What if it's not just about shaping?"

"What do you think it is?"

"Maybe there's no shaping in it at all," he said.

Tolan ran his hand along the furios. It had the strangely smooth surface with the runes carved in to it, and he wondered if perhaps that were true. If it didn't have anything to do with shaping, then how would he be able to re-create it?

Sighing, he looked up. "I don't know. Maybe this was a mistake."

"It's not a mistake for us to try to understand more about the element bonds, but when we start adding the knowledge of the elementals into it, I do worry."

"I'm not convinced we're adding a knowledge of the elementals into it," he said.

"But you're trying to take what you know and what you can do and put that into it."

"Maybe, but…" He wasn't sure exactly what he was getting at, only that he had thought there might be some link to the elementals in the creation of the bondar. At least, that was what Master Minden had suggested. Maybe there wasn't anything to it. And maybe she had only said that to him to convince him to do something he shouldn't.

Tolan flipped through the pages in the book before stopping at the end, where it began describing the draasin. There were pages upon pages of information about the draasin. Everything in it fit with what he'd seen when Jory had attempted to summon the draasin at the Convergence. That draasin had seemed large, but some of the pictures within this book revealed creatures even larger. For some reason, Tolan had the sense the draasin were a more tangible type of creature, less made of flames and more flesh and blood. If true, why—and how—had they been placed into the element bond?

Tolan replaced the book into his pouch along with the bondar. There was no point in continuing to work at it. He didn't know enough, and it frustrated him.

Taking the page marking the runes, he had begun to fold it up when something on it caught his eye. He unrolled it again and set it on the ground.

Where had he seen that symbol? It was one that was on the furios, he was sure of it, and had felt it pressing into his palm often enough to know it would have been, but there was another place he'd seen it.

Tolan removed the book on fire elementals from his pouch and flipped through the pages.

"What is it?" Ferrah asked.

He tapped on the marking. "This."

"One of the runes?"

He nodded. "I've seen it somewhere else."

"It could have been down near the Convergence. You said there were runes we had to get through."

Tolan closed his eyes, thinking of those markings. They had been different from these. He didn't think it likely he had seen them there. Where else would he have seen it? As he flipped pages in the book, he came across one of the stranger elementals, one for smoke that was called esalash and was different from shiron. On the page, there was a drawing for the elemental, but that wasn't what caught his eye. Rather it was the notation below the name for the elemental. There was a picture.

A rune.

Tolan's breath caught.

"There it is," he said.

Ferrah leaned close and looked at the book alongside him. "It's similar, but I don't know that it's the same," she said.

Tolan pulled the furios from his pocket and held it out, rolling it across his lap. "It is the same."

He pointed to the marking for the elemental, the same one he'd found in the book. That they were there and identical had to mean the marking was for that particular elemental. He chose another marking, this one a series of faint lines, and went flipping through the book. Near the middle, he found the symbol. This was for steam, ivay, and an elemental he had never attempted to summon, though he wondered if it would've helped when he had nearly drowned.

Rather than searching one by one, he went to the page for hyza. He found a picture of hyza near the front of the book. He had long ago memorized the wording about the elemental, no longer needing to read about how hyza was a mixture of fire and earth, a strange connection, and instead he looked at a part of the page that he'd never paid much mind to. There, like with the others, was a symbol.

248 | D.K. HOLMBERG

"Great Mother," he whispered.

"Is it there?"

Tolan nodded. "It's here. It's the same."

"Are you sure?"

He rolled the furios so she could see it. At the end of the furios, where his palm often rested, was the marking for hyza.

There had to be a dozen different marks, and so far, three of them represented elementals. Did that mean they all did? And if they did, were those the only elementals he could use the bondar to connect to? There was one for smoke and steam and for a mixture of earth and fire. He had used saa, so he suspected that was a part of it as well. Sparks—meaning iffin—would have to be there too.

All were various forms of fire, and all things he hadn't even noticed before.

He unfolded the page again and grabbed for the book on earth elementals. As he went through it, he found each of the symbols much the same way as they had been on the furios, each matching up with a picture in the book on the elementals.

"These weren't runes at all."

"They could still be runes, but they might just be runes that represent power."

Tolan shook his head. "I don't think that's what this is. These seem to be some way of connecting to these elementals. I don't see one for the draasin." He'd spent enough time reading through that section of the book that the symbol etched there remained fixed in place. Two outward-facing triangles with the line between, one he could practically imagine representing the draasin soaring high in the sky. "And I don't see any for some of the other elementals. There are only some of the elementals represented." He suspected that just as with fire, the elementals indicated by the golan would represent various forms of earth, probably making it so that earth shaping was even possible.

Why hadn't he considered that before?

"So, Master Minden wasn't lying to you about that," Ferrah said.

"Did you think she was?"

"I wouldn't have expected her to tell you how to create a bondar, but at the same time, anything to do with the elementals is a little tricky. People are touchy about them, especially if you imply you're using elemental power."

Tolan had seen that himself. There had been enough of that when it came to his offhand comment to Wallace to believe people would be odd and uncomfortable when it came to referencing the elementals, but there was something still troubling him.

"If these aren't runes, and they represent nothing more than the elementals, then where is the rune power?" Tolan asked.

Ferrah shook her head. "I don't know."

He sighed. Somehow, there needed to be some power from the rune magic. He believed that was a part of it, that it was somehow the key to how the bondar worked.

"We could go and ask those who have made replicas," he said.

"I'm not sure that's going to get us very far," Ferrah said.

"Even if we just ask nonspecific questions?"

"Anytime you raise a question about bondars, the masters get touchy. There's a fear that power will be abused, especially with something like the bondar, which allows people to connect so deeply to the element bonds. That's why they're guarded so closely."

He wasn't entirely sure why the bondar would have images representing the elementals if they were only designed to help people reach the element bonds. Why elementals in that case? Why not something that represented the power of the element bond?

Answering that meant another visit to the library, but he didn't know whether Master Minden would be willing to answer him.

Folding the sheet back up, he stuffed it into his pocket. It didn't matter quite as much. Now he had a sense of where those markings could be found, he didn't need to keep his document except for the fact it told him which elementals were marked on each of the bondars. And maybe if he uncovered something about the connectivity between the elementals more than what he already knew, he might be better able to use that knowledge.

"You're not going to give up on this, are you?" Ferrah asked.

"Why should I? I think we've figured part of it out."

"At least do it smartly."

"And what makes anything smart about it?"

"Making sure you're not just throwing yourself out there when it comes to this power," she said.

"Seeing as how I can scarcely do anything shaping-wise, I doubt you have anything to worry about."

She studied him, and as she did, he couldn't escape the concerned look on her face.

Tolan smiled, but a different question came to him. The bondar might not be critical for connecting to the elementals. What if it was only tapping into their power, tying them to the element bond rather than the elemental themselves?

There would be more testing, but he would need to do that himself. Ferrah wouldn't want to be involved in it, and he didn't blame her. She didn't have the same need to reach for power outside of shaping the bonds, not the way he did.

And if he could uncover some other way of reaching for power that didn't require the bondar, then maybe he wouldn't even need it, but the testing for the second level would be coming soon—and he wasn't ready.

"I don't like that look on your face."

"There is no look on my face."

"There is. And I don't like it."

Tolan looked away rather than meeting her gaze, not wanting to have to lie to her about what he was considering doing.

16

TOLAN TAPPED THE BONDAR ON THE TABLE. THE BONDAR for earth was solid, and he had no fear of breaking it. It was different from the bondars for the other elements. The furios was slender, and Tolan did fear the possibility he might break it if he weren't careful, but with the bondar for earth, the golan, he didn't think he could damage it.

"Would you stop?" Jonas asked, glancing over at him.

"I'm not trying to upset you," he said.

"Not that you're upsetting me, it's more that you're disrupting me."

"Then wrap it up."

"You want me to be finished?" He nodded toward the front of the classroom. "Master Shorav told us we needed to continue working at these shapings until we'd mastered them."

"Have you mastered them?"

"Well, this one I have. These weren't that difficult."

"I'm not going to master any earth shaping," Tolan said.

"You haven't even tried. You've been fiddling with that bondar the whole time we've been here. The least you could do would be to see if you could figure anything out."

Tolan glanced down at the bondar. In the time they'd been in class, he had attempted to visualize various elementals using what he knew of earth, trying to summon what he could, but nothing seemed to work. That didn't surprise him. He had done the same each time they were in their earth classes, and he didn't expect anything to change rapidly. Why should it? The only time he had seemed to have any effect with earth had been when he had been under stress. And that hadn't even required him to have the bondar.

"I don't think earth is an elemental I'm able to use."

"You mean element."

"What?"

"You said elemental. You mean element."

"It's not an element bond I can use. I've tried using the bondar, but it's not working for me."

They were able to leave when they were finished, and while Tolan would have loved to take all the time in the world to simply sit and experiment with the bondar, the fact it hadn't done anything for him made it so he didn't really care to stay. If he did, he would just grow increasingly frustrated at his inability to reach the element powers. There were other things he wanted to be trying, and if nothing else, he wanted to see if he could come up with some way of using the elementals with their symbols. He thought he was onto something, though didn't know if it would work the way he intended.

"You can go on. I'll catch up with you later," Jonas said.

Tolan nodded, gathering his things, and was making his way to the front of the classroom when Master Shorav arched a brow at him. "Are you already done?"

"I'm having an off day," Tolan said.

"An off day?"

"I'm not able to get the bondar to do anything for me. I've tried, but my connection to earth is weak."

Master Shorav glanced at the bondar Tolan held before looking up at his face. "You have the ability to sense earth."

Tolan nodded. "I do. That was the element I was most connected to." It wasn't a secret anymore that he didn't have much ability to shape before coming to the Academy. At least, not among the master shapers. There were still students who hadn't known that, and while Tolan didn't necessarily care if others knew, especially now he had a connection to fire, he didn't really want word to get out to some of the others.

"In the time you've been here, Shaper Ethar, you haven't managed to successfully reach any of the other element bonds. I question your motivation."

"I would like to reach the other elements," he said. "I've been working with Master Marcella, but she hasn't been able to coax that ability out of me."

"Master Marcella was a good student, but she is inexperienced as an instructor."

Tolan resisted the urge to say anything about her teaching methods. He couldn't imagine what she would try to do to pull earth from him. Would she try to crush him in some way? Maybe she would think burying him in a cave would somehow make him closer to earth.

When he was younger, his parents had attempted various tactics to get him to have a connection to earth, knowing that with his sensing ability, he should have some. They had taken a more loving approach than Master Marcella had tried with him, though Tolan wasn't sure what he would do if Master Marcella tried a loving approach. His neck started to get warm with the thought.

He turned away from Master Shorav before hesitating. "Have you ever lent a bondar to a student?"

"You understand the bondars are for classroom learning, Shaper Ethar."

"I understand, but I wonder if I had more time with it, I might be able to find my connection to earth. I know I can reach it." Success was infrequent, and certainly not often enough to feel confident with his ability. It was a minor miracle he had managed to use earth when they had been attacked on the Shapers Path. And with the testing coming—everyone agreed it would have to be soon—he needed something to prepare.

"You could petition the Grand Master, but I'm afraid I feel quite strongly the bondars must remain in class. They are far too powerful to be distributed within the school.

You are still learning, and if you attempt a shaping without having the expertise needed, it's potentially quite dangerous."

He smiled and set the bondar down. "I had to ask."

"You can spend more time here, Shaper Ethar. I'm willing to work with you outside of class if you are so motivated. You have a connection to earth; we just have to draw it out of you."

He should be reassured by that, and Tolan knew he should take Master Shorav up on the offer, but a part of him didn't really want to. Despite what he knew he should be doing, he would almost rather work on his own. He thought he might be able to uncover more about his connection to the elements that way, and certainly more about his connection to the elementals.

"That sounds good," he said rather than upsetting Master Shorav.

He turned away, heading out of the earth tower. Several other students had already left, though most of them were skilled earth shapers and didn't need the extra time. He wasn't surprised to see Draln and several of his buddies were already gone.

There was no question Draln would quickly advance through the Academy. It would be just his luck if Draln one day became an Inquisitor, and Tolan could easily envision him coming after him; Draln was the kind of person who would likely come after anyone he didn't like, regardless of guilt.

At the entrance to the tower, Tolan paused and looked

around. The various element towers were each ornate in their own specific ways. Some, like the earth tower, had intricately carved stone, and he couldn't even imagine how much effort—or earth shaping—had gone into creating it. There were carvings throughout, and Tolan had long ago realized those carvings seemed to indicate the various elementals, something that surprised him considering how the Academy trained the students to recognize the elementals and force them back into the bonds. But then, maybe that was the point of having the elementals carved into the sides of the walls. Being able to see them and recognize them was one way to be prepared for the possibility they might eventually need to counter them and force them into the element bond once again.

There was a pattern to them.

Tolan frowned as he stared up at them, realizing he hadn't seen it before. The orientation to the elementals took on a specific shape, and the longer he studied, the more he realized there was a distinctiveness to it.

Why hadn't he seen it before?

Tolan made a slow circuit of the tower. As he did, he pulled out a sheet of paper and then took a seat in the center of the entrance. Grabbing a pen, he started to copy the images of the elementals around the inside of the tower. He worked quickly, not needing to document the elementals exactly. He didn't think that was the key. But what he wanted to do was to see if there was anything about the shape that would give him any clues. It was similar to the shape and patterns within the spirit tower.

When he was there, he was convinced the spirit tower held a rune that marked a way of calling to spirit.

"Look at this guy," Draln said. Tolan looked up to find Draln with two of his friends in the entrance to the tower, looking out at him. He chuckled and sneered. "You look like a child sitting and drawing while his parents work."

"It sounds like something you have a lot of familiarity with," Tolan said.

"My parents included me in their work. What sort of work did your parents do, Ethar?"

The way he said it, and the disdain in his voice, led Tolan to wonder just how much Draln knew about him.

Tolan had been careful not to reveal too much about himself here. He didn't want anyone to question his allegiance to the Academy the same way they had in Ephra. Considering the fact he had so much experience with the elementals, there was even more reason to keep to himself.

"My parents were craftsmen," he said carefully.

"Craftsmen? I suppose at the border of Terndahl, you people think you need totems and other sort of magical items to ward off the Draasin Lord. Unless you're one of those who celebrates the Draasin Lord. I hear there are plenty like that out where you come from."

Tolan gathered his things and stuffed the page into his bag before getting to his feet. "Velminth isn't that much better, Draln. You come from a logging city."

"I might come from a logging city, but my family owns

the sawmill. My parents were both shapers who came through the Academy. What does your family own?"

Tolan glared at him, biting back any retort that would end up getting him into trouble. He didn't want to anger Draln any more than he already had, and would rather just have the other man leave him alone.

He glanced at the two with Draln, Horace and Nevern, both shapers of moderate skill who had the ability to easily reach two of the element bonds and were quickly working toward a third. He decided to head on his way. It was easier.

"We're going to have that duel soon, Ethar."

Draln laughed as Tolan left, relieved he didn't have to hear anything else they might say—for the time being.

He debated heading back to the student quarters, but there was plenty of time yet before he had to go to his session with Master Marcella. She would push him, and he didn't look forward to the way she might make him shape, so he would rather take some time to himself.

How long had it been since he'd been to the park outside the city? There had been no further rumors of disciple attacks, so Tolan believed they were safe. Why not go and relax, ignore everything else?

Tolan wound through the city, passing a few carts moving alongside the road, ambling quickly, and hurried past people working. Some of the storefronts were occupied by shop owners attempting to coax people along the street inside. Many had their doors wide open, inviting the warm breeze, and from some of them, Tolan noted the smells of food, leaving his stomach rumbling. The Academy fed him well, never leaving him wanting, but there were some foods out in Amitan that he couldn't find within the Academy.

Resisting the urge to go into some of those shops, he found himself heading toward the remains of the palace. Since the attack, he hadn't come here, and now realized he should have done so before. As he neared, he saw there was already construction, the palace rising up once again, shaped into existence. Five earth shapers worked, the power they were wielding incredible, and he was surprised to note Master Marcella among them. Tolan watched, noting how they pulled stone from the fallen remains of the palace and joined them together. The shaping caused the fallen sections to fit together perfectly, as if they had always been intended to go that way.

A hasty fence had been erected, preventing anyone from getting too close, but even with that, most people out in the city kept a generous distance, almost as if they wanted to avoid upsetting the master shapers.

What purpose would there have been in destroying the palace?

That was what troubled him most of all. The attack on the Shapers Path had been an attempt to destroy the protections around the city, but the palace didn't provide any sort of protection. The Academy served that role, but why then would the disciples of the Draasin Lord have attacked the palace?

He wouldn't get the answers. The Grand Master would

keep that from any student. Tolan continued to watch, amazed by how quickly the structure of the palace was rebuilt. Already, the central section had gained some form, resembling what had been before, though there were distinct differences. Whereas the previous palace had ornate and decorative features, this was smooth stone, though Tolan didn't know if they would add that decoration later or if were going to leave it off. The shape of it was different, too. While he hadn't visited the palace before, he had seen it from a distance. This was more of a circular shape, rather than a central structure with arms leading off it.

He continued to make his way around the boundary, watching as they continued to build. The power from the shaping reverberated, surging as the shapers worked. Were there only five earth shapers working on the palace? Maybe they were taking shifts. He'd have to ask Master Marcella about the palace when he met with her, though she'd likely view it as something he didn't need to worry about.

As he continued to make his way around the fence, a sense of shaping came to him, though it wasn't near the palace construction. Surprisingly, Tolan could tell it was a mixture of fire and wind, two unexpected elements so close to the building site—unless the shapers were using it to fortify the palace in some way?

He didn't think so. From what he could tell, it didn't seem as if the shapers were aware of it.

He still had time left in the day so he wandered,

deciding it was time to return to the park. It had been too long since he'd gone, and he wound the long way, sweeping out from the edge of the city and reaching the forest. He knew he probably shouldn't do this but continued meandering until he found the park and jumped over the wall to take a seat next to the tall finger of rock at the center.

He focused on a shaping. Fire, as that was what came easiest for him. When he'd come before, he had focused on his shaping but this time, he imagined a connection to saa.

The connection burst into existence, flames dancing around him much faster than before. Tolan released that connection hurriedly. He had shaped so easily—almost *too* easily. Had he been holding onto the furios? He didn't think so, but could have done so without realizing it. He'd intended to try it without the furious this time.

Reaching again for his connection to fire, he envisioned saa again. He'd not used the elementals when he'd come before, though why not? That was how he shaped.

This time, the elemental burst into view, dancing in front of him, a flame hovering above the grasses.

Tolan released the connection. That was *much* clearer than he expected.

He looked around but there was no one here, and certainly no one watching.

Was it him—or was it this place?

Once again, he started to focus on his shaping. As he did, he used saa to envision a shaping, and there came a fluttering within him. He'd felt that fluttering before when imagining elementals.

The fluttering seemed as if it were answered, like a bell tolling and reverberating.

The reverberations came from above.

Tolan looked up and realized the shape on the top of the tower had started to glow. He'd been to this park many times since discovering it, but this was the first time he'd seen anything change.

He released his shaping, getting to his feet and looking up at the tower.

What was that?

He hurried back to the wall and took a spot on top of it, looking toward the sculpture. As usual, the grasses had reformed, showing no evidence of his passing. He'd never given that much thought, though he probably should have.

Tolan focused on a shaping again, but from here, there was a much slower response. It came, but not quite as easily as it had when he had been so close to the sculpture. He reached for the furios, squeezing it, drawing upon the image of the elemental, and saa surged into existence, but much weaker than before. He looked to the top of the tower, but there was nothing. No sign of any glowing. Just the tower.

Tolan didn't think he'd imagined it.

Moving back to the tower again, feeling foolish as he did, this time, rather than focusing on a fire elemental, he focused on an earth elemental—not just a shaping. There were dozens of earth elementals he knew, and he tried to think about which one would be the least likely to cause any problems.

Oshal.

It was nothing more than a stack of rocks, and while it could be powerful, Tolan doubted he had the necessary strength to do anything with it. As he focused on it, the ground set off rumbling, and suddenly, the elemental started emerging.

There had been no hesitation, no delay as there usually was when he attempted to shape. It was just the appearance of the elemental.

Could the park be something more than a peaceful place to practice? Could this tower actually help him shape?

17

DARKNESS SURROUNDED HIM, A PITCH BLACK THAT enveloped him, and Tolan ignored it, focusing on the image of the elementals as he had been doing for the last hour. The tower pressed up against him, the sense of stone nearly overwhelming, and he thought about wind, letting it come to him.

A swirling gust spiralled around him, circling around the entirety of the tower, before he released it. The fact he had managed to succeed reaching wind had been a minor miracle. Reaching water had come as a shock, too.

That meant he had managed to reach each of the elements.

But then, he hadn't reached the elements at all, had he? He had reached the elementals. And he hadn't done it on his own. He had done it near this tower, the structure that somehow had given him a connection to those elementals. Maybe this somehow tapped into the Convergence deep beneath the ground, but he had nothing to tell him that was actually the case. The other possibility was that it was some sort of powerful bondar. With each elemental he focused on and called, his familiarity with it increased.

Why today, though?

It felt wrong to have such an easy time reaching those elements. Even more so than with the bondar, sitting here, drawing upon whatever power existed here, had allowed him to reach for a connection he had never known. Not only was it easy to come and reach for fire—and he had gone through every single fire elemental he could think of, other than the draasin—but it had become increasingly easy to reach the other elements.

There was some part of him that was tempted to see if he could summon a draasin.

Tolan wasn't even sure whether he was drawing real elementals or whether this was simply imagined. If it wasn't imagined, then he was actually shaping, connecting to the element bonds, something he wasn't even able to do in the Academy.

Continuing to practice, he went from elemental to elemental, sticking within one of the elements as he did. Right now, he focused on wind, summoning and releasing, getting familiar with the various forms of wind, then switching once again to water. It amazed him when a mist streamed down his face, drawn from the air itself. Even more so was when he had managed to make rain begin to fall from the cloudless sky. And then there was the water that bubbled up from the ground, causing him to jump to his feet. If he were anywhere else, close to the ocean perhaps, he might have wondered if he could control udilm, an elemental only found in the ocean.

Marcella had said he had no ability to shape water. This was more than no ability.

He leaned back. He was tired, both physically and mentally, drained from the hours he'd spent here. A part of him wondered whether he should reveal to his friends that he'd come here, but they would likely warn him against coming to a place like this.

Because it was hidden deep in the forest outside the city, they would have suggested he should have stayed closer to Amitan. Tolan didn't fear coming to the forest, though given the attacks that had taken place in the city, and the warnings the Grand Master had made, all suggesting people should remain within the city, perhaps he should. But then, there was nothing here that left him feeling as if he was in any danger.

Then again, if he hadn't come here, he would never have discovered this. And this left him feeling as if he could finally shape. If he learned enough, he *would* pass the testing.

Maybe this was nothing more than a dream. Maybe crossing over the stone wall had put him into some sort of trance, forcing him to believe he could do something he couldn't actually achieve. A spirit shaping, perhaps. If so, Tolan was content having it. More than anything else, he thought a dream like this would allow him to finally feel as if he had the ability to shape.

The stack of books he'd taken from the library depicting the elementals remained in his satchel. He had gone through them one by one, flipping through the various pages, using a shaping of fire he had been able to maintain in order to see in the dark.

There was one he shouldn't try.

Tolan glanced up at the top of the tower. He had discovered when he focused on one of the elementals, one particular pattern glowed. He wasn't able to tell which pattern it was, not without climbing up the side of the tower, and from the wall, there was no sign of what he had done. He suspected they were tied to each of the elements and wished he had an opportunity to tell which shapes represented which elements. Most likely, they were runes, and if he could uncover the key to them, maybe he could use that knowledge to help him understand the bondars? And then, the knowledge he was learning here could be translated to the bondars, and onward from there to being able to shape without them.

He shifted around the edge of the tower, reaching the section representing fire. It was the section that had glowed first for him, and as he sat there, he started envisioning the draasin.

It was dangerous, and the one he had never attempted before, but why shouldn't he try to reach for it? It was nothing more than his way of shaping, not as if he was actually freeing these elementals. Each time he released that connection, the power was tamped back down, as if this tower was simply allowing him to augment his imagination, or perhaps somehow allowing him to tap into some different power.

Ferrah would warn him against this, even more reason not to reveal to her or Jonas that this place existed. And he had wanted to bring her here, but perhaps that would have been a mistake. They didn't need a place like this to be able to shape. They had the bondars, and with those, they were able to do far more than he could. But then, with this place, he was able to shape more than they were able to do.

He focused, drawing upon the connection to fire. He had enough experience with fire and the way that the fluttering within him needed to coordinate. He needed to reach for the fluttering first, then began to visualize the draasin, though in this case, he focused on a smaller image, not wanting to draw forth a massive draasin that might escape control if it were real.

Slowly, the fluttering continued, power burning within him, and Tolan sat upright, watching as the shape softly glowed, taking form, growing larger and larger.

No. That wasn't what he wanted. He didn't want to create an enormous draasin.

He released the shaping but the draasin continued to emerge, growing larger and larger, the fluttering within him continuing to stir. Regardless of what he did, that fluttering continued, and he fought against it, trying to push it down.

Tolan began panicking.

If he was actually releasing a draasin, there would be

no way of controlling it. He had no idea what he was doing and feared he had made a mistake. He grabbed his books, everything he'd brought with him and went racing toward the wall. When he reached it, he jumped on top of it, and the connection suddenly was severed.

The stirring within him gradually abated, and he breathed out heavily.

He had almost released a draasin.

He had no idea if it would truly have been unleashed, but he needed to be far more careful with this place. Not knowing what this place was, or what power was actually available here, he couldn't risk the possibility what he was doing was real.

He jumped back down, heading back into the park. He didn't want to be done, not yet, but at the same time, maybe it would be better if he were. As he neared the tower, he looked up. The symbol for fire continued to glow, even though he was no longer holding onto a shaping, and he didn't feel that fluttering deep within him the same way he had before.

He continued to look around, worried he had made something of a mistake. There was no sign of the draasin, nothing that would tell him that whatever he might have shaped was real. As much as he might want to continue to practice, he needed to head back. He was tired, and shouldn't remain here.

As he backed away, he watched the top of the tower. The glowing began to fade, finally disappearing altogether.

At least that had happened. Thankfully, there was no more glowing, nothing that suggested he was still holding onto some shaping, and he continued backing up toward the wall. When he reached it, he climbed up to the top and scrambled over.

Tolan hesitated for a moment before turning and heading back toward Amitan. The path through the trees was easy to follow. As he made his way back to Amitan, he thought he heard a crunching.

Tolan spun, backing up toward the darkened trunk of a nearby tree. He pressed against it, and as he did, he scanned the forest, looking for signs of movement, but there were none. If only he had some connection to earth shaping, but out here, away from the tower, he didn't.

Could he use earth sensing?

Most of the time, his earth sensing came with being able to determine species of wood—something valuable when he had been working with Master Daniels. He had been slower than Master Daniels, and wasn't sure now would be much better. What he needed now was to know whether there was someone else in the woods with him.

Focusing on earth, testing his connection to it, he pressed through the ground, straining to see if he could pick up on someone.

At first, he detected the trees. There were hundreds throughout the forest, and surprisingly, it seemed as if the roots were all interconnected, but from there, he was able to detect something else. A nearby animal crept through the forest, although it did not come close to him.

There had been stories of the disciples, but there hadn't been any more attacks and he hadn't seen anyone outside the city.

Tolan continued to delve deeper into the sense of earth. He pressed farther than he had before, and as he did, he found himself reaching through the same strange fluttering he'd felt when near the tower.

Tolan retreated, afraid if he let himself push through that fluttering, he might draw out an elemental. But then, he hadn't been focusing on elementals. He'd been focusing on the earth itself, pushing through it, searching for some connection. If it didn't require an elemental, then did it mean he was actually shaping?

The fluttering within him, that strange stirring, was what seemed to be the key.

Tolan focused once again, realizing the connection to the trees, and from there, he focused even deeper, on the prowling animal. A wolf, though it was now heading away from him. There were other creatures, though they were more distant still. There was no one else in the forest with him that he could tell.

Maybe that wasn't true. There was a sense of an absence near him, something he should be able to detect with his connection to earth, but a void closed off to him.

Tolan started toward that sense, feeling ridiculous. There was no way there was someone this close to him who he hadn't detected, but there had been that cracking sound.

As he approached, he reached for his furios. If he

needed to protect himself, a shaping of fire was the only thing he might be able to do. Connecting to the earth in this way might allow him to sense, but that didn't mean he would be able to shape.

And then he found the sense of a void.

There was nothing here.

Tolan stepped forward, approaching the sense, and as he did, he searched, straining to see if there was someone here who was somehow masking themselves with a shaping, but there was nothing.

He was being foolish.

He turned and continued back toward Amitan.

It was long since time for him to return and he dreaded explaining to Marcella why he'd blown off his training with her. As he walked through the Academy's front door, he glanced toward the entrance to the student section before changing his mind and heading toward the library. He wanted to know more about the strange park and the sculpture within it, and there was only one person he thought he could ask.

He didn't know if Master Minden would share with him and didn't know if there was even anything she would know, but if anyone would know anything about that strange place, it would be her.

The library was empty at this time of day. Usually, there would be other students sitting at tables, but he had lost track of time, and while he thought it had only been an hour, as dark as it was, it probably had been much longer, meaning it was much later.

Thankfully, Master Minden was there.

He made his way to the dais and she looked up as he approached, a shaping building from her. He was no longer surprised when it happened, and it washed over him.

"Shaper Ethar. It's awfully late for you to visit the library."

"I lost track of time. How late is it?"

"Well after midnight."

"Why does the library have a librarian here at all hours?"

"This is our domain. We remain here to protect it and to serve the Academy if the need arises for research."

"Why is it always you in the overnights?"

"I need very little sleep," she said.

"I'm sorry if I'm bothering you during your research."

"The librarians are here to serve the Academy, Shaper Ethar. What is it you need?"

"I have questions about a bondar again." He would start with that and get to his questions about the park.

"You know I'm unwilling to share with you about the creation of a bondar."

"I know. That's not for student shapers."

"Not even for most of the master shapers," she said.

"Are there more powerful bondars?"

"More powerful than the ones the students use?"

Tolan nodded.

"There are other bondars, though they are the originals."

"The originals from when?"

"Unfortunately, little is known about the bondars other than that they have been here as long as the Academy has been here."

"And how long has the Academy been here?"

"The Academy has stood and trained shapers for well over 1,000 years, Shaper Ethar. As a student here, you owe it to yourself to understand the history of Terenhall."

It was a gap in his knowledge that he needed to fill, especially if he were to stay here and continue to learn, but at the same time, he had many gaps and trying to understand the history of the Academy wasn't high on his list of needs. Perhaps it should be, especially with as old as the Academy was. There were probably many things he could learn about shaping simply by attempting to understand the history of the Academy itself.

"I will spend more time on it," he said.

"I have many books that might be of interest to you."

He nodded, thinking those books would probably be far more interesting to Ferrah than they were to him, but he wasn't going to tell Master Minden that. "I was just questioning whether there might be larger bondars that might help me reach the elements more easily."

"More easily, or at all?"

"At all. I... I struggle to reach the other elements, and we have our testing soon."

"Many who came to the Academy never reached the other elements without a bondar, Shaper Ethar. There is no shame in that. You come and learn and try to maximize your potential. When you leave the Academy, you will do so as skilled as you can be, and you will be able to serve the Academy as well as you can."

"Are there any larger bondars at the Academy?"

She frowned. "You have already uncovered a secret of the Academy very few know about. If that's what you imply—"

Tolan shook his head. "That's not what I'm getting at. I'm wondering if there are any actual bondars. I thought the Convergence was something else. I didn't realize it was a bondar, too."

"The Convergence would not be considered a bondar, but the power is similar. It allows you to access the element bond more directly, similar to the way the bondars hone your connection. In the Convergence, there is nearly a direct connection to the element bonds. While the bondars allow for something similar, it's not the same."

That was his impression, too. "I'm just looking for a stronger connection. One that might allow me to reach for some of the other elements so I get more familiar with shaping them."

"More strength is not necessarily better. There are times when even working with the bondar is dangerous. It's the reason master shapers have restricted access to classrooms for the most part."

Her gaze drifted to his pocket and once again he wondered whether she knew he had the furios. As far as he knew, no one other than his friends knew about it.

Even having the furios hadn't allowed him to do anything dangerous. Not so far, at least.

"Do you know of any?" he pressed.

"There might be some, but they are restricted."

"Restricted?"

She nodded. "Any of the ancient designs are often restricted, especially as they are difficult to replicate."

"Why do you think the shapers from long ago had the ability to make things we don't?"

"We have master shapers quite capable of creating similar things."

"But I've been told they can't make bondars anymore. That they're only able to make copies."

"And those copies are effective. Don't mistake a change in knowledge, and evolution over time, for ignorance. The master shapers of today are incredibly capable, Shaper Ethar, and we have much knowledge the shapers of old did not."

"It seems to me they had knowledge we do not."

"You suggest knowing about the elementals would be valuable?"

"We can only read about them. Not experience them."

"I believe you have experienced the power of an elemental before. Would you like that power released upon the world?"

"I don't think so, but the elementals are connected to power the same way as shapers are, aren't they?"

"They are connected more directly to the elements, but your assertion would be correct."

"And if they are connected to the same power, then understanding the elementals and the use of that power would also be beneficial to us, would it not?"

"Which is why we study them."

"From what I can tell, we study the elementals so we can recognize them and suppress them, pushing them back into the bond, not trying to understand the various aspects of their powers."

"What have you uncovered about the elementals?" she asked.

Tolan realized he was heading into dangerous territory. He was pressing one of the master shapers about the elementals, and was alluding to how he didn't necessarily see them as dangerous in the way the master shapers typically did. It wasn't a far stretch to accuse him of sympathizing with the elementals, and from there, it wouldn't take much to accuse him of siding with the Draasin Lord.

He really needed to be careful with what he was doing and saying. And yet, he had a sense Master Minden knew something but was keeping it from him.

"Each of the elementals seems to have a different connection to the element powers. They seem to represent various aspects of the elements. I think of something like saa, and how it would be the power found within the hearth, the crackling flames of a fire. Then there is esalash or shiron, both of which have some different aspect of smoke, and there are examples of that throughout the elementals."

"You have been studying."

"You lent me those books. I thought you wanted me to learn about them."

"Many study elementals over the years, but very few take the time to grasp what that knowledge means. Most would try to recognize them, as you say, for the sake of being prepared to suppress them. There is benefit in that. The Academy trains shapers so we can be ready for the threat of the elementals escaping the bond, but very few seek understanding. I am surprised to find a student, especially a first-level student, looking for understanding."

Tolan wasn't sure if she was implying anything or if she was simply praising him. "I thought understanding would be the key to knowledge."

"It can be, but it can also be the key to persuasion."

"What do you mean?"

"A warning, Shaper Ethar. There is a difference between understanding and sympathizing. Be sure you know the difference."

He blinked, taking a step back and realizing what she was implying. She was suggesting to him he might be siding with the elementals. After everything he had seen and done, was that true?

He didn't think so. Everything he had experienced with that power had suggested he wasn't releasing any dangerous magic into the world. All he was doing was trying to master and understand his connection to the elements—and perhaps the elementals.

"I will be careful."

"And I would caution you not to pursue power you're not prepared for. That way lies danger as well."

Tolan nodded, and when she turned back to her writings, he headed out of the library, making his way back to his room and flopping onto his bed, doing so as quietly as he could so as not to wake the others. Even though it was late and he was exhausted from hours spent shaping in the clearing, he had a difficult time falling asleep. His mind continued to race, thinking through everything he had done and everything he had seen.

When sleep finally claimed him, dreams of elementals consumed him. One lingered most of all, the vision of the draasin as it continued to emerge from his shaping.

In the dream, the draasin escaped.

18

Days began to pass, one blurring into the next, and with each day, Tolan found himself heading out into the forest, to the clearing with the park and the sculpture, practicing reaching for each of the elements. It was his way of preparing for testing for the second level. Everyone agreed they would be tested soon, though no one knew when that would be. Even Marcella hadn't shared when, though Tolan had a feeling she knew.

He was no longer certain whether he was reaching for elements or elementals, and the steady fluttering he felt when he succeeded had become familiar. The longer he did it, the more control he had. It got to the point where he recognized the elementals he formed, solidifying the knowledge he had been studying in each of the books within his mind.

Tolan had not tried to summon a draasin again.

Mostly, it was because he wasn't sure whether the

summons was real or not, and if it was, he didn't want to be responsible for making a mistake in releasing a creature out into the world that he had no ability to control. The rest of the elementals were easy to suppress. He pushed them down, tamping out that connection, and had taken to looking up at the top of the tower to ensure the glowing stopped before he moved onto the next.

Each night when he came to the park, he found it empty, and there had never been another sense he wasn't alone. Had there been someone else here, he thought he would detect them, especially as he now felt a greater connection to earth, but there had been no others at the park. There had been no signs of the disciples.

His days were hurried through. He lost track of time and missed two of his classes, something that had gained the notice of Jonas and Ferrah. By the morning of the fourth day of heading to the park late at night, returning near morning, he woke to Ferrah and Jonas shaking him.

Both looked down at him, matching worried looks on their faces.

"What is it?"

"It's you," Jonas said.

"What did I do?"

"You've been gone. Where have you been going?" Jonas asked.

"We know you've been leaving at night," Ferrah said. "What we don't know is where you've been going and why."

"Does it matter?"

"It matters. We want to know what our friend is up to. And we're worried you're not preparing the way you need to for testing to the next level."

"I've been studying."

"Alone?" Ferrah asked.

"I've been trying to get a better sense of my connection to the element bonds," he said, rubbing sleep from his eyes. "I'm going to be ready for the testing when it comes." If he could master the elements at the park, he thought he'd be able to.

Ferrah studied him for a moment. "You haven't been going to the library. I've been waiting and watching, half expecting you will show up at any time, but you never do. So where have you been studying?" She lowered her voice. "You even gave up working on the bondar."

"Because I can't do it. And I shouldn't."

He yawned as he sat up. How late was it? He was still tired, though he wasn't nearly as tired as he had been when he had tumbled into bed the night before. Or maybe, this morning. Tolan wasn't sure how late it was, but the way his stomach rumbled suggested it was quite late. He had taken to heading straight to bed, though in reality, with some of the long nights, he should have been eating first.

"I've been studying outside."

"In the park?" Ferrah asked.

"Not in the park." He glanced from Jonas to Ferrah, meeting their gazes.

"Where, then?"

"There's a place outside of the city—"

"Tolan!" Ferrah started. "You know what the Grand Master said."

"I know what the Grand Master said, but I'm not going that far outside of the city, and it's not like it's unsafe."

"We don't know if there are other disciples of the Draasin Lord. You were there. Of all people who should be more careful about this, it should be you. You saw what they were willing to do and the way they were able to attack."

"There haven't been any other attacks."

"Besides the one on the Shapers Path. And the one on the palace. And then the three in the last week along the edge of the city."

Tolan shook his head. "What?"

"You didn't know?"

He sat up, reaching the edge of the bed. How could there have been attacks he hadn't heard of? He'd been along the edge of the city in that time. "What attacks are you talking about?"

"There have been three. Each has come along the edge of Amitan. The Academy has increased its shaper presence and master shapers have begun to patrol, though none has seen anything."

"What kind of attacks?"

"We don't really know. The master shapers are talking about them, and all we know is the rumors that have begun to spread."

If he had not been so distracted, he might have known

about them. It was possible he might've even detected them. Working at the sculpture, even his connection to sensing for shapings had changed.

"Have you gone to investigate them?" he asked.

"Have we gone to... Tolan," Jonas said. "The attacks came outside of the city. We're not supposed to be going outside of the city. So, no. We haven't gone to investigate them. We aren't master shapers." He turned to Ferrah. "I don't know what's going on with him. You see if you can figure him out." He headed out of the room, shaking his head as he went.

Ferrah scooted closer to him. The concern on her face was clear, and it gave Tolan a moment of pause. Had he been making a mistake? Shouldn't he have been sharing with his friends what he was doing? They deserved to know, especially as they would be concerned about him, and he didn't want to have them worried about what he was doing and where he had been.

"Are you... Are you okay?" she whispered.

"I'm fine," he said, getting to his feet. "I found something."

"What?"

He looked around the room, but Wallace was gone. With Jonas having disappeared, it left just the two of them. He met her deep green eyes, and she frowned at him.

"I found a bondar. A powerful one. It's larger than the ones we use in class and—"

"For what elements?"

"As far as I can tell, all of them."

Her breath caught. "All of them?"

"With this bondar, I've been able to reach and shape each of the elements, Ferrah. I've never experienced anything like it before."

"Why keep this yourself?"

"I guess I just wanted to see if I could understand anything about it."

"Have you talked to any of the master shapers?"

"I asked Master Minden about powerful bondars, but she warned me against using them."

"Because you can unleash power that is more than you can handle."

"Now *you* sound like one of the master shapers."

She shrugged. "Why, because it's true? That's the reason we aren't allowed to bring the bondars out of the classrooms. You've seen how powerful they are. With that," she said, nodding to where he kept his hand in his pocket, "you are far more connected to the elements."

He thought about telling her it wasn't the elements but the elementals, but after spending as much time as he had out in the park, he was no longer certain. All he knew was that there was the stirring within him each time he reached for that connection, and that with it, he had managed to shape.

"It's probably true," he said. "But it's strange. It's outside of the city. In a clearing. It's almost like I was meant to find it."

"Oh, Tolan…"

"What?"

"I don't like the sound of that."

"The sound of what?"

"You talking like that about a bondar. It was bad enough when you wanted to make one, and now you're sounding like you believe you were meant to find a powerful one. I don't like it."

"You don't want me to have access to this bondar?"

"I'd rather have you learn to shape without it," she said.

"That's just it," he said. "I wasn't learning to shape without it, and the more I continue to practice, the more useless my time in the various classes feels. Think about what Master Shorav has us doing. Most the time, he's having us work on after he talks to us about the elementals. I've done all the reading I can on the elementals, so anything he's teaching isn't anything I need to gain from him, and without an ability to use the bondar, any shaping I might try is useless."

"It doesn't have to be useless," she said.

"But it is. As much as I want to be able to perform the shaping he's trying to demonstrate, anything he's teaching is useless until I have a greater access to the various element bonds."

"Maybe you won't reach some of these element bonds," she said softly.

"It's possible I won't," he said.

"But you do with this bondar?"

"With this bondar—or whatever it is—I'm able to reach

each of the element bonds. I've tried not only fire, but earth and wind and water."

"What of spirit?"

"I don't know that it's meant to help reach spirit."

"You don't think this is dangerous?"

Tolan threw his hands up in frustration. "The entire thing is probably more dangerous than I should be doing. And at the same time, I don't know what else to do. All I want is to be able to shape, to do the things you do, but even with fire, my connection is so different than anyone else's."

"Show me."

"Show you my shaping?"

"No. Show me this bondar."

Tolan's gaze drifted to the door. No one had interrupted them. "It's time for our session on wind. Master Rorn would be disappointed if we didn't appear."

"Fine. We'll go to the wind class, and then after that, you can show me this bondar. If it's not dangerous, then you should be able to work with your friends."

He nodded. She was right. If it wasn't dangerous, he shouldn't be keeping it to himself. The others could shape the elements without needing the bondar all the time, but maybe they could do even more near the massive bondar.

She helped him to his feet and looked up at him. "It's okay that you don't have the same power as everyone else."

"Says the woman who has access to all of the element bonds."

"I would think that matters the most. I don't judge you in any way for not being able to reach certain element bonds. I recognize all of us are different."

Would she recognize that when he suddenly could shape elementals?

So far, she hadn't seen the elementals he had summoned, though he had, and he was certain that was what he was doing. Regardless of what Ferrah believed, elementals came from his shapings.

"How late are we going to be?"

"We woke you up early this time," she said.

"This time?"

"We tried waking you up yesterday, but you've been sleeping so soundly, we haven't been able to."

"Sorry about that."

"What time have you been getting in?"

"Late," he said.

"How late is that?"

He looked down rather than meeting her eyes. "I don't know. I've been focused on working through as much of the…" He smiled, shaking his head. He needed to be careful, not wanting Ferrah to know he had been working through trying to summon each of the elementals. That might draw the wrong kind of questioning. "Shaping as I could. I've been trying to work through the various lessons we've been taught in our classes."

"That's even more reason for you to have someone else with you. If nothing else, if the shaping goes awry, you need to have someone there who can help you correct it."

"Like I said, I'll bring you with me tonight."

"And you might need to talk to one of the master shapers," she said.

"I don't know that I want any of the other master shapers to keep me from this. I've been able to reach elements I haven't been able to even consider reaching before. At least with earth, I've had some ability on my own, but with wind and water... I've never had any potential with those, and all of a sudden, now I do. With this bondar, I'm able to reach for wind, use it to create a breeze, to swirl around me, so many things I have only imagined before."

"And water?"

"I've made it rain. I've felt mist spraying on my face. I felt water rising up from the ground."

"None of those are shapings we've discussed in class," she said.

"Those are the shapings I could think of," he said hurriedly.

She studied him for a moment before letting out a frustrated breath and heading out of their room. Tolan checked his pack and ensured his books were there, along with the furios. When he was confident they were, he followed her out of the room and down the stairs to the main section of the Academy. Some of the older students walked through the hallways, and Tolan nodded politely as he passed them, following Ferrah as she guided him toward the wind tower.

They snuck in the back of the class, but there was no

need to sneak at all. Master Rorn wasn't even there, so there wasn't any delay on their part. Tolan took a seat next to Ferrah and considered motioning to Jonas to join them. Usually in classes, he sat near Jonas, but maybe for today he could stay near Ferrah.

Slowly, some of the other students made their way in, and they all took their seats in the usual places. A shaped bell softly tolled and Master Rorn appeared, sweeping into the room, his robe practically floating. How much of it was shaped?

Master Rorn could be difficult for Tolan to read. He was a powerful wind shaper, thin and yet skilled, like so many wind shapers. Even Jonas was lanky and lean, yet strong despite that. Those who favored wind often took on those characteristics.

"Today, we will be talking about various elementals," he said, pulling out a board and starting to write on it. He used a shaping to document, leaving swirls of chalky letters on the board. The level of control Master Rorn displayed with his shaping awed Tolan. None of the types of shaping he had tried recently had involved that level of control. Maybe part of it was because he had been focusing on the elementals, rather than truly focusing on trying to follow the shapings instructed by the master shapers. If he were to attempt to copy those shapings, he might have more control, but instead, he was left with nothing other than making the wind move, fluttering it, swirling around him. Even that was enough.

"Take notes, students," he said.

Tolan dutifully pulled out his notebook and started copying the same things Master Rorn was documenting on the board, but surprisingly—or not so surprisingly— much of it involved information about elementals he had already known. There was some on ara, a powerful wind elemental, one that led to the heavy gusts that blew in out of the north. It was one of the wind elementals Tolan had experimented with and was now familiar with. There was the mention of foye, a wind elemental that had a different connection, not tied to the wind, but mostly to breathing and an interconnectedness between people. Tolan had experimented with this elemental as well. There was information about joil, and as Master Rorn documented, Tolan set his pen down.

"Aren't you going to take notes?" Ferrah asked, leaning toward him.

"This one is wrong," he said.

"You don't know that," she said.

"The book Master Minden let me borrow has information about the elementals. This one is wrong."

"There is more chatter than I'm accustomed to. Is there someone in the back of the room who would like to speak up?"

A warm flush worked through Tolan and he wiggled in his seat uncomfortably. He needed to be careful, especially in a wind-shaping classroom. Master Rorn would easily overhear him, and he didn't want to upset him when it came to his descriptions of the elementals. He had already learned there were many different descriptions of elementals than what he'd seen in the books. While what he knew might be one thing, the documentation within some of these ancient records was different.

For some reason, Tolan suspected the ancient records were more accurate.

No—he knew the reason. The ancient records were made by those who had a much closer connection to the elementals and didn't rely upon seeing them only when they were freed from the element bonds. They had known them almost on a personal level. The things he had seen and read about suggested that to him.

Ferrah shot him a look and Tolan stayed silent, choosing to say nothing. It was better to do that than to draw even more attention from Master Rorn. The other man continued to talk, documenting various elementals, and Tolan just sat with his hands on the desk, his pen set aside, the notebook resting next to him. He didn't need to take notes on this.

Ferrah documented, and with each note she made, she glanced over at him. He could practically read the irritation in her and suspected she wanted to tell him she had no intention of sharing her notes. At the same time, why would he need to take notes on this? He had the books that he'd borrowed.

After a while, Master Rorn replaced the board, sliding it out of the way, and pulled the tray with the bondars out and set it on the desk at the front of the room. "Today, we are going to focus on shaping the wind within you."

"Why?" somebody asked from the opposite side of the class.

"Because there are times when you must hold wind within you. Perhaps you are unable to breathe. Perhaps you want to maintain a capacity to hold your breath for longer. Or perhaps you have someone you care for who is unable to breathe on their own. This shaping will help with that."

Those who needed the assistance of the bondar all got up and made their way to the front of the class. Tolan went forward, grabbing one of the bondars, before taking his place back at the table.

Ferrah glanced over at him. "See? This is the kind you should be using so you can be ready for testing."

"I'm not disagreeing I need the assistance of a bondar," he said.

"You're just disagreeing that you need to do so in a regulated environment."

"It's not that, either."

"What is it?"

He raised a finger to his lips and turned his attention to Master Rorn. They had missed something while talking, and he could already tell Master Rorn had no intention of repeating it. Hopefully, Ferrah would share what he might need to know, but if she refused, he would have to just sit there for the rest of the class.

"Now is your turn, students. What I ask you to do is focus on the wind within you, and when you're successful, you can focus on the wind within your partner, but not before you master what is within you."

Tolan glanced over at Ferrah. "You already know how to do this, don't you?"

"It is one of the earlier lessons."

"Then why is he going through it now?"

"I don't know. Maybe he thinks we need a refresher on it? A lot of the lessons we've been going through these days have been somewhat basic. I think they're worried about the attacks and how prepared we are if we need to defend ourselves."

"Why would this help with defense?"

"Because if you can remove someone's ability to breathe, you can remove their ability to attack."

"This shaping allows you to stop someone breathing?"

"Of course. Think about how it's designed to have you focus on your own breathing. Once you do that, then you can begin to work on the breathing of someone else. If you can augment it and help them, it also means you can stop it."

Why was the Academy teaching first-level students this kind of lesson, unless they were preparing them for the possibility of an attack by the disciples of the Draasin Lord?

It was even more reason to continue to work with the massive bondar, trying to figure out what it would take to gain mastery over his connection to wind. The same thing could be said with water. He needed to have that connection so he could heal if it came down to it. He didn't want to lose his friends simply because he didn't have the ability to shape wind or water the same way they did.

Tolan focused on his breathing, reaching within him, searching for a connection to wind. It was there, he knew it was, especially as he now had felt it, but could he do so with a bondar?

He reached for the sense of wind. If it worked, it would come as a sense of fluttering, a stirring deep within himself. He had known that stirring often enough that he thought he should be able to reach it, but he'd never managed to do so with a bondar.

He held onto the sense of wind, letting that shaping flow through him. As it did, he felt the faint and familiar stirring deep within him that he had felt when near the massive bondar.

It slipped away from him.

It had to be the same, didn't it?

Tolan reached for it again, demanding a connection. He didn't know if it would work or if he could hold on to it, but he was adamant he'd find out.

The stirring came again.

Tolan latched onto it.

He focused on an elemental, choosing foye, as it connected the breath between people, and he focused on himself. It was there, the sense of the shaping lingering within him, and as it did, he continued to draw upon it, letting that sense rise more and more, ever more powerful, until with a burst of air, he let out a shaping.

"You did it," Ferrah said.

Tolan glanced over at her. "What did you feel?"

"I felt the shaping. Didn't you?"

"I wasn't sure what I felt. There was a burst of wind, and I felt a stirring within me, but I didn't know if it was going to work."

"What do you mean by a stirring within you?"

"That's what I detect when I shape. It's a stirring. I can latch onto that stirring and use it, but not all the time."

"Can you do it again?"

"I don't know. I wasn't even sure what I was doing this time."

Only—that wasn't quite true. He remembered the way he had felt the stirring and how the bondar had helped him summon it. When he focused on the elemental, drawing that image of power forward, together he had managed to bring a sense of the shaping.

He focused on shaping again, and this time, felt the stirring more rapidly. The bondar helped him connect to it, and now he knew what it was and how to reach it, he was able to grasp for it.

He strained, struggling for that connection to the bondar. He visualized the elemental again, and with a surge of wind, once more it came through him.

Now all he had to do was use it.

This time, he would add to himself like Master Rorn suggested.

With a flurry, it seemed as if the wind rushed down, filling his lungs, and his chest expanded, surging with the power of the wind that suddenly overwhelmed him.

"Tolan?" Ferrah asked.

"What?" His voice was loud, booming, and others near him laughed.

"Did you shape again?"

He breathed out, and with it, the shaping dissipated, the sense of wind leaving him.

He had succeeded. He had shaped wind. Not once but twice and using a normal-sized bondar. All he needed to do was try it again.

How many times could he be successful?

Better yet, was there any way to be successful with the other elements?

It wasn't so much earth, though he did wonder whether or not he would be able to shape earth more easily now he had connected to the massive bondar. It was more about water. There was so much that water would allow him to do, things he couldn't do without it. If he were somehow to be able to connect to that, to have that ability to heal, then he had to believe that attempting to use earth, wind, and water would change his shaping significantly.

"Now you need to let me attempt a shaping on you," Ferrah said.

"I'm not sure that's all that fair," he said.

"Why not?"

"Mostly because you are a significantly better shaper than me."

"That's not the point, and haven't I been talking to you about that? It's not so much the strength of the shaper as it is the way you use your shaping."

"I don't have any impressive way of using my shaping. I was lucky to do what I just did."

"That's not luck. That's you demonstrating an ability."

He waited. "What should I expect?"

"What do you want me to do? The shaping can be used in several different ways."

"I think I need to know how to use it in a more defensive way."

"I would agree. That's the entire purpose of learning to shape like this. If you can learn how to defend yourself against a shaping designed to suffocate you, you won't need to fear it."

These were the kind of things he needed to work on with her anyway, the kind of things he expected she wanted to teach him, to plan for the duel with Draln.

A shaping began to build from Ferrah.

He could feel it was a combination of wind, mixed with a hint of fire. Did she do that on purpose, or was the mixture of fire accidental and unintentional?

He braced himself.

When the shaping struck him, it did so with incredible force, sucking the wind from his body. As it did, he realized the purpose of mixing in the fire shaping. The fire sucked the wind from his body and he gasped, straining as he struggled to catch his breath, but there was nothing. It was as if her shaping pulled every bit of wind away from him, preventing him from reaching it.

Tolan tried to fight.

It was a dangerous and deadly sort of shaping, the kind he had never experienced before. Even when attacked by the disciples, the shapings hadn't been this brutal and this violent.

What he needed to do was maintain his focus.

He focused, holding onto the bondar, drawing through it. For a moment, there was nothing, only his heart hammering, his lungs gasping, and the rising panic that he was dying.

If he didn't do anything, he would need Ferrah to stop drawing wind away from him. He didn't think she wanted to harm him, but she would use whatever opportunities she had to teach him. In this case, the lesson was about wind, and the simple way it could be sucked away from him and he could die from just a shaping.

The lesson was well received.

He reached for his connection to wind. As he did, he could feel the faint stirring.

It was there. He focused once more on the same elemental, focusing on the power he could summon. All he needed was to reach for it, to draw upon it, and to replenish himself. He had done it once before.

The stirring continued and he grasped at it, clutching at the sense of the elemental. Pulling on the faint sense of foye, the sense came from deep within him, so faint he wasn't sure if that was what he was detecting or not. Then it surged.

Tolan drew the sense of the elemental to him, demanding help from it.

As it came, he sucked in a deep breath.

Power flowed through him. With a surge of the elemental, he took that breath and let it back out.

"Tolan?"

"I'm okay," he whispered.

"How did you do that?" she asked.

"What do you mean? I was using the shaping we were told to use."

"That wasn't the same shaping. Whatever you were doing was different than what I was using upon you."

"No. It was using the shaping Master Roln wanted us to use."

Ferrah stared at him for a moment, and then she shrugged. "Maybe it was. You destroyed my shaping, so I'm not really sure what exactly you did."

"What do you mean I destroyed it?"

"I mean you powered through it. I wasn't going to be able to hold onto it any longer. I was nearly ready to release my shaping in the first place and then you blasted your way through it. That was impressive."

He forced a smile and stared down at the bondar. How much more would he be able to do if he had an opportunity to continue to work with the bondar outside the city? Would he be able to finally shape the elements—*really* shape the elements?

"Let's try it again," he said.

"Are you sure?"

"I am."

"I think it's your turn to use it on me," she said.

"I'm not sure I have the necessary control to do that." He worried if he made a mistake, he would somehow draw away wind from Ferrah and end up hurting her. That was the last thing he wanted.

"Why don't you try it on me again," he said. "Let me practice reaching for wind a little bit more before you have me use it on you in that way."

"You don't think I can handle it?"

"I don't think *I* can handle it," he said.

She chuckled but nodded. "That's fine." Her shaping built again, and as it did, Tolan readied himself, preparing for the inevitability of the shaping as it sucked the wind out of him. When it did, he was more prepared than he had been before. It wasn't so terrifying, and as he lost the wind that gave him the ability to breathe, he began to shape, once again thinking of the elemental, using the bondar to summon that power. As it flowed through him, it filled him with a deep breath, tearing away the shaping Ferrah used on him.

Tolan gasped, but there wasn't the same sense of panic he had felt before.

"You did it again," she said.

"I did the same thing."

"It's not so much the same thing that you did. It's the way you destroyed it. I'm impressed."

"It's the bondar."

"I don't understand," she said.

"That's why I want to show you. You can tell me if you

think it's a mistake, but I don't know I would have been able to do this without having that experience."

Ferrah shook her head. "You want to keep practicing?"

"We might as well. As long as I have access to this bondar, I might as well keep working with it."

As he worked with Ferrah, as the shaping continued to build from him, he wondered if it was the bondar or if he would be able to do without it?

Eventually, he intended to find out, but for now, he would use the bondar, take the advantage it offered, and when the time came, he would see if he could eventually shape without it so he could pass the testing—whenever that would be. The problem was, he worried he was running out of time to be ready.

19

FERRAH KEPT CLOSE TO HIM, PRESSED UP AGAINST HIS ARM as they reached the edge of the city. She stared around, flicking her gaze from one place to the other, her eyes wide.

"I don't like coming out here like this," she whispered. "What if there are disciples out here?"

It was late. Night was beginning to fall, though it was much earlier than Tolan had come recently. Most of the time, he had come well into the darkness, at a time when there were very few people out in the city, and certainly no one who would comment on the fact he was leaving the Academy.

"It's okay," he said.

"You're only saying that because you want to do this, but I'm still not sure this is the right thing," she said. "There have been the attacks—"

"I've come the last several nights," Tolan said. "And I

can assure you it's okay. Nothing is going to happen to us. There's been no one here."

That didn't change the fact that Ferrah continued to shape, wrapping herself in some protection, though Tolan wasn't entirely sure what sort of shaping she used. Was it a barrier of wind? It couldn't be that, especially as she was pressed up against him and he didn't feel any sense of wind. Did she fortify herself with earth? Shapings of earth were known to give shapers incredible strength, and that would be a fitting shaping for a time like this, especially if she was scared.

They reached the edge of the city and Tolan pointed to the forest in the distance. There was a gap before they managed to reach it, and he hurried across, unmindful of who else might be out and watching. There shouldn't be anyone out at this time of night, and he was doubtful there would be anyone watching. Ferrah grabbed his arm as he hurried from the edge of the city and reached the boundary of the forest.

"I didn't take you for the scared type," he said.

"I'm not normally, but after what we've gone through lately, I think it's prudent to be cautious."

"We can be cautious, but I don't think we have anything to worry about. I don't feel any sense of shaping as I did."

"What if you wouldn't?"

"My ability to detect shapings hasn't failed me before," he said. It sounded arrogant to make that claim, and yet it was true.

"Tolan, you're a first-level student, and while you have some interesting talents, that doesn't change the fact you are still a student. It wouldn't surprise me if there were master shapers able to mask themselves from you. What makes you think you would even know if one of the master shapers was using their abilities near you?"

Tolan didn't know, and yet, his experience with shaping told him he would. Everything he had experienced suggested he would be fully aware of a shaping. When the master shapers used their abilities within the Academy, he was aware of it. It wasn't something he struggled with.

Would he know if an elemental was nearby?

When they had been at the edge of the waste, he had felt the rumblings of earth coming from the elementals, and he had felt the stirrings of wind, but he hadn't felt any power from them.

Maybe he wouldn't know if it was an elemental.

But if there was an elemental, it would be unlikely there would be any shapers nearby. The shapers would likely run, disappearing if there was the threat of an elemental appearing.

"I think we're okay," he said. "Besides, you wanted to see this bondar."

"I still think we should have brought Jonas," she said.

"I would've brought Jonas, but I think he's angry."

"He's just upset because of everything you've been keeping from us."

"I haven't been keeping anything from you. If anything, I've been sharing the things I was told not to share."

"I know that's how you see it, but from our standpoint, it's a matter of learning we've been shaped, and there are things we don't remember but should. It's strange knowing you've experienced something but have no recollection of it."

"I think it's strange I should have been shaped alongside you and yet somehow I haven't been. Somehow, I've managed to avoid the shaping."

"Maybe you're destined to become an Inquisitor."

Tolan shot her a look, and she shrugged.

They made their way onto the path that would lead deeper into the forest, and as they went, Tolan realized he was connecting to earth without even knowing he was doing it. After the first few times coming here, he had begun using that connection to earth in order to give himself a greater sense of strength, and with that, he was better able to detect if they were alone or not.

As far as he could tell, the only other person with him was Ferrah. He could feel her through the earth connection, but no one else. There were the trees, and they were strangely powerful through that connection.

He slowed when they neared the park.

"What is that?" Ferrah asked.

He nodded at the wall. "That's where we're going."

"It looks like the ruins we have in Par."

"I'd wondered if you'd say that."

"The ruins are places that existed long ago. Many were

shaped, so they have lingered far longer than most, and even now they stand sturdy, despite the ravages of time that should have claimed them, but many are for structures with a purpose we don't really understand."

They reached the wall and Tolan climbed on top of it, taking a seat. He had sat on the wall or stood often enough that he was comfortable here, and now he was here, now he waited, he stared out toward the center of the park clearing, studying the statue.

Ferrah climbed up and sat next to him. She remained close, pressing her body up against his, and the sense of shaping building from her continued to radiate, a comfortable sense.

"That's the bondar?" she asked, staring at the sculpture.

"I think so. Whatever it is, it has a connection to power that's different than anything else I've been around."

"What if it's not a bondar?" she asked.

"I don't know what else it might be."

"Well, you described the Convergence, and seeing as how you've been there, maybe this is connected to it in some way, which allows you to use it."

"Maybe." It was something he'd considered. The Convergence was difficult to reach and hidden deep beneath the Academy, while this was out in the open, for anyone to use.

"I want to know if it augments your shaping," Tolan said.

"What happens if it doesn't?" she asked.

"Considering how much it augmented mine, I suspect

it'll do the same to you, which is why I want to see what you can do with it."

"But that's my point, Tolan. What if it doesn't work for me?"

"Why wouldn't it work for you?"

"Because it's something else. Look at it. I've been shaping at it ever since we appeared, and I haven't been able to get anything to happen."

"What do you mean you've been shaping at it?"

"Just that. I've been shaping at it, trying to see if I could figure out how that bondar works, but nothing has happened."

Tolan thought about his experience with it and shook his head. "I don't know that it works from the wall. I've tried doing something similar, and it's never managed to work from here, either. I have to be right up next to it."

Ferrah's mouth wrinkled in a concerned line. "You want me to go through that mess?"

"Don't tell me you're afraid."

"Do you know what's in there?"

"Grasses. Some flowers. It's really quite lovely in the daylight."

"I thought you said you only came at nighttime."

"Most of the time, but the first visit was during the daytime."

"How did you end up out here again?"

"I was wandering."

"How did you *wander* out here?"

"Fine. I was looking to see if I could uncover anything

that would indicate Master Daniels was in the city and had anything to do with the destruction of the palace."

"Tolan, you know you shouldn't be going after that. We don't know enough about shaping."

"You keep saying that, and yet we were the reason the attack on the Academy was stopped. It wasn't master shapers. At least, it wasn't the master shapers to begin with. It was us. You and me and Jonas."

"I really wish I could remember it."

"I really wish I could remember my parents better."

"Why is that?"

"I've begun to wonder if perhaps memories of my parents were spirit-shaped away from me."

"Why would memories of your parents be spirit-shaped from you?"

"I don't know. It's just the memories I have of them are different. They're hazy. Not quite the same as what I would expect I should have. The more I think about my parents, the less I'm able to come up with the memories I think I should have."

The strongest memories he had now came from the Selection, and other than that, he didn't really have any. They were vague, memories involving them taking him places, working with his ability to shape, testing to see what connections he might have, but in none did he remember specific details. Shouldn't that be different?

The more he thought about it, the stranger that seemed.

"I thought you couldn't be spirit-shaped."

"What if I can't be spirit-shaped *now*, but maybe I could before?"

"That doesn't make much sense. It's not as if your abilities have improved."

"You seem to think I have some sort of protection placed on me. What if there was a spirit shaping placed upon me that protects me?"

"I don't think that's likely," Ferrah said.

"Probably not," he said.

He hopped off the stone wall and headed through the grasses. As he went, he continued to stretch outward with his earth shaping, letting his connection to earth call to him, searching for anything that might be out in the night. Once he was within the walls, he found it more difficult to do.

And then he neared the sculpture. As he did, there was a familiar weighty sense to it. It was difficult to put words to, other than he felt power near it. As he stood, he ran his hand along its surface, waiting for Ferrah to join him. She approached cautiously, frowning, her gaze lingering along the base of the tower.

"Look at the top," he said.

"What do you see up there?" she asked.

"When I shape, something glows up there. I'm not exactly sure what it is, but I think a rune represents the element I'm shaping."

"All of this is quite strange, Tolan."

He nodded. He took a deep breath, focusing on fire. As he did, he pulled upon the connection, feeling the stirring deep within him, and summoned a connection to saa. The elemental was powerful, but not as powerful as some, and not one he feared the way he feared others. As the elemental came to him, he held onto it, letting it flow away from him. Flames flickered, hovering in the air. Tolan was able to feed those flames, holding onto them with much more power than he usually did. Ferrah stared at the flames until Tolan pointed.

Her gaze followed his. The peak of the sculpture glowed, the symbol not one Tolan recognized. Without any way of seeing it clearly, he couldn't tell if it was a rune or not.

He released the connection to the elemental and it took a moment, but the flames started easing and finally disappeared altogether. The heat in the air faded and so, too, did the glowing at the top of the tower.

"What was that?" she asked.

"That was a shaping."

"That wasn't a shaping, Tolan."

"That was a shaping," he said.

"If that was a shaping, it's not one I recognize."

"I've told you how I have to shape."

"You told me you use visualizations of the elementals, but that... that *looks* like an elemental."

"That's my point."

"Are you trying to convince me that when you shape, you call elementals into existence?"

"I don't know if I'm calling elementals into existence

or if I'm merely imagining the elementals, which creates a shaping tied to them. I just don't know."

"If that's what you're doing, that would be an incredibly complicated shaping. And if you're shaping an elemental into existence, maybe that's not something you should be attempting."

"None stays" he said, but the memory of the draasin came to him and he wondered if maybe he should say something about it to Ferrah. He had very nearly drawn a draasin into the world. While he didn't know if it was real or not, the power surging from it had felt real enough.

"Even if they don't stay, I worry what this means," she said.

"Like I said, none of them stays."

"Is that what you've been doing out here?" She turned to him, her arms crossed over her chest, and she frowned. "Have you been spending your time out here trying to reach each of the elementals, using the knowledge within the books Master Minden gave you?"

"Not entirely," he said.

"Tolan!"

"I'm trying to see what sort of shaping I might be able to do," he said.

"What if you're not shaping at all? What if what you are doing is drawing elementals? We've seen how dangerous they can be."

Tolan had expected this argument and didn't know how he would justify what he'd been doing, especially not to Ferrah. She was a traditionalist, and he worried he would have to explain himself more, but at the same time, she also had an open mind; with her interest regarding the strange powers found in Par, he wondered if perhaps she might be more open to the possibility he had some unique method of shaping.

"We've gone through this," he said.

"I know we've gone through this, but I just didn't realize."

"I know you didn't realize, and I know you were thinking I was doing nothing more than imagining elementals. This is my shaping."

She continued to stare. "How did you shape in the wind classroom?"

"I used a shaping through the bondar," he said.

"No. How did you shape? Did you use this connection to the elementals?"

Tolan didn't want to deceive her. She deserved that much, and especially deserved him telling her that his ability to shape came from the elementals, but she looked at him with an expression reminding him of the way people had looked at him when he was younger. It was the same expression others within the city had worn, the one that cried out that he was a follower of the Draasin Lord.

"Tolan?"

"It was the elemental. The more we study them, the more I've realized the elementals represent the aspects of shaping the master shapers are trying to teach us. Think about it. Today, we were asked to use a shaping so similar to the elemental foye. How else do you think I was able to overpower your shaping?"

"Well, I had thought you were shaping, not realizing you were summoning elementals."

"I *was* shaping, but at the same time, also connecting to what I know of the elementals."

She looked at him for a while before turning her attention to the sculpture once more. "Can you show me another?"

"Are you sure?"

"I think I need to see another."

"No judgments?"

"I can't promise that, but I will try to understand."

He nodded. As he commenced shaping the next one, he again focused on fire. He used fire for several reasons, not least being that he felt as if he had the most control over it. This time, he focused on smoke, letting the elemental fill the air with traces of steam, rising higher and higher as it swirled around the outside of the tower before dissipating.

"I'm not familiar with that one," she whispered.

"Sure, you are. That's one Master Sartan has taught us. Esalash."

"I didn't realize it was the same elemental. What he talked about in class is not nearly as potent."

"What is talked about in class isn't the same. That's what I've been trying to say. I don't think the elementals they've been teaching us about are the same as the elementals this book has."

"Why wouldn't the master shapers know about the elementals in the book?"

"Maybe they do, or maybe their knowledge is different because they've never seen them before."

"Maybe you're only creating an image of an elemental the way you've seen it in the book," she said.

Tolan shrugged. "That's entirely possible." He didn't think so. When he imagined the elemental, he focused mostly on the power in the connection to the element, not so much on the shape of the elemental itself. That seemed to come naturally, suggesting whatever it was he did was real, it came from the power of the elemental and not so much from anything he actually did.

"What else can you show me?"

"I've spent quite a bit of time working with various elementals," he said. "Some of them are exactly what you'd expect, but some are unusual. Not all are the way we were taught."

He focused on earth, calling one elemental after another. The ground shifted, rumbling as elemental after elemental surged forward, revealing itself. There was a part of Tolan that wanted nothing more than to show off, to reveal to her the various elementals he could summon, and as he worked, he held them for a moment before releasing them.

"None of those looks like what I was expecting," she whispered.

"What were you expecting?"

"I don't know. I guess I was expecting something else.

The fact you have summoned this makes me wonder what else you might be able to summon."

He met her gaze. He knew of her interest in the draasin, and knew that with the spirit shaping, she had forgotten what had happened at the Convergence. It was something she had longed to see.

"There's something else I can show you, but…"

"But what?"

"But I worry I don't have the necessary control over it," he said.

"Why wouldn't you have the right control?"

"Because it's the only elemental I felt as if it took on a life of its own."

She gasped. "The draasin."

He nodded. "When I try this, one of the elementals I attempted was the draasin. I… I knew I shouldn't, but I couldn't help myself. I wanted to see if all elementals would work with this place."

"And?"

"And it worked," Tolan said.

"What do you mean, it worked?"

"What I mean is when I was focusing on the draasin, I saw it."

"You saw one?"

He decided not to say anything about seeing a draasin when they were at the Convergence. That one had been larger than the one he had focused on, but then, the one he had accidentally started to summon had started off small and continued to grow. If he had lost control of it, it would continue growing, and he worried what would have happened at that point.

"I summoned one," he said.

"Can you show me?" she whispered.

It was the first time she said it without any hesitation. There was no sense of judgment, only a yearning.

It was the same yearning Tolan understood. It was the yearning he had experienced when he had begun to pull upon the sense of shaping, the sense that had allowed him to reach for wind and then water. It was a yearning that filled him, one that left him compelled to continue to try to shape. It was that yearning that drew to him, demanding he try again and again. It was that yearning, that desire to understand, that had compelled him to try to reach for power he had never known.

Ferrah deserved to know what that was like.

He started to shape.

Fire came so easily to him these days, but more so in this place. As he shaped fire, feeling the stirring deep within him, latching onto that sense of warmth that came with it, he focused on the image of the draasin, thinking of the characteristics that made it unique. That was what was required for the summoning, and as he focused, as he drew upon that power, he continued to feel the stirring.

When Ferrah gasped, he realized something was happening.

Tolan looked around, and it wasn't until he looked up that he realized the draasin—small as it was in this first, earliest stage—was beginning to form. It took shape over his head, small at first but gradually beginning to elongate, and then it spread its wings.

Its wings were enormous. From there, Tolan continued to push power, though letting it flow from him in a steady trickle, careful, afraid if he unleashed too much, he would release the draasin. He was afraid of doing that, afraid of that power, and afraid of that elemental. The others didn't worry him the same way the draasin did.

Perhaps that was a mistake on his part. Maybe he *should* be more afraid of the other elementals, as there were plenty of others tied to the other element bonds that were equally powerful, as noble and frightening and terrifying as the draasin.

He thought about what they had experienced on the edge of the waste, the power that had taken over a dozen master shapers, and that power had been mostly earth and wind and water. There was no power of the draasin within it, and even that power had been terrifying.

"It's magnificent," Ferrah said.

Tolan eased back on his connection, not wanting to push too much strength into it, but even as he eased back, he felt the power drawn from him.

It was the same thing he had felt before, the same sort of power he had experienced when he had attempted to call to the draasin, and much like then, the connection to it was incredible, the kind of power that attempted to steal from him, to unlock the power of fire, to force its way free.

"Ferrah—"

Tolan grabbed her arm and pulled her back toward the wall. He released his connection to the shaping, but as before, the draasin continued to hover in place, the wings continuing to spread. The sides of the draasin continued to expand, more and more power flowing into it. The creature was becoming enormous.

Now it was easily as large as Tolan, and was not done growing. The wings were each the size of his entire body. And the draasin moved them, flapping them in the air, and heat slowly filled the space around them. Tolan tried to tamp down his connection to fire, pushing it deep within him, but it continued to surge. Everything he did to resist the draasin growing and flowing failed.

Ferrah cried out.

Tolan grabbed her and raced toward the wall. He climbed up on it, and once he was there, he tried to push down the sense of fire, trying to push away the shaping, but it continued to come, practically drawn from him, as if demanded by the power of the shaping.

There was nothing Tolan could do to stop it. It continued to flow from him, and everything he did, every attempt to push that power down, failed.

Ferrah began shaping. It pulsed toward the center of the clearing, toward the sculpture, but it wasn't successful.

"What did you do?"

"This is what happened the last time," he whispered.

"Then why did you try again?"

"Because you wanted to see the draasin."

"Are you freeing a draasin from the element bond?"

"I... I don't know."

Tolan tried to sever the connection, but it continued to build, rising within him. He heaved against it, trying to force it back, but the power surged.

Ferrah started shaping, pushing earth, mixing water, and the combination wasn't enough. Tolan decided to try the same thing, adding a shaping of earth, feeling that surge within him, focusing on that stirring.

The draasin stabilized.

"I don't know if I can stop this," he said.

"We *have* to stop it," she said. "If you are somehow releasing this creature, we need to stop it."

Tolan stared at it. It continued to get larger and larger. With each passing moment, he could feel the heat rising. If he did nothing, would there be any way of suppressing it without going to the masters?

"Can you help?" he asked.

"I've been trying." Shaping built from her again, this time focused on the draasin. She used a combination of earth and water, mixing in a hint of wind. "Nothing seems to work."

"Maybe this isn't even real," he said. And yet, the longer he stared at it, watching as the draasin continued to appear, the more he felt there was something quite real about it.

And here he had thought Jory was the one who would release one of the draasin, but no—it would be him. All because he had wanted to show Ferrah, thinking after everything she had done to try and know what they were like, she deserved this opportunity.

"Why isn't it retreating?" he asked.

"I haven't been able to get anything to work on it," Ferrah said. She continued to shape, but she had retreated to the other side of the wall and now was shaping across it. Tolan knew that wouldn't be effective.

As he watched, the draasin set off circling.

20

Tolan took a step back, moving toward the wall, and as he did, his heart continued to pound. The draasin swirled, circling, continuing to move toward them. Much longer, and the draasin would reach the edge of the park, and Tolan feared what would happen if it managed to break free.

The draasin swooped toward him.

Tolan ducked, rolling, forced away from the wall and out toward the center of the clearing once again.

He wasn't going to be able to stop it like this. It would take something more, perhaps him remaining willing to throw himself out there, but how?

"Get going," he hollered at Ferrah.

"I'm not leaving you," she said.

"I'm not going to let you stay here while this attacks."

"What makes you think you get to decide what I do?"

"Please."

He stared at the draasin as he begged. It was all flames, fire swirling along its length, and even its wings were made of fire. Power radiated from it and the larger it got, the more solid it seemed to become, almost as if separating from the bond—however this was possible—made it more tangible than it had been otherwise.

The draasin swooped again, and once again, Tolan dropped to the ground, rolling off to the side. Why did the draasin come at him in this way? Did it think that by attacking him, it could be free?

He didn't have any control over it. With the other elements, when he had shaped them, summoning them out of his imagination, there had been a belief he could dismiss them. Whether that represented control or not, he didn't know. It had always worked.

Maybe there was another way.

Rather than dismissing the draasin, could he ask the draasin to disappear?

There was no reason that should work. There was no reason anything should work, much less freeing a creature out of legend, and yet, that was where he was.

Tolan focused on the draasin, holding his hand out in front of him. As he did, the creature continued to swirl, though never flying all that high. It seemed like that was important.

The draasin kept his eye on him, fixing him with a dark gaze as it circled.

Something within the draasin's eyes triggered the stirring within him.

Tolan reached for that sense and focused on the draasin, but this time, he focused on trying to reach it.

There was no reason it should work, no reason other than his desperation.

Please.

He begged within his mind. As he did, there came that fluttering sense again.

He focused on fire, the connection he had focused on before, and tried to encourage the draasin to return to the bond. That was what he imagined, at least.

Tolan had no idea whether it would be effective, but there was nothing else that had succeeded.

The draasin continued to swirl around him, but it seemed as if the flying was slowing.

"Tolan!"

He didn't dare remove his attention from the draasin, fearing if he were to look away, he might lose control—whatever control he had—from this creature. For now, it seemed as if he had some measure of control over it, and he needed to maintain it.

The strange stirring within him persisted. Tolan tried to beg, trying to ask the draasin to return to the bond.

For a moment, there was nothing, but then there came a sensation, one he could only describe as fear.

The draasin was afraid.

Why should a creature like that fear?

The sensation gave him reason to hesitate, and in that hesitation, he once again begged, pleading with the connection to fire, afraid if it failed, if *he* failed, the draasin would escape, and if it did, he would be responsible for freeing an elemental.

Please.

As he sent the request again, it seemed as if the draasin changed its focus.

Rather than attempting to pull upon him, pull upon his connection to fire, he felt the fluttering, that stirring within him, begin to retreat. There was once again that sensation of fear, but along with it came a sort of reluctant acceptance.

Why should he be aware of that?

The draasin began to disappear, fading, first growing smaller and smaller before eventually, power from it flickered out. He stared for long moments, terrified he still hadn't been successful, but the longer he looked, the more convinced he was the draasin was no more.

Letting out a shaky breath, he started to back up, and as he did, he realized Ferrah wasn't where he thought she would be.

Tolan stood on the wall surrounding the park.

She wouldn't have left. He didn't think she would have simply abandoned him with the draasin, though he *had* attempted to send her away, so maybe she had decided to do as he had asked.

Tolan jumped down and then commenced a search for her using his connection to earth sensing. There was an emptiness, as if she had disappeared, or perhaps someone had shaped it so she would disappear.

A void.

He had experienced that before when he had felt convinced there was someone else out here, and now he detected it again. That couldn't be a coincidence.

Tolan hurried off into the woods, racing after the sense he suspected came from where Ferrah had disappeared. He hurried forward, heading toward that distant sense of the void. Racing into the darkness, he tried to see if there was anything with the void he could understand. For a moment, he thought he could sense something, but then it passed.

Straining with his earth sensing ability, he grabbed the furios, running his fingers along the runes but not finding any reassurance from them.

"Ferrah!"

It probably wasn't a good idea to call out in the darkness and reveal his location or the fact they were here, but at the same time, it wasn't a good idea to have come out here in the first place. He wasn't going to be the reason something happened to Ferrah.

Maybe it was nothing more than that she had headed back to Amitan and the Academy, but why would she have done so without letting him know?

Could she have been so afraid of the draasin?

That might be all it was. It could be she worried about unleashing a draasin and might have gone to one of the masters for help. Even then, he still didn't know if that was what he had done.

The draasin hadn't attempted to escape from the center of the park. None of the elementals had. He had no control over them outside of the park and away from the sculpture, suggesting perhaps whatever effect he had while there was limited.

There was no denying he had been able to understand wind more effectively after having experienced the shaping near the sculpture. He hadn't tried the other element bonds in class, but earth should be easier for him.

Tolan strained for earth. He imagined the elemental, using that to reach for the power of earth, to connect with it. As he did, there was only a faint sense.

He was aware of earth around him but reaching for it and somehow summoning the power of it felt as if it were beyond him.

If only he had a bondar.

Ferrah claimed it was a crutch and he depended upon it far too much, but there was no shame in using his connection with whatever was required to shape.

He paused again to see if he could reach for earth, but there still was nothing.

Had he used too much energy while trying to both summon and then suppress the draasin?

Continuing into the trees, he made a steady circle of the park. When he reached the path that led toward the park, he raced along it, heading back toward the city. He plunged out of the darkness of the trees and stood on the hillside overlooking Amitan. As he stared, he searched for any sign of movement.

He should've done this from the beginning. If Ferrah

had gone this way, she would have been easy to find. As he stood in place, he could not find sign of any movement.

It was late enough that he should have been able to see anyone heading through the streets, especially someone racing toward the Academy, but there was no sign. More than that, there was no sense of shaping, nothing more than what he would have expected.

Without any sensations, he had to believe she was still within the trees.

And if that were the case, then had something happened to her?

Tolan turned back, moving more carefully. He ran his hand along the furios again, tracing his fingers on the runes. If he was right about them and they were a marker of some sort for the various elementals, then would he be able to summon one of the elementals by focusing on that particular rune? Most of the time, he thought of hyza, but there were other elementals he'd summoned, though with varying degrees of success. As he walked, swinging his head around, he tried to think of which elemental might allow him better vision in the darkness.

If there were others in the forest, then he needed to exercise some caution. Could there be some way of using the elementals to reveal others around him?

Pulling the furios from his pocket, he thought there might be one elemental that might work, but it would be difficult.

The elemental ashla would create sparks, and he had demonstrated that once before, so he knew he could use it, but would it be enough to be able to generate the kind of light needed to reveal Ferrah?

Squeezing the furios, he focused on the elemental, and with a faint pull of power, he sent it into the furios and out into the night. Sparks began to shoot out from the end of it, streaking off into the forest.

In a panic, Tolan suppressed his connection to the elemental. That wasn't what he had wanted at all. It would do nothing more than reveal his presence here and would make it easier for him to be found rather than easier for him to find her.

He raced back toward the park, straining to think of whether there were other elementals that might be more effective. If ashla wasn't going to work, that didn't mean there weren't other elementals that might be more effective. Tolan wasn't able to come up with what they might be.

He skidded to a stop, looking around. The forest and the trees were nothing more than patches of darkness, streamers of moonlight parting between them.

When he neared the park, he discovered other shapes.

He stopped near one of the trees, staying as much in the shadows as he could, afraid he had made a huge mistake.

Voices drifted out into the darkness. "Are you sure this is it?" someone said.

"This is it. Can't you feel it?"

"I can't feel anything. Why would it be so close to Amitan?"

"They built the city near this. They thought to conceal it, and it was concealed until that fool decided to attack."

This place had been concealed? That at least explained why Tolan had never seen it before, and might explain why there hadn't been any of the master shapers around it. He expected someone would have been here, but there had been nothing and no one.

"How do we get in?"

"Ask her."

Tolan realized there was a figure lying on the ground, motionless.

His breath caught. Ferrah.

How had they captured her? What did they intend to use her for?

"She won't know anything. Look at her. She can't be anything more than a student, and considering how young she is, probably not a very advanced one, either."

"She was here, wasn't she?"

The other man grunted and one lifted Ferrah, jerking her to her feet. She gasped but didn't say anything as they forced her closer to the wall.

"How do we enter?" one of the men asked.

"I don't know what you're talking about."

"I think you do. I saw you coming from here. You discovered something about this place."

"I didn't discover anything. I—"

Something jabbed Tolan in the back. He tried to glance over his shoulder, but a firm grip on his other shoulder kept him from looking behind him.

"Move," a deep voice rumbled. There was anger within the voice, and he felt compelled, though not in such a way he suspected he had been shaped. This was more of a command, a man who was used to others obeying him. This was the kind of man who was not to be trifled with.

Tolan took a step forward, his feet squishing along the soft ground. It took a moment before the other two realized Tolan was there along with his captor.

"What is this?" the man holding Ferrah asked.

"This is the key to understanding."

"This boy?"

"He's a little older than a boy," his captor said.

"What makes you think these students know anything about reaching beyond the wall?"

"Because I knew his parents. And I know what he is capable of."

His captor shoved him forward and Tolan staggered, rolling off to the side to look up. In the thin shafts of moonlight, he caught a glimpse of a face that didn't fit with the voice he heard.

Master Daniels.

21

TOLAN TRIED TO TEAR HIS GAZE AWAY FROM MASTER Daniels, but he couldn't. All he could do was stare. He looked so different than when he had seen him the last time. The heavy beard on his round face was thicker than it had been, and more gray-peppered than before. He remained a muscular man, like most who favored earth, the tattered cloak he wore barely covering him. There seemed to be something almost menacing about him that Tolan didn't remember. Dark eyes pierced the blackness of night, staring at him.

Ferrah remained motionless, lying on the ground where they had thrown her, and if she was still awake and alert, there was no sign of it.

"Tolan Ethar. I would ask what you're doing here. But seeing as how you're wearing what you are, and are with her," Master Daniels said, nodding to Ferrah, "I assume that means you were selected?"

Tolan could only nod. He wanted to yell. Cry out. Anything, but there was nothing for him to do. Even if he could summon a shaping, Master Daniels was a skilled enough earth shaper that he would be able to counter anything Tolan might try.

"Why are you here?" Tolan asked.

Master Daniels fixed him with a hard-eyed stare. Gone was the warmth he had once displayed when looking upon Tolan. After his parents' disappearance, Master Daniels had been one of the few willing to take him in and claim him. Tolan owed him so much, but right now, it was difficult to remember anything he might owe him. Right now, all he could think of was the way Master Daniels looked at him, the heat within his gaze almost making him unrecognizable.

"How were you selected?"

"I don't know. I just was."

"You should never have gone to the Selection. Your parents made sure of that."

Tolan stared. "My parents did what?"

Master Daniels turned away from Tolan, looking at the others. "What did you do with her?"

"She tried to escape us, but we subdued her. She's quite skilled," one of the men said.

Master Daniels glanced over at Tolan before turning his attention to the others. "This is it. We've been looking for this."

"We have, but we can't enter. They placed some sort of

protective shaping around it that prevents us from crossing."

"There is no protective shaping. All you need is the right influence," Master Daniel said. He walked up to the wall and pressed his hands on the stone.

At first, there was nothing, but then a steady rumbling grew louder. As it did, Tolan realized he had felt nothing. There was no sense of shaping taking place, only the incessant noise and trembling.

How was Master Daniels making the earth shake in that way without shaping?

Elemental magic.

He gasped, and one of the men glanced down at him before turning his attention back to Master Daniels. As the wall continued to rumble, it parted, a door appearing. Slowly, the door opened, each side pulling outward before stopping altogether.

"We wouldn't have been able to enter without you?" one of the others asked.

"Me, or someone who can speak to them," Master Daniels said. He strode forward, and once he was inside, the rumbling began again, the wall surging back into place. Master Daniels turned to it and whispered something softly, something Tolan couldn't even be certain he heard, and the wall stopped moving. "Grab them and bring them with us."

"We don't need them in here," one of the others said.

"We also don't need them running away. If we leave

them, who is to say the protections on this place wouldn't relax, allowing them to escape?"

He stared at the others for a moment before turning on his heel and heading deeper into the park.

The other two grabbed Tolan and Ferrah, hoisting them. As Ferrah was lifted, Tolan was relieved to see she was awake, though he didn't know if she was somehow bound by a shaping to prevent her doing anything. From the blank stare in her eyes, it seemed something had happened to her.

"Ferrah?" he whispered.

The man guiding him jerked on his arm and shot him a glare. "Quiet."

"What did you do to her?" Tolan asked.

"The same thing that will be done to you if you're not careful."

Tolan quietened down but focused on a shaping. All he needed was the opportunity to get free—and to get Ferrah free. Tolan didn't have any interest in trying to stop Daniels. He had no idea what Master Daniels was after. All he wanted was for his friend to get free and get to safety.

In the distance, the large bondar loomed into view. It was near enough that Tolan could feel its presence.

Master Daniels approached the bondar and kept a respectable distance, nearly a yard, as he paced around it. He held his hands out in front of him, and it almost seemed to Tolan that he was whispering something. A steady shaping sense began to build, different than what he had detected from the wall around the park.

The others stood off to the side, letting Master Daniels work. He pushed out with power, and it flowed toward the bondar before dissipating. Trying again, another shaping built, this one even more potent the last. As it built, Master Daniels continued to focus on the bondar. He paused in front of one section—the earth section, Tolan noted—and this was where he focused his effort.

He was trying to use it.

The ground rumbled for a moment, but then ceased.

Master Daniels tried again. With each attempt, Tolan noted it as a surge of connection to his shaping sense. Power flowed out of Master Daniels and into the bondar.

While he watched, Tolan wondered if this was the way it seemed when he attempted to shape at the bondar or whether this was something else? His shaping worked differently. It came from his mind, connecting him to the bondar, and from the stirring from somewhere deep within him. Was that what Master Daniels did?

Master Daniels looked at the others. "Unfortunately, the key to this lock has been lost."

"Are you sure?" the man holding Ferrah said. He jerked on her arm and forced her forward. She stood, swaying in place, her eyes still glazed. "This one seems to think otherwise."

Master Daniels made his way over to Ferrah and brought his finger up underneath her chin, forcing her to look up at him. A shaping built, but it was subtle.

Different than what Tolan had detected from him before. Ferrah gasped and looked around.

"Tolan?" she asked when she met his gaze.

Tolan's heart skipped a beat. "I'm here, Ferrah. I don't know what—"

Pain suddenly wrapped around him.

It felt as if narrow bands of fire swirled around him, confining him, and all he could focus on was getting rid of that pain. It burned within him, coursing through his entire body. He cried out, collapsing to the ground.

The pain eased slowly. As it did, the other shaper stood over him, staring at him with eyes that seemed almost black.

"You will talk when we ask you to talk," the man said.

Tolan took shallow breaths, trying to keep his mind clear. If it came down to it, he might need to shape, and in his experience, he wouldn't be able to without having a clear head. First, he wanted to understand what these people—including Master Daniels—were after. Once he understood, then he could figure out what he might need to do.

"Don't worry about Tolan," Master Daniels said. There was an energy in the way he spoke that came with the sense of shaping he'd detected before.

Spirit.

He was a spirit shaper?

Why would he have remained in Ephra all that time if he was a spirit shaper? Why wouldn't he have used that to join the Inquisitors?

Unless he had.

Could Master Daniels have been an Inquisitor all along?

Tolan had never really understood why Master Daniels had been sent back to Amitan and the Academy for additional training. He'd never heard of that happening before, and ever since coming to the Academy, there had been no others Tolan had heard of who had been forced to do the same. Maybe Master Daniels had been an Inquisitor but had somehow neglected his responsibilities? That might explain why the Grand Inquisitor had been there in the first place.

"You know the secret of this place?" Master Daniels asked.

For a moment, Tolan hoped Ferrah would resist. She was a strong shaper, and with her control over each of the elements, she should be able to withstand it.

She blinked and turned her gaze to Tolan. "I don't, but Tolan does."

Master Daniels kept his hand lingering on Ferrah for a long moment before slowly turning to Tolan. A shaping built, starting slowly, steadily, and it directed at Tolan.

Nothing happened.

"What do you know of this place?" Master Daniels asked.

"I don't know anything," Tolan said.

Master Daniels cocked his head to the side, frowning. The thick beard on his face gave him a more intimidating appearance than he'd had before. When Tolan had been apprenticed to him, Master Daniels had always been welcoming, warm, not terrifying and intimidating, the way he looked now. While he had some shaping skill, Tolan had never known him to be what would have been considered a powerful shaper. Everything he was feeling now, everything he'd learned since coming to the Academy, suggested his understanding of Master Daniels and his shaping ability had been wrong.

"You know something, Tolan. You need to share that with me."

"I don't know anything. And I don't need to share anything with you, either."

The man nearest Tolan began to shape, but he was prepared for it this time. Bands formed around Tolan, but Tolan had his hand in his pocket, holding onto the furios, and began a shaping, focusing on hyza. All he needed was enough of a burst of flame to startle the shaper.

Power burst from him, and it slammed into the shaper nearest him.

Tolan jerked his arm free and dove.

The other shaper who had been holding onto Ferrah rolled out of the way and shaping built all around him.

Tolan reached Ferrah, grabbing her and tossing her to the ground, and leapt to his feet, pulling the furios from his pocket and pointing it at Master Daniels.

"Release your shaping of her."

"Release what shaping?"

"I can feel the effect of your shaping. Release it." Master Daniels took a step toward Tolan, and Tolan pointed his furios at him. "No closer. I know you're spirit-shaping her. You need to stop."

Master Daniels grinned at Tolan. "You know nothing, Tolan Ethar. You know only what the Academy has allowed you to know. Unfortunately, none of that is what you should know, not someone with your background."

"And what background is that?"

"I can help you. It doesn't have to be this way," Master Daniels said.

"What way is that?" Tolan asked.

He realized almost too late that Master Daniels was attempting to distract him.

He spun, pointing the furios at the other shaper, and focused on an image of hyza.

Power burst from him, surging out of the end of the furios, and now with the bondar out of his pocket, the furios was able to unleash the full light of the formed elemental that Tolan imagined.

An enormous elemental—at least, what appeared to be one—surged outward, and slammed into the other shaper. The man was tossed to the ground and Tolan focused his shaping, guiding it toward Master Daniels. The elemental shape went toward him.

Spinning back to Daniels, he kept the bondar pointed at him.

A dark smile crossed Master Daniels' face. "Had I known you were so useful, I might not have left Ephra."

"I'm not going to be useful to you all."

"Oh, I think you're mistaken." Master Daniels took a

step forward and held his hands outward, a shaping building.

It was nothing like what Tolan had experienced from the disciples of the Draasin Lord. This shaping seemed to soothe the elemental, and the flames relaxed and suddenly dissipated, disappearing into nothingness.

"Had you more control over what you summoned, you might actually have some potential. In time, I suspect you could be taught how to handle this. For now…"

The ground rumbled again, and this time, it surged up on either side of Tolan as if the earth itself intended to hold him. It was a shaping that reminded him of ones he'd been taught in the earth classes, but Tolan hadn't detected anything. No sense of shaping had come with it.

That meant elemental power.

Master Daniels was able to control the elementals.

"There aren't supposed to be any elementals freed," Tolan said, trying to jerk his feet free but failing.

"I wouldn't have expected that amount of cleverness from you when you were working with me. You were useful, but no one would ever have accused you of any particular intelligence."

"Why are you doing this?"

"Because this lock holds the elementals from our world."

"What lock?"

"We've been searching for it. There's been quite a cost, but those of us who understand recognized the benefit."

"The Draasin Lord," Tolan said.

"Do they let you speak of him now? When I was here, they feared speaking of the Draasin Lord, almost as if saying his name would summon him. While he is powerful, I doubt even he could come on a summons like that."

"I thought you served Terndahl," Tolan said.

"I serve what needs to be served. And I have done so long enough to recognize the mistakes Terndahl has made. They seek to control and subjugate when they should seek understanding. Unfortunately, they would conceal this from young shapers like your friend."

"Not from me?"

"Are you a young shaper, Tolan Ethar?"

"I'm at the Academy, aren't I? I was selected, wasn't I?"

Master Daniels grinned. "You were selected, and I'll be honest, I am surprised you managed to make it to this point." He stopped just in front of Tolan, unmindful of the furios Tolan gripped, though his gaze occasionally drifted down toward it, a smile spreading more widely across his face. "What is the key?"

"I don't know what you're talking about."

"I don't need to be a spirit shaper to tell you're lying, so I will ask you again. What is the secret to unlocking the key? Don't mistake our past experiences for an opportunity for compassion. When it comes to what must be done, compassion is irrelevant." He grabbed Ferrah, lifting her with the force of an earth shaping. He held her outward and twisted her so she was brought in front of Tolan. "This is your last opportunity to share with me what you know."

Tolan looked over at Ferrah, attempting to will her to alertness. If she could wake up, she could shape herself free, and with her strength, maybe she would be able to free him as well, but there was no inkling she could come around.

"What do you intend to do with it?"

"Do? I intend to control them."

"Why?"

"You haven't been at the Academy long enough to understand, but eventually you will learn that there are those who deserve power, and those who are born to it. I intend to bring power to those meant to control it."

"The elementals aren't supposed to be controlled," Tolan said.

"Is that right? You would find compassion for the elementals?"

"I would find compassion for creatures that have been trapped for thousands of years."

"Interesting. I would have thought the teachings of the Academy would have managed to convince you there is no torment within the bond."

"I've seen the elementals that are freed. They don't want to return."

"I would suggest you are reading far too much into their motivations. Now. Tell me what I need to know or your friend will suffer."

Ferrah moaned. It started softly, but it built, pain causing her back to arch. Her eyes shot open and she screamed, her cry splitting the night.

Tolan couldn't look at her like this. She was here because of him, because of what he had discovered, and he hadn't realized that was the very thing the disciples had been searching for ever since coming to the city. And if he did nothing, if he continued to refuse Master Daniels, she would continue to suffer.

"I don't know how to do it," he said.

"But you do," Master Daniel said.

"It's something about connecting to the elementals. I imagine them, and that somehow connects to something and draws them out."

He released his hold on Ferrah. She sagged, her head rolling off to the side. The glazed look on her face faded and tears streamed down her face. "Tolan..."

He shook his head, looking away from her. If he didn't say anything, he knew what Master Daniels would do to her. He wasn't able to free himself from the shaping of earth—or the elementals that were here—and without any help, they would be trapped.

He was determined to ensure nothing happened to Ferrah because of him.

Another shaping began to build, this one increasingly powerful.

Tolan looked over his shoulder. The shaping came from outside the park.

"You have very little time remaining," Master Daniels said.

Could it be the master shapers were coming?

The shaping continued, but there was something in it

that Tolan recognized. It wasn't shaping from the master shapers. This was more similar to what he had experienced from the disciples of the Draasin Lord.

As he stared, dark shapes dropped from the sky. All were dressed in black, the cloaks reminiscent of what he'd seen from the disciples before. Each carried a sword unsheathed, and when they landed, their shaping built, converging on the park.

There would be no rescue.

"Like I said, you have only a little time remaining," Master Daniel said.

What would happen if he did nothing?

He had seen the way the disciples had attacked the city before, and with as many as were here now, he had little doubt they would be tormented, and perhaps worse.

There was a possibility, but it was dangerous. Considering how difficult it had been the last time he had connected to the draasin, he wasn't sure he was willing to risk it, but if nothing else, he might be able to distract them long enough to get himself to safety.

"I'll show you," Tolan said.

"Show me?"

Tolan nodded. "I'm... not a very strong shaper." He glanced down at the furios. "I need to use a bondar for shaping all the element bonds. I managed to figure this part, but I can only show you with a weak elemental."

The shaping power continued to build behind him. Somehow, the park managed to hold them back, but Tolan didn't doubt they would find some way to get inside. The disciples were all powerful shapers, and maybe they were more like Master Daniels, able to somehow connect to the elementals, to use that power to get inside.

His only hope was eyeing a dangerous approach that might deter them, or might free a deadly elemental upon the world.

The ground retreated, and Tolan was able to move.

"Hurry."

Tolan raced toward the bondar, practically feeling Ferrah's eyes on his back.

He ignored the question in her gaze, ignoring everything else around him, focusing on the draasin. All he needed to do was imagine the draasin, to use that power to call it forth, and when he did, he could take that distraction and run.

Once outside, separated from the park and the power that could find it, he would be able to suppress the draasin again. He had to be able to.

"I focus on the elemental I intend to summon and then I do," Tolan said.

"And what elemental do you intend to summon?"

"I'm most connected to saa," he said. If Master Daniels knew the elementals well, he would recognize Tolan was connected to a different elemental, but he had to hope that either he was not paying close attention or maybe the fact Tolan had no shaping ability would make it difficult to pull on the connection to anything else.

"Saa will be a good example," Master Daniels said, looking around. He kept his gaze darting all around him and a shaping built, but it mixed with a rumbling within the ground. That rumbling rolled outward, heading toward the wall.

He was freeing the disciples, allowing them inside.

Tolan didn't have much longer. Once the disciples were here, any chance they had at escape would disappear.

What he needed was the distraction the draasin would create.

Tolan imagined a moderate-sized draasin, using that image, holding it within his mind, sending a sense of urgency deep within himself.

As he did, there came the fluttering. The stirring.

He wasn't sure whether it would respond or not, and relief swept through him as he felt it. He pressed his hand onto the bondar, focusing on the draasin. As he did, he sent a silent plea through the bondar to the draasin.

Help me.

There was no reason that should work, no reason other than the fact he had connected to the draasin—at least what he imagined of the draasin—before.

Heat built up.

"What are you doing?" Master Daniels asked.

"I'm using what I can imagine of saa and connecting to the elemental," Tolan said.

"Saa is nothing but flame. This is something more."

"It's not. This is just—"

Master Daniels slammed his hand into Tolan, throwing him back. He landed on the ground next to Ferrah and held tightly onto the furios, rolling toward her.

"What did you do?" she whispered.

"The disciples are coming. We need to get out of here."

"Tolan—"

Tolan shook his head. "There's no time. If this works, I will have bought us some time. But I don't want to be here when the disciples appear. We need to go warn the master shapers."

He started to crawl, and as he did, the ground rumbled, reminding him of the elemental attack that had converged around them before.

No!

The thought came as a silent explosion. With his hands pressed on the ground, his mind imagining the various earth elementals, the rumbling within the earth eased.

Tolan grabbed Ferrah and started toward the far wall. All they needed to do was reach it, throw themselves over it, and run. Once they were free, he hoped Ferrah would be able to find some way to shape them more rapidly than they were able to so far.

Heat continued to swirl around them, flowing from behind them.

Ferrah gasped. "What did you do?"

"What I had to do."

He glanced over his shoulder as the draasin faded into sight. It started slowly, little more than a faint glowing, but that glowing intensified rapidly, quickly taking on form. As it did, additional heat built, radiating.

Master Daniels focused on the draasin, his eyes wide,

and he held his hands outward. There was no attempt to shape, not at first, but slowly, a shaping developed.

Tolan stared at the draasin for a moment. *Help us.*

For some reason, he had the belief that speaking to the draasin—and really, all of the elementals—had somehow helped. When he had spoken to the draasin before, there'd had been a sense it had understood and been willing to cooperate.

The draasin began to flap its enormous wings. It made its way around the bondar, swirling around the enormous structure, going higher and higher. Heat surged outward from the draasin, and as flames came to form around the bondar, Master Daniels was forced back, pushed away.

He changed his focus. Rather than holding his hands outward as if pleading to the draasin, he raised his hands into the air and earth began to rumble, forcing its way up, curling around the enormous bondar.

No!

Tolan smacked the earth as he said it, and with a sudden surge, everything went quiet.

The draasin continued to swirl, rising ever higher into the air, and then it dove.

As it did, it headed straight toward Master Daniels.

He scrambled back and Tolan raced toward the far wall, away from Master Daniels and the disciples, eager to get anywhere but where he was.

Ferrah stayed with him, and when he reached the wall, pressing his back against it, he surveyed the inside of the park.

This was a different place than where they had entered before, but all parts of the park looked similar. He'd never noticed it before, but there were runes on the walls. They were enormous and made of a slightly darker stone, enough so that he had not paid any attention to them before. But then, when he'd come to the park previously, he had been mostly focused on the bondar, trying to understand its purpose and what it might mean.

The rune nearest him looked to be one of earth, and he wasn't surprised to see fire on the opposite side, but was taken aback to see fire glowed softly from the peak of the bondar, the top of the sculpture finally glowing brightly enough to make out the shape.

Was there some significance in that?

It would be something he'd have to come back to later —if there was a later.

Scrambling up the wall, he helped Ferrah, and they jumped across.

"What about the disciples?"

Tolan hadn't given them any thought, focusing mostly on escape. "Can you shield us?"

"Against powerful shapers like that?"

"We have to try," Tolan said.

Ferrah nodded, and her shaping began to build, leaving him wondering what exactly she was doing. Not for the first time, he wished he had the same talent and could shape with the same skill.

"Let's get moving," she said.

"Is it done?" he asked.

"As well as I can, but I don't know if—"

The roar of the draasin split the air, the sound thundering and exploding near them.

Tolan looked up to see the draasin continuing to race higher and higher into the sky. From the ground, Master Daniels was shaping, focusing his effort on the draasin, power continuing to build.

"He's trying to shape the draasin," Ferrah said.

"What?"

"I can feel the direction of it," she said.

As Tolan focused, he was aware of what she was sensing. Master Daniels *was* trying to shape the draasin, but why?

"Great Mother!" Ferrah whispered.

Tolan turned to see one of the disciples approaching the wall. He remained motionless, terrified, but commenced building a shaping, holding on to the furios, prepared to release hyza if it came down to it. In this place, where the elementals seemed to be more freely released, he wasn't sure if it would be easier or harder. Either way, he was determined to do it if it came down to it.

The disciple moved past him and reached the wall. From what Tolan had seen before, the wall had prevented the others entering. The disciple rested his hand on the wall and held it there a moment before climbing quickly over and landing on the other side.

Tolan's heart skipped.

What would happen to this place with the disciples here?

"We can't let them take over this place," he said.

"Tolan, we don't have any way to stop them. These are powerful shapers, the kind even the master shapers struggled against."

He breathed out. "Can you, I don't know, *signal* to the master shapers in some way?"

"I can try, but I'm not sure that shaping out here would be noticed."

"Perhaps not but see if there's anything you can do."

"What are you going to do?"

"I'm going to see if there's any way I can keep them from abusing the bondar."

"Tolan—"

He ignored her as he started off, reaching the wall and hurrying over. Once inside, he crouched, resting his back against the wall—and the rune, he realized.

With his back against the rune, feeling it pressing up against him, he wondered if there were any way to connect to shaping the same way as he would near the bondar. If so, then maybe he wouldn't need to approach the bondar. Maybe he could shape from here.

Tolan focused on earth, especially as this was an earth rune, and sent a summons to jinnar. It was the most powerful earth elemental he could find, one he had dealt with before, and in this place, he hoped it would create a distraction.

A steady rumbling built and suddenly, the earth elemental appeared.

It turned its manlike face toward him. *Help me. Stop them.*

The ground rumbled and the elemental turned away, racing toward the center of the park.

Had that actually worked?

It made no sense. There was no reason for the elemental to have listened, and yet... it seemed as if it had.

Tolan sat back and had begun to relax when Master Daniels suddenly appeared in front of him.

It was almost as if he shook free from a shaping, the masking he'd used to hide himself dissipating. "There you are. I must say, that is quite impressive."

"Leave me alone!"

Help me!

Master Daniels stalked toward him. "It's time for us to go before *they* decide to intervene."

"The master shapers will be here soon," Tolan said, hoping it was true.

"I don't fear them, but I do worry about the others."

Tolan frowned. What others? Who would Daniels fear?

"And here I thought you would never have been useful despite your connection to your parents. I'm only disappointed I didn't identify it sooner."

"What do you know about my parents' disappearance?"

Master Daniels grinned at him. "Did you think I took you in out of compassion? No. I wanted to know whether you knew what they knew. Unfortunately, it seemed as if you never did. A shame, really. Had I known, we would not have needed to stay in Ephra all that time. I could have used you long ago."

Tolan continued back up, pressing against the wall. As he did, he felt the ground rumbling.

What was Master Daniels doing now?

The draasin continued to circle, and he didn't know if the shaping Master Daniels had attempted to use on it had succeeded or not. If it had, it was possible Master Daniels was in control of the elemental.

"Unfortunately, it's time for me to go, but I think I will take you with me. You will be quite valuable."

"Valuable to whom? The Draasin Lord?"

Master Daniels glanced over his shoulder. The dark shapes of the disciples moved within the park, and one was grabbed by the earth elemental and thrown back. The disciple managed to correct himself, righting himself in the air and landing, and Tolan noticed he was holding his hands outward the same way Master Daniels had when it came to the elementals.

"The Draasin Lord *would* find you quite the prize. Unfortunately, that's not where you're going."

Master Daniels reached for him and Tolan jerked back, slamming into the wall. As he did, he let out a soft call for help.

Stop him!

He tried to back away, but earth grabbed him the same way it had near the bondar. Master Daniels continued to stalk toward him, moving carefully, and a shaping built that wrapped around him the same way it had when Master Daniels' men were trying to hold onto him.

He couldn't move.

What had he been thinking, trying to come back into the park by himself?

A shaping built, and it came from behind him. He managed to look back. Ferrah stood on top of the wall, holding her hands outward, a blast of wind swirling from her as it slammed into Master Daniels.

He looked up at her. "You really would have been a powerful student. It's a shame you never will have the chance."

A shaping built. With a sudden realization, Tolan could feel it was spirit.

The only reason he knew it was spirit was because it felt so different than any other shaping he had ever known. Once it hit Ferrah, he had little doubt it would destroy something about her.

"No!"

He lunged forward.

The earth released him, and he slammed into Master Daniels. He jabbed the furios at him, releasing a shaping. Both hyza and saa poured free from the furios and into Master Daniels. Tolan rolled free, springing to his feet, and backed up.

Master Daniels pressed his hand to his chest, the elementals trying to reach for him, but the earth shaping he summoned was powerful enough to push them back.

As he sat up, he looked at Tolan. "That is about enough—"

Jinnar—the summoned earth elemental—grabbed him and lifted him in the air, throwing him to the far side of the park.

The elemental looked at Tolan, watching him, and turned, heading toward where he'd thrown Master Daniels.

With a burst of shaped power, the disciples—along with Master Daniels—lifted into the air. The draasin snapped at them, but it seemed tethered to the bondar, held in place, and the disciples continued to rise higher and higher into the air before eventually disappearing.

22

"WHAT NOW?" FERRAH ASKED, LOOKING AT THE WALL surrounding the park.

"I—"

Tolan didn't get the chance to finish. The Grand Master appeared, his gaze taking in everything in a heartbeat before settling on Tolan and then on Ferrah.

"You can release your shaping, Shaper Ethar," the Grand Master said.

"I can do what?"

The Grand Master nodded toward the park. "Your shaping. It's no longer necessary."

"I..." Tolan glanced over his shoulder and realized he still had a connection to fire and earth, and through that connection, both the draasin and jinnar remained. He tamped down the connection to both, finding as before that his connection to the draasin was much more difficult to separate from, though this time, the earth elemental was more difficult than he remembered as well.

"Shaper Ethar?" the Grand Master asked.

"I'm trying. It's just that this bondar or key or whatever it is makes it difficult for me to separate my shaping."

"As it should," the Grand Master said. "This place is one of the many that helps us maintain the elementals within the bond." He paused and turned to Tolan. "You called it the key. Why is that?"

He breathed out before turning his attention back to the Grand Master. "The shaper who was here. I knew him. I didn't realize he was one of the disciples."

And he still wasn't sure what to make of it. How had Master Daniels managed to hide among the Academy so long? It seemed impossible to believe, but then he also had believed Master Daniels had taken him in, agreeing to work with him all those years ago because he had been friends with Tolan's parents. To find out that was all a lie left him feeling empty.

There was something more, though he wasn't sure what to make of it. Master Daniels had made a comment about something his parents had done, some way they had tried to prevent him from getting selected. If only he'd had a chance to ask more questions.

"I'm not sure he was with the disciples."

"He was the one who's been attacking the city," Tolan said. What else would he be but one of the disciples? Then there was what Daniels had said. Could Tolan have been wrong? "I recognized him after the palace attack. I knew he'd been called back to the city for additional training, but didn't know more than that," he said.

"Called back?" the Grand Master asked.

Tolan nodded.

"And you saw him near the palace?"

"I'm sure of it. Was he looking for this all along?"

"There have been many attempts for many years to find the Keystone. One of the things the Shapers Path does is create protection, but the other is to create a shielding for this. When that was damaged, the shielding protecting the Keystone failed. And then the palace fell, another piece of the shielding. It was why they released the elementals around Terndahl. They thought they would be drawn here, but that's not how it works."

"Why would the palace be a part of the shielding?"

"Do you think it should be the Academy?" the Grand Master asked.

"The Academy has shapers, and I just thought if there was something that needed to be protected, there would be a reason to do so there."

"The Academy is not always safe," the Grand Master said. He turned his attention back to the park. "A Keystone. Not many have a connection to the Keystone, Shaper Ethar."

"I thought it was something like an enormous bondar."

The Grand Master chuckled. "Perhaps, but in this case, this enormous bondar is what separates us from the elementals stored within this place."

"Stored?"

"Not all of the elementals were forced into the bond. There are some that remained, though confined to places like these Keystones. The reason behind that has long been lost, though only the Grand Master and several of the master shapers even know this place exists near the Academy." He looked at Tolan and then Ferrah. "And now the two of you."

"Do you intend to have us spirit-shaped?" Tolan asked.

The Grand Master studied him, running a thumb beneath his chin. "I'm not certain a spirit shaping would be successful on you, Shaper Ethar. And I believe I can trust Shaper Changen."

Ferrah nodded.

"What happens now?" Tolan asked.

"Now you have revealed the presence of the Keystone and used the power here?" The Grand Master asked.

"I suppose," Tolan said.

"Now it must be suppressed once again. The power of this place is dangerous and needs to be controlled. Now we know this was their target, we can conceal it again."

"But they saw it."

"They saw it, but the power will be moved," the Grand Master said.

"You can *move* it?"

"You can move a great number of things," the Grand Master said. "You only need the right connections."

The Convergence. That was what he meant, though Tolan wondered why he would tell him that.

"I think it's time for you to return to the city," the

Grand Master said. "As a first-level student, you must continue training for your testing."

"I haven't suppressed the earth elemental and the draasin."

"I believe I can manage," the Grand Master said. "And besides, Shaper Ethar, I don't want you to be here when the other master shapers arrive, as they may feel differently than I do about you maintaining a memory of this place."

"Will we ever see it again?"

The Grand Master stared at the sculpture. "Unfortunately, I can't promise such a thing."

Tolan sighed and Ferrah took his hand, starting him away, but he paused and looked back. "Are there others?"

"There are others."

"Why?"

"If there weren't, our land would become like the waste." He paused and turned away from Tolan. "Go on, Shaper Ethar."

Tolan looked back, his gaze lingering on the draasin. It was never in danger of being released. The draasin was confined, though Tolan didn't know quite how, other than the fact it seemed bound to this place. And when they left, the Grand Master would force both the earth elemental and the draasin back into the bonds, securing them once more.

"What is it?" Ferrah asked as they disappeared back into the trees.

"I… I just can't shake the feeling I was supposed to find this place."

"Supposed to? Tolan, you heard what he said. This is a place where the elementals were able to remain, and with that being the case, you coming here—untrained, I might add—is incredibly dangerous. We're lucky we weren't killed when this place was attacked."

They were lucky, but something troubled him. The more he thought about it, the more he wondered why Master Irina had brought Master Daniels back to the city. "Do you think she knew?" he whispered.

Shaping built around them, and he glanced up to see shapers soaring high overhead, heading toward the park. How long would it be before they moved it? How long before he no longer had the ability to access the bondar?

Not long. Tolan doubted the Grand Master would wait, especially now the disciples knew about it.

"Who knew?"

"The Grand Inquisitor. Do you think she knew?"

"Knew what?"

"That Master Daniels was a spirit shaper. She would have to have known, wouldn't she?"

"What are you getting at?"

"Only a concern, though I'm not sure what to make of it."

Ferrah slowed, and as they were still holding hands, he slowed too, looking over at her.

"Are you suggesting the Grand Inquisitor was somehow a part of all of this?"

"I'm suggesting she brought him back to the city. She gave him a reason to come. There has to be something behind that."

"Oh, Tolan."

"What?"

"I'm concerned you are bringing me into something I want nothing to do with."

"Even if it threatens the Academy?"

"That's why I'm afraid. Why didn't you say something to the Grand Master?"

"I said something, but I'm not sure he thought it as significant as I did."

They started walking, and as they did, power built around them. It was an enormous shaping, and Tolan wondered if he would've been aware of it had they been in the city. It was the kind of power he remembered from when he was in the Convergence. The shapers had to be drawing upon that power and moving the Keystone.

Would he be able to determine where they were moving it?

"Come with me," he said.

"Tolan…"

She didn't argue, though, and as they traced the sensation, Tolan felt the movement. Surprisingly, it drifted toward the Academy.

Didn't the Grand Master say the Academy wasn't a good place to hide the Keystone?

As they reached the Academy grounds, a familiar face greeted him at the door.

"Master Minden."

She looked at him with the milky gaze she had, and her mouth was pressed in a tight line. "Shaper Ethar. It's an interesting night for you to be out."

"I—"

"You should return to your quarters. You will have a long day tomorrow."

Tolan glanced at Ferrah and realized that any desire he might have to follow the shaping and determine where the Keystone would be moved would be thwarted by Master Minden, a master shaper he had never seen outside the library before now.

"Go on." When he started past her, she whispered something soft, faint, and perhaps only in his mind. "You can ask questions about the Keystone tomorrow, along with your questions about the Grand Inquisitor."

Tolan lingered a moment before Ferrah pulled him on. He glanced back, but Master Minden continued to stare out into the courtyard. The air swirled around her, but Tolan felt no shaping emanating from her, not as he should.

Elemental magic.

He started to smile. Whatever was taking place within the Academy was much more than he had imagined. He didn't know whether the Grand Inquisitor was a part of it, but he was determined to find out. He only had to decide whether he would trust the Grand Master or Master Minden first.

For now, he was able to shape. His connection to the

Keystone had given him an ability to reach shaping that he hadn't before. And with that ability, he was going to be able to remain a student. That would tie him more tightly to the Academy, but it would give him an opportunity to try and understand what else might be taking place here. And it might help him understand the elementals better.

"Tolan?"

He glanced over to see Ferrah watching him.

"Are you coming?"

"What else can I do?"

23

Once back inside the Academy, Tolan paused. They still had the testing for promotion from first level to second level, and with all the time he'd been spending out in the park near the Keystone, he hadn't prepared.

Which meant he likely wouldn't pass.

After everything else, surviving the attack from Master Daniels, now he wouldn't even be able to stay here.

"What is it?" Ferrah asked.

"It doesn't seem fair."

"What doesn't seem fair?"

"I feel like I've done everything we're supposed to do, and we've stopped dangerous attacks on the Academy several times, but that's not going to be enough."

Ferrah glanced over. She took his hand, squeezing it gently. "You're going to do fine."

Tolan stared straight ahead. "I don't know how. The testing is more than I'm ready for."

"After what you've just gone through?"

"That's different, and we both know it. Out near the Keystone, I had access to a powerful bondar."

"Then use a bondar."

"We both know that won't be enough."

He had his furios but would need more than that in order to pass the testing from first level to second level. None really knew what was involved, only that there was a testing. At least he had stayed at the Academy this long. After his Selection, he hadn't really expected to have lasted. He had expected to find himself thrown out before now.

A hulking figure heading up the stairs caught his attention in the distance and he groaned.

"What is it?"

"I just realized I have more than just the testing to worry about."

"What else?"

"Draln."

She squeezed his hand and they reached the stairs leading up to the first-level student quarters. At this point, all he wanted was to rest, but his mind was racing. There were so many questions. What would happen with the Keystone? What would the Grand Master do? Would there be any way for Tolan to find it again?

It was that power he wanted to understand, and yet if the master shapers moved it, he doubted he'd ever be able to find it again.

Once inside the quarters, he had started back to the rooms when he heard his name shouted.

Tolan turned slowly and stiffened.

Draln watched him, arms crossed over his chest. For some reason, he had a heavy cloak thrown over his shoulders, as if he'd recently been traveling. A nasty gleam shone in his eyes. "Ethar. You've been avoiding me long enough."

"I'm not avoiding you at all, Draln."

"You skip off from classes. It's almost as if you don't want to face me in a shapers duel."

Tolan took a deep breath, straightening his back. He wanted nothing to do with the shapers duel, but feared it was going to be required, regardless of what he wanted.

"Let's get it over with then," he said.

"Tolan," Ferrah hissed.

He shook his head slightly. What did it matter, anyway? If he wasn't going to pass the next level, the least he could do was confront Draln. With his furios, he had to believe he had enough fire strength that he should be able to withstand anything Draln might do. The other man might be able to manipulate the elements, but Tolan was able to connect to the elementals. Whether or not that was safe to do was a different matter.

"In the morning. In the park."

The others standing behind Draln all laughed, and Tolan shot them a look before turning his attention to Draln. "Fine. In the morning."

The other man turned away, already starting to laugh with his friends, and Tolan headed back to his room, sighing heavily. At least Draln wasn't going to force it right now. He wasn't sure he had the necessary strength to do anything. After having faced Master Daniels, he wasn't sure there was anything he *could* do. All he wanted was rest.

"You should have refused," Ferrah said.

"What does it matter?"

"If he does something that hurts you—"

Tolan shook his head. "Even if he does something that hurts me, it really doesn't matter. I'm not likely going to be here much longer."

"You can't talk like that, Tolan."

"Because it's true?"

"You know as well as I do that's not true."

He let out a sad sigh. "I don't know anything."

He reached the bedroom and dropped back on his bed, rolling off to his side and ignoring Ferrah. He ignored it when Jonas came in as well. As much as he wanted to sleep, it didn't come easily. He lay there for a long time, struggling, and when he did sleep, dreams of elementals fluttered through his mind.

When morning came, he was up earlier than he had been in quite some time. He sat on the edge of his bed, his hand in the pocket of his cloak, gripping the furios. He traced his fingers along the surface of it, feeling the runes that were there, wishing he had some way of reaching the other elements. Fire would be useful, but it would be more useful to not be limited to only fire when it came to facing Draln. The other man had enough control over fire that he probably would be able to counter anything Tolan did.

"Tolan?"

He looked up and saw Ferrah already awake and dressed. She had brushed and braided her bright red hair and she leaned on the doorframe, watching him. Concern shone brightly in her eyes.

"You don't have to do this."

He forced a smile. His dreams had been filled with the possibilities of what he might have to face, but he'd come to one conclusion. "I don't think Draln intends to face me to the death."

"And if he does?"

Tolan shook his head. "He's not going to. He wants to stay at the Academy. The worst he is going to do to me is—"

"Hurt you badly," Ferrah said.

Tolan smiled slightly. "If he does, then maybe I'll have a little bit more time before my testing."

Ferrah watched him, and it seemed as if she wanted to say something, but bit it back. "You want to get food before you do this?"

"Why not? A last meal, as it were."

They headed down the stairs to the kitchen. It must be early, as there was no one else out in the halls.

"What are you doing up so early?" he asked Ferrah.

"I would've asked you the same thing."

"I couldn't sleep."

"I couldn't, either."

Once in the kitchens, they grabbed some food and took a seat at one of the counters. They ate in silence. As they did, Tolan worked through what he might try, the various shapings he thought might be effective against Draln. He worked through all of the various elementals. That was going to be his focus. If nothing else, he could intimidate Draln. Seeing as how he wasn't going to be at the Academy much longer, he thought that approach would be best.

When he was very nearly finished eating, the door to the kitchen opened and Master Sartan entered. He glanced from Tolan to Ferrah, nodding at them both.

"Shaper Ethar. It's time."

"It's what?"

"It's time for testing."

They couldn't really expect him to be tested so soon after what happened the night before, could they? The Grand Master would have known, and Tolan thought if anyone would have helped support him, to ensure he wasn't subjected to testing before he was ready, it would've been the Grand Master.

"Both of us?" Ferrah.

"Your testing will be later, Shaper Changen."

She reached for Tolan's hand.

"I will be fine," he whispered.

"Good luck," she whispered.

"Make sure Draln knows I didn't avoid him."

"Do you really care about that?"

Tolan offered a hint of a smile. He wasn't sure if he did, but more than that, if this testing went the way he suspected it would, it probably didn't matter at all. If he failed—as he would almost have to fail—there would be no reason to even need to face Draln. He would likely be exiled from the Academy.

The only worse thing that would happen would be if he were forced to stay and serve in the Academy. But then, he thought punishment was reserved for those who failed to pass the first testing. As he had managed to pass that, he wouldn't be confined to the Academy itself. Tolan still didn't know what would be required of him, but perhaps that didn't matter.

He followed Master Sartan, who led him through the Academy, out the main doors, and into a central plaza. From there, he nodded, looking up. The master shaper burst into the air on a shaping of fire, taking to the Shapers Path. Tolan hesitated a moment, reaching for the bondar before following. He drew upon that power as he followed Master Sartan.

Once on the Shapers Path, he trailed along after Master Sartan, wondering where the other was going to take him.

"The testing takes place outside of the city?"

"It's often safer that way," Master Sartan said.

"Why?" There were plenty of places within the Academy where they were protected from shapings, so he had to wonder why it would be necessary to travel beyond now.

"At your stage and training, the type of shaping we will ask of you is difficult. There can be a lack of control, and we want to ensure it is safe."

They followed the Path until Tolan was sure they were no longer anywhere near Amitan. He pointed, motioning to what appeared to be a rolling grassy hillside. When Master Sartan shaped his way down, Tolan followed, reaching the ground. As he did, he hesitated. It reminded him of the park.

Much like with the park with the Keystone, there was a low wall surrounding it. It had a weathered appearance, and he noticed one of the symbols on the wall.

He frowned to himself. That couldn't be coincidence, could it?

"Why here?"

"This is a place pre-dating the Academy," Master Sartan said. "The earliest shapers placed protections upon it. It allows us to work incredible power and ensures that power does not escape beyond the borders."

It was similar to the Keystone.

"Why not have earlier-level students come here and work?"

"As it is a place of ancient power, it's dangerous for those not fully trained. If you pass beyond the second level, you would be granted an opportunity to come here. Until then, you will require a master shaper to attend."

Master Sartan approached the wall, and Tolan noticed one difference from the Keystone. A narrow opening led inside. It was an archway that curved overhead, and

Master Sartan had to duck beneath it, avoiding the stones, and when Tolan followed, there came a tingling sensation across his skin.

He paused. He wasn't alone here.

"Shaper Sar will be finished soon," Master Sartan said.

Tolan looked toward the center of the grassy space. The park was not nearly as wide as the one with the Keystone, and yet, as he looked around, there were the similar walls framing it, and symbols marked those walls. They had to be symbols of power. Would he be able to shape the same way as he had within the Keystone Park?

He had to push those thoughts away. Draln worked in the center of the park, an enormous shaping of fire spinning in a funnel as it tore out of the earth. The shaping built with immense power, and Tolan didn't need to be able to reach each of the elements to know that somehow, Draln was pulling on earth and wind and fire at one time. The only one missing was water.

It was an impressive shaping, and he knew whatever else might happen, he wouldn't be able to replicate that.

At least he didn't have to worry about Draln thinking he had abandoned the duel.

Draln's shaping twisted and the flames turned to smoke before fizzling out.

It was a level of control he hadn't seen Draln possess even within the classrooms.

That surprised him.

The other man was a skilled shaper, and Tolan worried about what would happen when they did have a shapers duel, but he also knew he was still inexperienced, much like they all were. To do a shaping like that required power Tolan had not yet seen from Draln. And having spent the last year in classes together, Tolan had enough experience to know what Draln was capable of shaping.

"What's the nature of the test?"

Master Sartan glanced over, and Tolan suspected he wouldn't answer. They had been friendly, and Master Sartan had never been unkind to him, especially since Tolan had demonstrated some predilection toward fire—however artificial that might've been.

"You have been taught many shapings in classes over the last year. You are asked to demonstrate some of them."

"That's it?"

"That's it? Shaper Ethar, I believe you have some difficulty with reaching various elements."

"I have had some difficulty. I guess I was just expecting the testing to be a bit more."

"It's always a bit more," Master Sartan said.

Almost as if in point of emphasis, the shaping Tolan had been watching struck Draln, throwing him back.

It wasn't Draln's shaping at all.

The other man scrambled to his feet and the shaping changed, earth erupting from the ground, wind whistling. There was an attempt at fire, but he wasn't able to use it. Tolan could feel the attempt, but there was a sense of resistance.

It was an attack.

Not just use what they had learned in class, but they were expected to be able to defend themselves.

And here he thought he was getting out of a shapers duel.

Another blast struck, the ground rumbling, and Draln was tossed into the air. He crashed down, and at the last moment, wind whipped up, catching him.

Draln sat up. He was managing far better than Tolan would've expected. Reacting like that involved keeping a clear mind, knowing the nature of the shapings, and being prepared for whatever might come their way. In this attack, he wondered if he would be able to do something similar.

"Why do I get to watch?"

"Do you think it will help?" Master Sartan asked.

It seemed unnecessarily cruel. "No."

A circle of fire surrounded Draln, and a shaping built from him. As it did, the fire continued to press inward with more and more force and Draln scrambled, spinning in place.

He wasn't going to be able to escape.

Earth shook, and from where he stood, Tolan could see the panic on Draln's face.

Everything pressed in upon him.

The other man continued to fight, but he was overwhelmed by the nature of the shaping.

And then it blinked out of existence.

Draln sank to his knees. There was a hint of ash smeared across his cheek and sweat streamed down his brow. Three master shapers approached, one of them Master Marcella, Tolan realized. They whispered something to him, and one of the master shapers helped pull Draln to his feet. He headed away, reaching the wall with Master Sartan and Tolan.

Draln shot Tolan a look. "Good luck, Ethar."

Tolan met the other man's eyes, and he couldn't tell if he was being serious or not.

"Did you pass?"

"I don't know."

Tolan stared at the three master shapers. They were moving away from the center of the clearing and taking up space once again around the outskirts of the park. If Draln hadn't survived, what chance did he have?

Master Sartan nodded to Tolan. "It's time."

Tolan nodded, starting forward.

Master Sartan reached into his pocket and pulled something out, handing multiple things to Tolan.

Tolan took them, frowning. All were slender rods, and all had symbols he recognized marked along the sides.

Bondars.

There was one for each of the elements, including fire. They were shaped differently than the bondars they used in the classroom, but there was no doubt in his mind they were bondars.

"What is this?" he asked Master Sartan. He flicked his gaze to Draln. The other man carried a set of bondars as well.

"To pass through the second level, one must demonstrate mastery of shaping. It does not require you to reach that shaping on your own. You may use the bondar if you feel it will help. Not all choose to do so, but the expectation is that you will be able to reach each of the elements."

Tolan's heart started to hammer.

Had they tested him only a few weeks before, he doubted he would have been able to do this. Even now, under this situation, he wasn't sure if he'd be able to.

"You will be tested until you fail," Master Sartan said.

"Until I fail?"

The master shaper nodded. "Good luck."

Tolan started toward the center of the park. Once there, he looked around, half expecting to see some residual effect of what had taken place when Draln had been here, but there was nothing. The shaping had been completely smooth, eliminated, leaving the ground unmarked.

He squeezed the bondars.

What was the best way to hold them?

He didn't even have a chance to process. Power built.

It was a strange thing facing an attack again. After facing Master Daniels and the others the night before, he was battle tested, but in this case, the stakes were equally high. With Master Daniels, it had been a desire to ensure he would survive. In this case, it was a matter of wanting to stay at the Academy.

And he did want to stay.

He gripped the bondars in one hand, turning in place.

What technique would he need?

He tested fire, pulling on various shapings he could think of, drawing upon his image of the elementals as he did. They came one after another.

Shifting to earth, he worked through the various shapings he had practiced while in the Keystone park. Once again, he was able to reach them.

What about wind and water?

There was no chance to test them.

The earth heaved, tossing him into the air.

Tolan took a deep breath, gripping the bondars. He pushed off with a shaping of fire, using the same sort of shaping he used when he reached the Shapers Path. It was a blast of heat, and it carried him up, letting him twist in the air. He noticed Draln watching from the far side of the park and wondered what the other man was thinking. He was likely already planning his attack for the duel.

He didn't have an opportunity to see anything else.

The flames holding him in the air faded.

He started to crash and Tolan shaped, using an image of cilika to catch him, cradling him softly toward the ground.

When he landed, he solidified the earth again, stepping forward.

As it had with Draln, a circle of flame worked around him.

This was one Tolan thought he could manage. At least with the bondar.

He ignored the furios Master Sartan had given him, reaching for the one in his pocket. He was familiar with the shapes upon it, and he focused, searching for which elemental would absorb those flames. Earth might do it, but if you used the right shaping of fire...

He focused on lisinar and it swept through, circling him, practically swallowing the flames.

Wind struck him, threatening to knock him over.

He needed some way of burning that off.

He could use fire as well.

He shaped, this time using saa. It was an easy elemental to burn off the wind, and the heat flowed up from the ground, an enormous shaping, and it swallowed the wind.

He had to demonstrate the other elements. If he were to pass the test, he would need to do so.

When sharp shards of ice started batting at him, Tolan focused on what he could remember of water. He needed to change it. Could he turn it to mist?

Masyn.

The elemental drifted into the front of his mind, and he focused, thinking about what he knew. The ice continued to batter him, and he turned in place. When he did, he saw Master Marcella staring at him.

This was her shaping.

She had already tried to hurt him once, drowning him, and though she had intended it to try to draw out his shaping ability, the fear of death had been real.

He wasn't going to let her succeed when it came to this.

Tolan squeezed the bondars.

Had he not shaped the night before, had he not experienced that terror, he wasn't sure he would have been able to react.

But he knew what was needed.

Focusing through the water bondar, he shaped, drawing upon masyn.

The ice shifted. It twisted, becoming something else.

There was resistance to his shaping through the bondar, and as he looked up, Master Marcella gritted her teeth, trying to oppose him.

Tolan scanned the inside of the park, and his gaze fell upon a wall behind Master Shorav.

Water was there.

He used that rune, focusing. Whether or not this place was like the Keystone didn't matter. He thought the power was similar.

He pulled upon that, drawing even more power.

The shaping exploded out from him. He directed it toward Master Marcella.

Wind slammed into him again, and again he reacted, pushing out with saa but he twisted it, using his connection to the bondar, sending out a pulse for ara.

As the wind elemental swirled, he directed it outward, forcing it toward each of the walls. He was determined to overpower the shaping used on him.

It continued to build.

Tolan forced more and more power through the shaping, through the elemental, unmindful of the fact he was drawing upon elemental power. In this place, he could argue he was doing something else.

He needed to be careful, not wanting to harm the master shapers, but then, Tolan wasn't sure he even would be able to do so.

The pressure continued to build.

Suddenly, his hold on ara faded, and heat and wind and water and earth all slammed into him. They swirled around, forming a cage, and as they did, he was pushed backward. Tolan tried to fight, pushing outward with fire and earth. He added what he could of water and wind, but was still exhausted from the night before. Missing sleep the night before, he hadn't had the opportunity to fully recuperate. Although he continued to attempt shapings, he was stuck. The power built around him, squeezing, and he resisted, trying to fight, but couldn't.

It pressed in upon him.

Pain squeezed his chest, filling him.

Tolan collapsed.

When he dropped to his knees, his hold on the bondars faded and he dropped them. All he had was his furios—and the runes around the park. He reached for that power, feeling the faint stirring deep within him, and he tried to push outward.

For a moment, there was a reprieve. The power pressing in upon him waned, but briefly.

And then it pressed in upon him again.

He lost track of time. The pain was intense. And then it faded.

He crouched there for a moment, trying to gather himself, steadying his breathing.

The bondars that had slipped out of his hand lay useless on the ground.

Master Shorav was the first one there. He reached out, offering his hand, and Tolan took it, getting to his feet.

"The testing is complete."

"That's it?"

"You will learn of your results later today."

Tolan looked at the others. Master Marcella had a streak of dried blood down her nose, and she watched him. He had expected there to be anger, but that didn't seem the case. It was almost as if she had pride shining in her eyes.

He took a shaky breath and turned back toward the entrance to the park. Master Sartan waited, but Draln had already left.

Master Sartan escorted him through the archway, and once through, a powerful shaping burst from him, holding onto Tolan. He carried him to the Shapers Path, guiding him back along the Path and toward the Academy. Tolan was thankful for that. He wasn't sure if he would have had the strength necessary to return on his own.

When they lowered once again to the courtyard outside the Academy, Master Sartan tipped his head.

"How did I do?" Tolan asked.

Master Sartan cocked his head, watching him for a moment. "I'm not at liberty to discuss until your results are known."

With that, the master shaper took to the sky again, disappearing along the Shapers Path.

Tolan took a deep breath, which meant he hadn't done well enough. He thought of some of the creative shapings he'd seen from Draln, and the way he had used various elements, twisting them together. He'd shaped all of them at one time, something Tolan hadn't managed to do. He might have demonstrated each of the elements, but had it been enough?

He found his way through the Academy, trudged up the stairs, and paused in the main room. Draln sat in one corner, alone for the first time Tolan could remember.

Tolan took a deep breath before heading over to him.

The other man glanced up and nodded. "That wasn't what I expected."

"What did you expect?"

"I knew we had to shape each of the elements, but..." He looked back down at his hands.

"I don't think they were trying to hurt us."

"It felt that way."

"You did well. I watched, and you were mixing each of the elements—"

"Do you think I need your approval, Ethar?"

Tolan took a deep breath before standing. "I just wanted you to know I thought you did well."

Draln glanced up, glaring at him for a moment. He opened his mouth as if he was going to say something but bit it back.

Tolan turned away, heading back to his room. Once

there, he found a folded slip of paper resting on his bed. The seal of the Academy held it closed.

He stared at it. The other beds in the room were empty, which meant Ferrah, Jonas and Wallace were off somewhere else—possibly even at their testing.

Grabbing the piece of paper, he held it.

What was he waiting for?

Tearing open the paper, he unfolded it. His gaze skimmed across, and five words were all that stood out:

Promotion to the second level.

Tolan looked up, holding the page in hand, and smiled to himself.

Click now for book 3 of Elemental Academy: The Water Ruptures

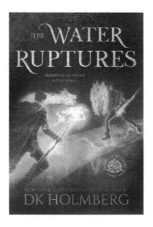

The Disciples of the Draasin Lord have again been

defeated, yet a traitor remains within Terndahl. The Inquisitors have come, and their presence has everyone on edge.

With the help of the Keystone, Tolan has discovered the ability to shape each of the element bonds. Now that he's passed testing to the second level at the Academy, he finally feels as if he belongs.

Still, he can't shake the feeling that his shaping is different than others—and tied to the elementals. Discovering the reason why leads him to ask dangerous questions. Between that and knowing someone works against the Academy, Tolan finds himself in the middle of a dangerous plot on the Academy itself.

Only this time, with Inquisitors involved, he might not be able to escape.

ALSO BY D.K. HOLMBERG

Elemental Academy

The Fire Within

The Earth Awakens

The Water Ruptures

The Wind Rages

The Cloud Warrior Saga

Chased by Fire

Bound by Fire

Changed by Fire

Fortress of Fire

Forged in Fire

Serpent of Fire

Servant of Fire

Born of Fire

Broken of Fire

Light of Fire

Cycle of Fire

The Endless War

Journey of Fire and Night

Darkness Rising

Endless Night

Summoner's Bond

Seal of Light

The Elder Stones Saga

The Darkest Revenge

Shadows Within the Flame

Remnants of the Lost

The Coming Chaos

The Shadow Accords

Shadow Blessed

Shadow Cursed

Shadow Born

Shadow Lost

Shadow Cross

Shadow Found

The Collector Chronicles

Shadow Hunted

Shadow Games

Shadow Trapped

The Dark Ability

The Dark Ability

The Heartstone Blade

The Tower of Venass

Blood of the Watcher

The Shadowsteel Forge

The Guild Secret

Rise of the Elder

The Sighted Assassin

The Binders Game

The Forgotten

Assassin's End

The Dragonwalker

Dragon Bones

Dragon Blessed

Dragon Rise

Dragon Bond

Dragon Storm

Dragon Rider

Dragon Sight

The Teralin Sword

Soldier Son

Soldier Sword

Soldier Sworn

Made in the USA
San Bernardino, CA
25 May 2020